Linda Gillard lives on the Black Isle in the Scottish Highlands and has been an actress, journalist and teacher. She's the author of six novels, including STAR GAZING which was short-listed in 2009 for *Romantic Novel of the Year* and *The Robin Jenkins Literary Award* (for writing that promotes the Scottish landscape.)

HOUSE OF SILENCE became a Kindle bestseller and was selected by Amazon as one of their Top Ten *Best of 2011* in the Indie Author category.

D0205488

Also by Linda Gillard

Emotional Geology
A Lifetime Burning
Star Gazing
House of Silence
Untying the Knot

www.lindagillard.co.uk

THE GLASS GUARDIAN

Linda Gillard

First published as a Kindle e-book in 2012
This paperback edition 2012

ISBN 978-1481170901

Cover design by Nicola Coffield

www.lindagillard.co.uk

For my daughter Amy

Prologue

When I was a child I nearly drowned. In a pond. Nothing dramatic, apart from the fact that I nearly died. I fell into a big pool at my Aunt Janet's house on the Isle of Skye.

I fell from a wooden bridge over the pool. At least, I *think* I fell. I don't remember falling. All I remember is drowning – *almost* drowning – and then I remember being very cold and so sick, I thought I must have vomited up my insides.

I was rescued – well, *obviously* – but I don't remember being hauled out of the water. Such memories as I have of the event are just what my aunt told me afterwards, about how I lay gasping and retching on the grass, black with mud and slime, covered in pondweed, like some sinister water sprite.

I do remember one thing though. I remember Aunt Janet shouting at my little playmate, the child who must have rescued me from the pond. She shrieked at him, over and over, 'Who was it? Did you *see* him?' I think she wanted to know who'd pulled me out. Or pushed me in. I remember her screaming (was it in anger or terror?) at the boy who'd apparently saved my life, 'You can't have! You're not even wet! *Who was it?*'

After she'd given me a good scolding and forbidden me to play on the bridge ever again, Aunt Janet never mentioned my near-drowning. I suppose it was something too terrible to talk about.

But I used to dream about it. I still do.

It's a black, choking dream in which I feel so cold, it seems more likely I'll freeze to death than drown. Then something moves through the water, something very pale. And strong. It pulls me, drags me upwards, toward the light. The strange thing is, in the dream, I don't want to go. I want to stay down in the darkness. I want to die. Or rather, I don't *mind* dying.

But despite myself, I rise upwards, then just as I'm about

to break through, into the light, I wake up. I wake up soaked with sweat, drenched and cold, almost as if I've actually been in the water. It's a horrible dream. So real.

I didn't drown, but every time I have this dream, I feel as if I did, but that I was given a reprieve. Another chance. Another go at life.

I didn't have that dream last night. What happened last night was worse. *Far* worse. But you won't understand unless I start at the beginning. And even then, you still might not understand.

In the end I decided it wasn't so much a case of understanding, but *believing*. Believing it was possible. Because not believing just wasn't an option.

Chapter One

I wasn't sorry to leave London. It was high time. People have short memories when it comes to TV programmes, but occasionally someone would accost me in a supermarket aisle.

'Excuse me, but didn't you use to be Ruth Travers?'

I would stand tall, pull my tummy in and say, 'Actually, I still *am*.'

Undeterred, my tormentor (usually female) would peer at my face, as if I were an unusual specimen in a zoo. 'You looked *younger* on TV,' she would say, accusingly. 'Fancy seeing *you* in here. "Delia of the Delphiniums"!'

'You know, in five years I only made one programme about delphiniums.'

'Suppose you'll turn up on Hallmark eventually. There's so many channels now, they don't know how to fill up the schedules, do they?'

'Really, I have no idea. I don't even watch TV these days, let alone appear on it.' Glancing ostentatiously at my watch, I would form a startled O with my lips and exclaim, 'Is that the time? You must excuse me. I'm going to be late for a meeting with Prince Charles. He wants to pick my brains about growing comfrey as green manure. Sorry! Must fly!'

Ignoring a belated request for an autograph, I'd make my escape, diving into the nearest tube station, anxious to resume the life of anonymity and quiet desperation I'd known since losing my lover, my father and the woman I'd regarded as a mother.

I called it The Year of Deaths. 2010. My *annus horribilis*.

It began with David dropping dead on New Year's Day as he shovelled snow. He was fifty-four. I wish I could say he died a happy man, but two hours earlier, I'd finally summoned up the courage to tell him I thought our relationship was going nowhere. Unable to process the information, he'd gone out to clear the drive as a displacement activity and suffered a fatal heart attack.

I was given leave of absence from my TV gardening show and was gearing up for a return in the spring when my irascible and difficult father was diagnosed with an inoperable brain tumour. He was a widower and I was his only child, so I turned my back on a lucrative television career and the horticultural work I loved, in order to spend more time with my father and eventually to nurse him.

I took his ashes to the Isle of Skye. Dad had spent little time there himself, but I knew it well. I was only eight when my mother died, but my father virtually gave up on the real world and retreated into academia, his first love and great consolation. He sent me to Skye every year to spend the summer with his sister-in-law, Janet, while he stayed behind in Cambridge to research and write.

Aunt Janet did her best to fill the breach and became mother, father and friend to me. It was she who taught me to grow things and to love the natural world, so after I'd scattered my father's ashes, I decided to stay with Janet for a while, hoping to recover from the combined shock of the loss of my partner and my father's sudden decline.

But there was to be no let-up for me. Janet had one of her dizzy spells in the garden and fell down a small flight of stone steps. She broke her arm and collarbone and never recovered. She was eighty-two and, confined to bed, her mental and physical decline was rapid. Her GP advised me to prepare for the worst.

I'd borne up pretty well losing David and then my father, but when Janet died I went to pieces. Smithereens. I was inconsolable and thought I would go mad with grief. (Perhaps I did. That would account for what happened later. Or *seemed* to happen.) Janet's kindly GP looked after me and said my reaction wasn't just about losing my aunt. It was pent-up grief that had accumulated during that terrible year.

I couldn't face a return to London and my stalled career,

let alone the prospect of dating at the age of forty-two. Nor could I face clearing out *Tigh-na-Linne*, Janet's beloved home, which now belonged to me. So I shuttled back and forth from Skye to London, collecting my things, tidying up loose ends, shutting up my flat, finally returning to *Tigh-na-Linne*, where I spent my time in a sort of daze, grieving, resting and tending Janet's beautiful garden.

Then something unaccountable happened.

One day, I went into the study, determined to make a start on sorting out her personal things. I should perhaps point out that, unlike me, Aunt Janet was obsessively tidy. Since her death I'd tried to keep the house in good order, with everything in its place, just as she would have wished. I think I must have been scared of letting her go, of forgetting her, and this was my way of keeping her with me for a little while longer.

As I sank into the battered leather chair behind Janet's desk, I noticed the top was off her gold fountain pen. Pen and pen-top lay on the blotter, leaking fresh ink. Beside the pen, Janet's RHS gardening diary (my Christmas present to her every year) lay open. Glancing at the blank page, I registered with a pang that the diary was open at the week of her death. Puzzled and not a little unnerved, I scanned the rest of the desk. My eye came to rest on the brass perpetual calendar which Janet hadn't been able to alter since the day of her fall. It said Thursday, October 21st.

Today's date.

Janet had been dead for about a month. She employed no cleaner or any other domestic staff. There had been a gardener who put in a few hours a week, but once it became clear I was staying, Janet gave him notice, insisting (for my own good, I think) that I took responsibility for the garden.

As far as I knew, no one had keys to the house apart from me. Janet's nearest neighbours were currently in Australia. Dr Mackenzie had looked in on me two weeks ago, but I'd had no visitor since, unless you counted the postman. No one and nothing had disturbed my hermit's existence. I was quite alone. At least, I *thought* I was.

I put it down to strain. I'd been in a bad way after Janet died and Dr Mackenzie had had to prescribe a tranquilliser to get me through the funeral, so I concluded I must have had some sort of delayed reaction to the drug, some drastic memory lapse that prevented me from remembering that I'd wandered into Janet's study and messed about with her things.

Or perhaps I'd taken to sleepwalking. Wasn't that supposed to be a reaction to stress?... I'd never done such a thing in the two years I'd been sleeping with David, but with all my loved ones wiped out in less than a year, who knew what sort of reaction might set in? And if it *was* a reaction to grief, I might well have touched my aunt's precious things, arranged her desk to look as if she'd just popped out of the room. (Except that Aunt Janet would no more leave the top off her pen than leave the house in her underwear.)

I tidied these troubling thoughts away, along with Janet's pen and diary, which I put into the desk drawer, shutting it firmly. My enthusiasm for making a start on her papers had evaporated, leaving me feeling unsettled. I decided I would go to the music room instead and sort out her sheet music.

In her youth, Janet Gillespie had been a fine pianist. She'd hoped for a performing career, but she'd never fulfilled her early promise and, in such a competitive field, it was easy for a woman (rather a plain woman, it has to be said) to be overlooked. Janet eventually abandoned her performing career and channelled her energies into teaching and composing. After an inauspicious start – a chamber opera that flopped and a set of piano pieces that critics condemned as "trite" – Janet seemed to find her voice in the 1950s and began to enjoy some success, notably with a romantic song cycle, *In Memoriam*, a poignant and pacifist response to the First World War, in which several of her forebears had died.

In Memoriam made Janet's name and she never looked back. Success seemed to unleash her creativity and her new compositions met with acclaim. Since her death I'd received emails from academics asking if I wished to sell Janet's musical archive. One persistent but polite musicologist from Toronto University had asked if he could visit *Tigh-na-Linne* to make a study of her manuscripts as he was writing a book about female composers. Since Janet would have loathed the idea of being relegated to such a ghetto, I'd said no.

So far I'd ignored all other requests, but I knew I'd have to deal with them eventually. Janet's musical legacy was important. It was probably also valuable. So I decided I'd spend a pleasant morning in the music room, her favourite room in the house and the one with the best view.

On Janet's death I'd become the owner of *Tigh-na-Linne*, (Gaelic for "the house by the pool"), a large Victorian country house on the Isle of Skye in the region of Sleat (pronounced "Slate".) Sleat was known as "the garden of Skye" on account of the lushness of its vegetation. It was appropriate that Janet should live there since she divided her time and energy between her two great loves: music and gardening. Hers was a seasonal existence. She composed in winter and gardened from spring (very late on Skye) until the end of autumn.

Tigh-na-Linne was draughty, leaky and, as the estate agents say, in need of refurbishment. (To judge from some of the wallpapers and carpets, I don't think Janet had decorated since the 1980s.) But because it was largely unmodernised, the house retained a lot of period features: marble fireplaces, wooden shutters and sanitary ware of surprising loveliness. When I used to come and stay as a child, I felt as if I'd wandered in to the pages of one of the classics: *The Railway Children* or *The Water Babies*. There was even a big mirror over the mantelpiece, like the one in *Alice Through the Looking-Glass*. Standing on a chair, I'd attempted to penetrate it by pressing my hands against the glass, but I'd found it unyielding. (So was Aunt Janet when she saw the grubby fingerprints I'd left on the mirror.)

Modernised and refurbished, *Tigh-na-Linne* would be worth a tidy amount. What was impossible to value was the house's location. Rattling windows, water-stained ceilings and idiosyncratic plumbing paled into insignificance when one looked out of the big windows at the view over Loch

Eishort, a sea loch, to the Black Cuillin mountains beyond and the distant islands of Canna and Rhum.

Janet had spent most of her life at *Tigh-na-Linne*. She'd been born there and so had her mother, Grace, only surviving child of James and Agnes Munro, who lost their three sons in the so-called Great War. Not long before she died, I asked Janet if she'd ever grown tired of her incomparable view, or if she'd just become inured to it after eighty years. Without pausing to think, she announced, in that abrupt way she had that sounded impatient but really masked an essential shyness, 'Och, you never get used to beauty, Ruth. Never! All that happens is you become increasingly intolerant of *ugliness* and wonder why on earth folk put up with it.'

Now with Janet gone, all that beauty was mine to enjoy.

Alone.

Having discovered Janet's desk in disarray, I was a little nervous as I entered the music room and made my way toward the cabinet where she stored all her music. I hadn't entered the room since her death. Before that I'd only come in once a week, at Janet's request, to dust. She couldn't bear for the Bechstein grand piano to stand unused, but as I couldn't play and she had a broken arm, it had to remain untouched, but not entirely neglected. I dusted it carefully and always left it as Janet would wish to find it: open and ready to play.

I didn't notice the piano until I turned round, my arms full of sheet music and sheaves of manuscript paper. As soon as I saw it, I cried out and dropped all the music. As it fell to the floor, loose sheets fluttered upwards, then sank again with a sigh. I stood and stared, open-mouthed.

The piano was *closed*. The lid was down and the keyboard was shut away. Not only was there no music open on the elaborately carved music stand, the stand itself had been folded away inside the piano. Never had I seen Aunt Janet's piano in this sorry state. It was a point of honour that her beloved Bechstein – her partner in life almost – should always stand ready to play. To close it up would have been a kind of sacrilege.

But closed it was.

Stepping over the piles of music on the floor, I headed for the sitting room where I poured myself a brandy, my mind reeling. Someone was playing games with me. But who? Dear old Dr Mackenzie? Surely not! Could it be the gardener Janet had laid off, unemployed and nursing a grudge? It surely couldn't be a random intruder, shutting up a grand piano and leaving the top off a fountain pen. It had to be someone with malicious intent who knew both Janet and me very well. But who knew *both* of us? Only Dr Mackenzie. And why would he do such a thing?

The brandy wasn't helping, but I needed a distraction and I liked the feel of the heavy bottle in my hands, like an improvised weapon. I took a deep, calming breath and considered. Gardener-with-a-grudge had to be Suspect No. 1. Perhaps Janet had once lent him a key, or he'd seen one hanging up somewhere. Perhaps he knew of a secret way in to the house. I decided I would check every door and window, after which I would speak to the man whose name and number were recorded on the kitchen notice board.

Despite the mildness of the October day, I was shivering as I drained my glass.

Chapter Two

I found all the windows locked or impossible to open from the outside and all the doors locked, apart from the back door, which was my concession to local custom. This was the Isle of Skye where trusting souls paid scant attention to security. Nevertheless, I now locked the back door, which would annoy the postman who was used to opening it without ceremony and dumping the post on the kitchen worktop. Too bad. He would have to knock. Perhaps *he* was my mysterious intruder. I was taking no chances.

The scrap of paper on the kitchen notice board said only *Howard – gardener*, followed by a mobile number. The writing wasn't Janet's and I had no idea if this was the man's surname or his first name. I picked up the phone and tapped in the number. After a couple of rings, he answered.

'Hello?'

'Mr Howard?' I asked uncertainly.

'Speaking.'

'Hello. This is Ruth Travers, Janet Gillespie's niece.' I paused, wondering how to continue when Mr Howard cut in.

'May I offer my condolences? Miss Gillespie was a grand old lady and she'll be much missed.'

'Thank you. She'll certainly be missed by me,' I replied, swallowing down a lump in my throat.

'So,' he prompted gently. 'Can I be of assistance in some way?'

'I'm not sure. I just wanted to clarify something really. I believe my aunt used to employ you as her gardener?'

'Yes, that's right. As a matter of fact, I wanted to talk to you about that, but I haven't liked to call. I didn't want to disturb you. I'm sure it's been a very difficult time.'

'What did you want to discuss?' I asked, bracing myself for a possible altercation.

'My employment.'

'I see. Did Janet owe you money?'

He laughed. 'No, rather the reverse. I wonder, are you at home at the moment? Because I'm at your road-end now. Could I drop by? It's actually a bit of a delicate matter. You might prefer to discuss it in person.'

My mind was racing. Was I talking to my intruder? Should I perhaps indicate there was someone else in the house? Or, when he arrived, refer to a large, occasionally vicious dog shut in the scullery?... A dog that didn't bark at new arrivals wouldn't seem very intimidating. I decided if I received Mr Howard in the kitchen and hovered near Janet's comprehensive *batterie de cuisine*, something would come to hand that, in an emergency, I could use as a weapon.

But the man sounded harmless enough. It was so hard to judge on the phone. He was English and his polite solicitude suggested someone older than me, rather than a young thug. Unless he was one of those vigorous "active retired" types, I was sure that, at 5' 8", with the unladylike biceps I'd developed heaving bags of compost and shifting paving stones, I could take him on, armed with the *Le Creuset* omelette pan I'd spotted sitting handily on the hob.

Feeling more confident now, I said, 'Yes, I'm at home. By all means drop by. But—' Inspired improvisation! 'I'm expecting an estate agent to call any time to value the house, so I might have to curtail our conversation.' Especially, I added mentally, if you try any funny business.

'That's fine, I won't keep you long. I just wanted to explain something that I'm sure your aunt won't have mentioned to you.'

Intrigued, I suggested he come to the back door. He said he'd be with me in a few minutes and hung up, so I unlocked the door again, filled the kettle and switched it on. Boiling water would come in useful, either for coffee or for causing grievous bodily harm.

The kettle had just boiled when there was a knock at the back door. I hadn't heard a car draw up so I assumed Mr Howard must have been on foot. I heard a voice call out 'Hello!' and then the door swung open to reveal my visitor.

11

He stared and I stared.

I'd no idea why *he* was staring, but I stared because Mr Howard wasn't "active retired". He looked as if he could take me on, frying pan notwithstanding, without breaking sweat. A blond giant; tanned and obviously fit; forty-ish, I supposed, with crinkly brown eyes that looked a little sleepy, or perhaps just amused. By me? Had I got a smudge on my face? Something stuck in my hair? Was that why he was staring?

He extended a large weathered hand that completely enveloped mine and said, 'Tom Howard.'

'How do you do?' I said faintly.

I admit I was thrown. Partly because it's not every day you entertain an attractive man in your kitchen, especially one this big. (The man, I mean, not the kitchen.) But also because something about Mr Howard seemed familiar. And the way he was smiling at me now seemed *over*-familiar. Swivelling my eyes toward the hob, I checked the omelette pan was still in position. When I looked back, he'd released my hand but was still smiling.

'You don't remember me, do you?'

'Should I? If we'd met before, I think I would have remembered!'

Damn. That didn't come out quite the way I intended. Was his smile now one of smug conceit?

'I used to call you Ruthie. And you used to call me Tommy. When you were ten, you promised you'd marry me. But, don't worry, I'm not going to hold you to that.'

'*Tommy?*' He nodded, then grinned. Suddenly I was a child collecting shells, scrambling over rocks, plunging into the freezing sea. '*Tommy*! Oh, no, I don't believe it! My God, you've *grown*!'

He laughed, threw his arms wide and folded me in a hug which yanked me straight out of my lonely childhood and back in to my lonely present, where I realised just how long it was since a man had held me in his arms.

Tommy Howard had been a pale, skinny boy with corrective spectacles, sometimes held together with Elastoplast. For years he and his mother spent the whole of the summer school holiday on Skye. I never knew if he had a father. Tommy and I had an unspoken agreement. I never asked about his father and he never asked about my mother. I suspect we both sensed what the other lacked and steered clear of a painful subject.

Tommy stayed with his mother in a little house right by the sea, *Larachbeag* – "The Wee Ruin". Janet let it out to holidaymakers all year, but for the summer it was always let to Tommy's mother, Patricia – I suspect so that I'd have the luxury of a playmate for the whole of my stay. And Tommy was the perfect playmate. He was the same age as me, biddable and always happy to fall in with my games. I'd forgotten about my precocious marriage proposal, but I did remember how I used to look forward to seeing him every summer and how disappointed I was when, at about twelve or thirteen, he lost interest in me and took up climbing and canoeing with local boys. Aunt Janet did her best to compensate and we hiked, picnicked, watched birds and pressed wild flowers. She tried and failed to teach me the piano, but taught me to love gardening by giving me a patch of my own to cultivate and a copy of *The Secret Garden*. In the evenings we played card games and backgammon and took turns reading to each other. Apart from missing Tommy, I was very happy.

Now I was mortified to think I'd forgotten all about him. Since there was no resemblance between young Tommy and his beefy adult incarnation, I supposed I could be forgiven for not recognising him. Nevertheless, I'd sensed something. Eyes don't change. Not much. The squint was gone now, but I'd known those liquid brown eyes with their drooping lids, even though they looked very different on a man.

'Sit down,' I said, indicating the kitchen chairs. 'Let's have some coffee. Or would you prefer tea?'

'Whichever you're making,' he replied, pulling out a chair.

I re-boiled the kettle and set two mugs and the sugar bowl on a tray. As I warmed a jug of milk in the microwave, I cast a sidelong glance in the direction of my visitor, who was removing his jacket and hanging it on the back of his chair. He had a slightly unkempt air. His curly fair hair was rather long and untidy and his face was frosted with golden stubble. I noticed a button hanging by a thread from a shirt that had seen better days and he wore no wedding ring. He screamed "bachelor" to me. Divorced perhaps?

Spooning coffee into the pot, I wondered guiltily if I'd always assessed men in terms of their availability, or was that something that had developed since David died? Did I not look before because I was unavailable? I couldn't remember. It wasn't as if I was actually *looking* now. I just... noticed things.

And what would Tom have seen if he'd scrutinised me in the same way? That chubby little Ruthie Travers had grown tall and slimmed down. That her chestnut hair had dulled a little with age, but as yet showed no grey. If he'd looked closely, Tom might have spotted shadows under her grey eyes and tense lines around her wide mouth, a mouth not quite as ready to smile now as when she was a girl. Adult Ruth was physically fit, yet emotionally frail. Would Tom's intelligent brown eyes have noticed all that?...

'So, should I call you "Tom", then?' I asked, as I poured hot water into the coffee pot.

'That's generally what people call me. You and my mother were the only people allowed to call me Tommy.'

'I forget now – what did Janet call you?'

'Tom. Thomas when she was cross with me.'

'Tricia's well, I hope?'

'She died a few years ago. A stroke.'

'Oh. I'm very sorry to hear that.'

'I gathered from Janet you lost your father earlier this year.'

'Yes. He had a brain tumour.'

Tom winced and said, 'You've had a hell of a year then.'

I decided not to mention David's sudden demise and changed the subject. 'So you've settled on Skye permanently then?'

'Well, it's home for now. Tricia came to live here when I went off to uni. She bought *Larachbeag* from Janet – you remember the house we used to stay in? So I used to come here during the uni holidays. Then when Tricia died, I decided I'd keep the house. It really wasn't worth much, it needed so

14

much doing to it. But it suited me. I'd been working for the Forestry Commission on the mainland and then a job came up here. I applied and I got it, so I moved in. Janet seemed glad to have me around again. She'd taken Tricia's death quite badly. They were good friends.' He paused, then said, 'Sometimes I wonder if they were more than friends.'

'Janet and Tricia?'

'Yes. Why not?' I must have blinked in astonishment because Tom added hurriedly, 'Sorry, I didn't mean to offend you.'

'I'm not in the least offended. Just surprised, that's all. I'd love to think Janet's life wasn't as lonely as I thought.'

'Well, it's just a little theory of mine. They were certainly very close. And I'm damned if I know how Tricia was able to afford to buy *Larachbeag* from Janet. We lived a hand-to-mouth existence. My guess is, Janet gave her the house. So they could be together perhaps, once I was out of the way.'

'How romantic! I hope you're right.'

He shrugged broad shoulders. 'I suppose we'll never know now. But I always wondered about my father. I gathered the marriage was short-lived and unhappy. Tricia said I was the only good thing that came out of it. And that's pretty much all she ever said on the subject.'

I poured two mugs of coffee and set one in front of Tom. 'But that wasn't the "delicate matter" you wanted to discuss, was it?'

'No, there's another one.' He reached into his jacket pocket and pulled out his wallet. 'I want to repay some money I owed Janet.'

'Oh. Well, I think you can forget about it now. Janet's death cleared the debt as far as I'm concerned. Unless...' I looked at him doubtfully. 'Was it a very large amount?'

'No, but I'd rather give it back. And now she's dead, I *can* give it back.'

'Sorry, I don't follow.'

'Janet insisted on continuing to pay my wages after she'd laid me off.'

'Why on earth did she do that?'

'Because she hadn't wanted to fire me, but she thought if

she did, it would get you involved with the garden. Give you a sense of responsibility. Something to do.'

'Well, she was right about that.'

'She thought it would help you cope with losing your father. Obviously she didn't think I'd be laid off for long, so she refused to cancel the standing order. Then she had her fall. And you stayed on. So the money mounted up. And now I'd like to return it. I didn't feel right taking it and I certainly didn't feel right about you not knowing. I thought if you looked at Janet's accounts, you might think I was blackmailing her or something.' He removed a folded cheque from his wallet. 'So who shall I make this out to? You?'

'Tear it up, Tom. Janet obviously wanted you to have the money, so there's no way I'm taking it back. I'm sorry she laid you off, but her instincts were sound. The garden has been a life-saver for me. It's given me a sense of purpose. Something to think about that isn't death-related.'

'Well, perhaps I could donate the money to a charity Janet supported?'

'*No*, she wanted you to have it! And you're not telling me you couldn't use it.' The look he gave me would not have disgraced a kicked puppy. 'Oh – I'm so sorry! That was unforgivably rude of me.'

'That's OK. It's true. I'm self-employed now. Tree surgery, garden maintenance, that sort of thing.' He shrugged those shoulders again, in a gesture that was fast growing on me. 'The money's not good and the work's irregular. So, yes, you're right, Janet's money would come in very handy.'

'Well, I apologise for speaking out of turn. I can see that's going to happen.'

'What's going to happen?'

'I'll slip back into treating you as if we're ten. Don't stand for it. Keep me in line.'

He shook his head and laughed. 'You used to get so mad at me when I called you "Bossy Boots". But, you know, you *were*.'

'Oh, I'm sure. I bet I was insufferable! I can't imagine why you put up with me. No one else to play with, I suppose.'

'Rubbish. We had a brilliant time. And I *liked* being bossed about. It meant I didn't have to think. You were the brains and

16

I was the brawn.'

It was my turn to laugh. 'As I recall, you had arms and legs like pipe cleaners!'

He smiled. 'I suppose I have filled out a bit.'

As he put the cheque back in his wallet, I said, 'If it makes you feel any better, I could use some help in the garden now, so it would actually suit me to re-instate you as Head Gardener.'

His brows lifted and those wide brown eyes met mine with a hint of challenge. 'With you in charge, surely I could only ever be the gardener's boy?'

Did I imagine something speculative there? Was he testing the ground? For what?... Tidying our mugs on to the tray, I reflected that young Tommy Howard had never been this inscrutable. Or attractive.

'Would you like to come back to work here?'

'Very much.'

'Were you happy with your previous terms of employment?'

'Yes. Janet was very generous.'

'Good. Then let me know what those terms were and we'll carry on as before. If you could just keep things ticking over for now – the autumn clear-up, general maintenance. We'll put our heads together next week and come up with a plan for the winter.'

'Are you going to stay on here?'

'I don't really know. I've got a flat in London, but my TV career is stalled, possibly over and I'm having to re-think. You know I did a gardening makeover programme for years?'

'Oh, yes. I used to watch it. You were very popular. And influential. "Delia of the Delphiniums", wasn't it?'

'Oh, please – don't remind me!'

'I was surprised when you were replaced with that other woman.'

'I'd asked to be released. On compassionate grounds. I'd had a very sudden bereavement. Someone close.'

I said no more and sensed Tom was about to ask a question, then I saw him think better of it. He murmured, 'I'm sorry,' and the conversation dangled for a few moments until he said, 'Which agent's coming to value the house?'

I stared at him blankly, then remembered my ruse. 'Oh, I forget which one it is now. Actually, I've no intention of selling up yet. I just want to get the house valued. I can't cope with deciding what to do with all Janet's stuff. It's still too soon.'

'I can understand that. But you'd like me to start work straight away, I imagine? There's always a lot to do at this time of year.'

'If that suits you?'

'Yes, that's fine. Could you let me have my keys back?'

With a jolt I remembered why I'd wanted to talk to "Mr Howard". 'You don't have a set?'

'I used to have a key to the shed and one for the garage. I've never had a key to the house. Never needed one. Janet didn't lock doors. I used to keep the shed and garage locked because they were my responsibility. I wasn't quite as trusting as Janet. I've found tools & machinery have a nasty tendency to go walkabout.'

'Do you know where she put your keys?'

'No idea. But she was a very tidy person, so I'm sure they'll be somewhere sensible, clearly labelled. Janet ran a tight ship.'

'Yes, I know,' I replied, my heart sinking at the thought of her fountain pen and diary lying open on the desk. 'Do you know if anyone else has keys to the house? Did she leave a set with neighbours?'

'She never mentioned it. But she wouldn't necessarily have told me. Are you concerned about security? You don't need to be, you know. There's no crime here to speak of, apart from the odd drunken fight or car smash. Occasionally a bit of vandalism. You're much safer here than on the streets of London. But if you're worried, why not change all the locks?'

'That's a good idea. I hadn't thought of that.'

'Would you like me to do it for you?'

'Oh, that's very kind of you, but—'

He raised a hand in protest. 'My remit was to perform general handyman tasks around the house, as well as garden maintenance. I probably know more about how this house operates than you do.'

That, I realised, was exactly what I'd been afraid of. But clearly, there was nothing to worry about with regard to Tom. He held no grudge and had no reason to. And he was my childhood friend. What possible motive could he have for wanting to frighten me? But if Tom wasn't my intruder, then who was?...

He stood up, surprising me again with his height and said, 'Thanks for the coffee. I could come back on Monday and make a start on the garden.'

'That would be great. I should have found your keys by then.'

'If you're passing, stop by and take a look at *Larachbeag*. I've smartened it up a bit. Well, I had to. It was practically falling down.'

'It always was a bit ramshackle. But that was part of its charm.'

'Charming for kids, maybe. I decided a few more creature comforts wouldn't go amiss.' He sighed. 'Does that mean I'm getting old, I wonder?'

'We're the same age, so I couldn't possibly comment.'

He opened the back door, then suddenly turned round and said, 'By the way, whatever happened to Heckie?'

'*Heckie?* Who was Heckie?'

Tom looked at me, surprised. 'You've forgotten *Heckie*? Poor sod... You women – you're so damn fickle!'

'What on earth are you talking about?'

'Heckie was your friend. Went with you everywhere. Shared our games. And our meals. For all I know, he shared your bed.'

My hand flew to my mouth. 'Oh my God...'

'It's coming back to you now?'

'*Heckie!*'

'Your imaginary friend. Except you swore blind he *wasn't* imaginary, it was just that *I* couldn't see him. You even used to set a place for him at meal-times. You were one weird kid, Ruthie. Sometimes you even had me believing in him.'

'I'd completely forgotten! When did I stop all that?'

'I don't remember. You used to talk about him all the time

19

when we were young. Then I think you started keeping him to yourself. You no longer shared him with me, but I knew you were still thinking about him. *Seeing* him. I think I got a bit jealous. Round about the time I was ten or eleven. Hormones, I suppose. They must have started to kick in then. I dismissed you as a crazy girl who imagined things. But *that* was why your games were so good. You made it all real. Because for you, it was.'

'You killed him.'

'*What?*'

'You killed Heckie. Well, you said you did. We had a terrible fight – I can't remember what it was about – and you said you'd *killed* him. You said you'd stolen a knife from the kitchen and stabbed him.'

'*Did* I?'

'Yes. I was beside myself. Completely hysterical. I said I hated you and never wanted to play with you ever again.'

'You really believed me?'

'Of course I did! Heckie was real to me, so why shouldn't he be dead?'

'But... didn't you see him again after that?'

'No. It was as if he really *had* died. God, I can't believe I'd forgotten all that! At the time, it was as if I'd lost my mother all over again.'

'Jesus, I'd no idea. Well, for what it's worth, I'm really sorry. I was just jealous, I suppose. You had so much that I didn't. You even had invisible friends.'

'Oh, don't be sorry! We were just kids with overactive imaginations.'

'Maybe. But it must have been bad for you if you blotted it all out afterwards.'

'I suppose so.'

'Poor old Heckie,' Tom said, thoughtfully. 'Was that short for Hector?'

'I don't know... He never said,' I added solemnly.

Tom looked at me, open-mouthed, then burst out laughing. 'OK, you had me there for a minute! Look, I'd better be on my way. If you have any problems or need help of any kind, just give me a call. If I can't sort it out, I'll know someone who can.'

'Thanks. That's very kind of you.'

We stood facing each other and I could tell he was thinking whether to kiss me goodbye. I saw his body lean in toward me for a moment, then he seemed to change his mind. Standing in the doorway, he turned toward the garden and said with a contented sigh, 'You know, I really love this place. If it was mine, I could never bear to part with it.' He turned his head and said over his shoulder, 'It is yours, I suppose?'

'Yes. Janet said she'd leave everything to me apart from some small bequests to friends. She had no other family. Her brother died of scarlet fever when he was a child and her sister, Kathleen – that was my mother – died in 1976. I think it must have been quite a lonely old age.'

'Unless, of course, I'm right about my mother. Let's hope so, for both their sakes.' He looked down at me, then bent his head and kissed me on the cheek. 'Bye, Ruth. It's been great to catch up. I'll see you Monday.'

'Bye. It's been good to see you again.'

It was one of those beautiful October days with a cloudless Mediterranean blue sky, the kind you rarely see in the Highlands, even in summer. As I watched Tom stride along the path, covering the ground quickly with his long legs, the autumn sun burnished his hair so it glowed like old gold. Beyond him, the limes, yellows and russets of the turning leaves formed a glorious patchwork backcloth. As I watched him go, feeling an odd mix of pleasure and pain, I saw something move quickly in a thicket of shrubs and trees. A reddish-brown shape that almost blended with the decaying foliage, but which moved through it easily, as if branch and trunk offered no impediment. A red squirrel? Of course. What else was that distinctive auburn colour?

Tom turned the corner, which took him out of sight, so I closed the back door and turned the key.

As I was putting the coffee mugs into the dishwasher, it suddenly occurred to me that there are no red squirrels on Skye, only grey. Whatever it was I'd seen moving through the shrubbery – at about head height, now I came to think about it – it wasn't a squirrel.

Chapter Three

After Tom had gone, I went upstairs, threw myself on the bed and indulged in a shameful bout of self-pity, during which I got through half a box of tissues. I hadn't really cried since Janet's funeral, so it was perhaps overdue, but I wasn't crying for Janet. Well, not just Janet. I was crying because I missed them all *terribly*. Janet, David, the father who'd never really wanted to know me and the mother I could hardly remember. And now I'd remembered him, I missed Tommy, my childhood friend. That scruffy, skinny kid who – until puberty distorted his judgement – thought all my ideas were good ones and who hung on my every word.

Maybe it wasn't Tommy I missed. Maybe it was Heckie. Or just my childhood self, the self who could forget loss and loneliness collecting the fluffy heads of bog myrtle to stuff dolls' pillows; who thought sunflower seeds were magic because something taller than a man lived inside, waiting to spring to life. Just add water. The water of life... *Uisge beathe*...

That's what I needed. Whisky.

I peeled myself off the bed, filled the waste paper bin with sodden tissues and headed downstairs in search of a bottle of Janet's Talisker. It was something of an acquired taste, but I was bent on acquiring it. The only whisky distilled on Skye wasn't cheap and my aunt – optimistic soul – had died with five bottles in stock. I hoped Tom liked Talisker. I didn't propose to get through it all on my own.

I went down to the sitting room and poured myself a dram, registering that this was my second strong drink of the day and it wasn't yet four o' clock. Island-itis was getting to me already. But the circumstances were exceptional: a possible intruder and an unexpected reunion with a cherished childhood companion. This wasn't just *any* old Thursday.

I switched on my laptop and made myself comfortable in an armchair by the French windows. The light was starting to fade now, but I surveyed the garden, hoping to spot my mystery bird or mammal (a pine marten?), but nothing moved apart from the wind and the dying leaves as they abandoned their struggle to cling to life and fluttered, vividly, to the ground.

I turned my gaze back to my laptop and studied my Inbox. Athelstan again. The guy didn't give up easily, I'll say that for him.

Dr Athelstan Blake was a musicologist at Toronto University. He was writing to tell me he'd had second thoughts about his proposed book on female composers. He said the interest occasioned by my aunt's demise had made him realise Janet Gillespie merited a book to herself, in which gender issues in music could be raised without undermining her standing as an important composer, not just a *female* composer.

'Now you're talking, Athelstan,' I said, raising my glass to the newly enlightened Canadian.

The rest of his email consisted of the same old request: could he come (at my convenience) and sift through Janet's manuscripts, letters, cuttings, photos, etc? I emailed back, with possibly more enthusiasm than prudence. (All I'd consumed since breakfast was brandy, coffee, then whisky, so I was feeling a bit light-headed.) I informed Dr Blake that I felt sure Janet would have approved of his planned study and that I would – eventually – do my best to co-operate, but it was still far too soon for me to make the archive available to him, so I would be in touch at a later date. That seemed a tad discouraging, so to make the old boy's day, I added a PS saying, if he'd like to give me some indication of his interests, I would be happy to enter into preliminary email correspondence.

Well, I thought that was handsome. If he sent me a list of questions or research topics, it would motivate me to make a start on clearing out the music room and then the house. Once that was done I could go back to London and resume my life. What was left of it.

Gloom threatened to descend again, so I went to the kitchen and threw together a cheese omelette. As I ate, I stared at the chair Tom had sat in and thought how nice it would be not to have to eat alone... Maybe I should invite him for dinner. No, *supper*. That sounded more casual. Because it *was* casual. I might be lonely, but I wasn't desperate. It would just be nice to spend an evening in a man's company, chatting. And there was a lot we could chat about, apart from our childhood. The garden, of course, and what to do about the house. As a local, Tom's advice would be invaluable.

So that settled it. I would invite him to supper.

After I'd tidied the kitchen, I sat slumped in front of the TV, conscious I wasn't taking in a word. Eventually it dawned on me, this was because the programme was in Gaelic. I couldn't even summon the energy to change channels, so I decided it was time for bed.

I dreamed of sex and death. I woke in the early hours, more exhausted than when I'd turned in. Nightmares were normal for me. I'd witnessed the passing of three loved ones in the last nine months. I coped pretty well during the day, keeping negative thoughts on a tight leash, but when I slept, my subconscious took its revenge and I often woke feeling wrecked.

I'd woken in a sweat, with my heart thumping, but this time I was pretty sure my racing pulse had little to do with fear. As I surfaced, I tried to analyse the confused elements of my dream. Tom Howard's face was the first to be identified. So was his body. Flushed with embarrassment, I sat up in bed and turned on the light. The alarm said 04.10. I reached for the glass of water on my bedside table and gulped it down. Feeling slightly calmer and cooler, I turned off the light and lay down again.

I know I didn't dream it because there wasn't time to fall asleep. In fact when I first heard the noise, I assumed *I* was making it, fidgeting about in the creaky double bed. But after I'd been lying still for a minute or two, willing myself to go back to sleep, I heard the noise again. A dragging sound. As if furniture was being moved. Slowly.

I switched the light on again, sat up and listened.

It's at times like these that you wish for noisy neighbours. Someone to blame. This wasn't mice. Or rats. Or bats. It wasn't an owl in the roof. The noise was coming from outside my room.

Burglars? Well, if it was, they'd been extremely clever getting in through locked doors and windows, which I'd double-checked before going to bed. And if they'd broken in through the back door, they'd somehow avoided triggering my improvised alarm, which consisted of a pile of baking trays and cake tins piled on top of each other in a cunning Leaning Tower of Pisa construction, designed to collapse noisily if the door opened.

Would burglars who'd managed to sidestep a DIY alarm system drag furniture about? Was I being burgled by Pickfords? And what could they be looking for? Janet's valuables were helpfully in all the obvious places: her desk and jewellery box and the silver was still in the sideboard.

I'd like to pretend I was brave; that, like Jane Eyre, I threw a shawl around my shoulders and ventured out into the corridor, ready to do battle with a madwoman, but the truth was, I needed to pee. I'd had too much excitement for one night, both at the conscious and the subconscious levels and I needed the loo. So, as I got out of bed and pushed my feet into my slippers, I told myself I was just suffering from stress. Or tinnitus. Or hallucinations. And if I didn't get a move on, I'd soon be suffering from incontinence.

As I emerged from my bedroom into the hall, I saw a pale figure standing at the end of the corridor. I let out a scream guaranteed to drive any burglars from the premises, not to mention owls, rats and bats. I clutched at the door handle for support. As I did so, the ghost copied my movements *exactly*.

I was staring at my own reflection in the huge mirrored wardrobe at the end of the corridor.

My subsequent laughter was a touch hysterical. By now any self-respecting burglar must have assumed there was a maniac on the loose and scarpered, so I dived into the loo opposite my bedroom and luxuriated in an all-pervading sense of relief.

I was back in bed, assuring myself the strange noise had been caused by *Tigh-na-Linne*'s ancient plumbing, when it started up again. Something heavy was being moved an inch at a time. At least that's what it sounded like.

I switched the light on again and my eye fell on my mobile. I could ring Tom. Then what? Ask him to come round in the middle of the night? Just because I could hear a peculiar noise? And supposing he got the wrong idea? I remembered my dream and blushed.

I decided I had to cope alone. Again, this wasn't bravery. I just wasn't prepared to let Tom see me in my shapeless fleece pyjamas. Nor was I prepared to change into something more flattering. And just how terrified could I be if I was considering this sartorial point? Mad, possibly; terrified, definitely not. Misery makes you reckless, but it can also make you brave. I'd lost my lover, my father and my beloved aunt. Two out of three had expired in my arms. As long as something *living* was making that damn noise, I didn't care what it was.

I threw back the bedclothes and got out of bed again. It had to be a rat. Or a squirrel. Or a pine marten. I didn't care if it was the Hound of the bloody Baskervilles, I needed to get some *sleep*. I strode over to the bedroom door, flung it open, stepped in to the hall and switched on the light.

The wardrobe had moved.

I knew it had moved because I wasn't in the same position. I mean, my *reflection* wasn't in the same position. The mirror had moved. It had moved because the wardrobe had moved.

I don't remember deciding to walk along the corridor. It was as if I was being drawn. My feet seemed to have a will of their own and they took me toward the wardrobe. I stood in front of my own reflection, white-faced and open-mouthed. The wardrobe was a massive Victorian double-fronted affair and it would have taken several men to move it, but it was now no longer parallel to the wall. It had been pulled out a few inches on one side, away from the wall. I couldn't see what, if anything, was behind because the wardrobe filled the short wall, being as wide as the passageway itself.

Then I noticed the smell. A garden smell, not unpleasant. Damp earth... Rotting vegetation... Then something else. *Not* a garden smell. Not an outdoor smell at all. And not pleasant.

Something made me look down. At this end of the corridor the light was dim, but I could see there were marks on the polished wooden floorboards. I knelt to examine them and found a patch of what appeared to be mud. Beside it were drops of something dark and liquid, a spillage of some kind. I stood up and reached for the switch on a table lamp nearby. Blinking in the light, I turned back to the marks on the floor.

There's nothing else that looks like blood, is there? Claret doesn't, nor does Ribena. And red ink is too bright. The only thing that looks like blood, is blood.

This was blood.

I opened my mouth to scream, but nothing came out.

And then I fainted.

I woke up in bed, with a pounding head, as if I had a hangover. (Talisker was heady stuff, but one little glass?) It was beginning to get light and I lay there, trying to remember The Awful Thing that had happened last night. There *had* been an awful thing, hadn't there? Or was it just one of my nightmares?

So far, I couldn't remember any details, but I had that sickening sense of dread I used to have as a child, the fear that something not very nice was lurking outside the bedroom door and might try to come in. Heckie had been good for that. Obliging chap, he'd spend the night on duty at my door, like a guard dog, making sure I came to no harm. As details began to emerge from the foggy depths of my memory (dragging noises... mud... blood... Oh my god, *blood*?), it struck me, I could do with Heckie now.

Obviously, I told myself, as I struggled out of bed, it had all been a very bad dream and I should avoid the cheese/Talisker combo in future. The bedclothes were proving intractable for some reason and I had to kick at them to free my legs, so I could get out of bed. I groped with my toes for my slippers but couldn't locate them, so I stood up and bent to look for them.

They were the wrong way round. My slippers were placed, side-by-side, with military precision, well under the bed. I had no idea how they could have got there. I always let my slippers fall off my feet as I sit on the bed and I leave them there, ready for me to slide my feet into in the morning with minimal effort. I can do it with my eyes closed and frequently do. I would *never* put my slippers neatly side by side, the wrong way round. That's what other people do when they tidy up after you.

I wasn't liking this train of thought.

Somewhat agitated now, I looked round the room. I didn't see anything suspicious until I looked back at the bed. Uncomfortable with the constriction of Janet's cotton sheets and blankets, I always slept with them loose, like a duvet, but now the bedclothes were *tucked in*. Tucked in all the way round, except where I'd got out of bed.

I backed away from the bed and sank onto a chair. What exactly had happened last night?... The last thing I remembered was seeing drops of something that looked like blood and then everything going black. But if someone had picked me up, carried me back to bed, tucked me in, then tidied my slippers away under the bed, *this* would be the result.

The other, much simpler explanation was, I was losing my mind.

The truth of the matter was easily ascertained by venturing into the corridor now and examining the floorboards in question. So I put on my dressing gown, doing up all the buttons *and* the belt as a delaying tactic, then I flung the bedroom door wide and sallied forth. I might possibly have been humming.

There was, of course, no blood.

Nor was there any mud.

But the wardrobe was still in its new position.

Breakfast was a cup of tea and two paracetamol. It was all I could face. When I thought it was a respectable hour to call, I rang Tom and said with studied casualness, 'Hi, Tom, It's Ruth. Sorry to bother you. I've got a rather strange query about furniture. Have you got a minute?'

'Of course. What's the problem?'

'Well, I'm not sure it's a problem, exactly. Not yet. I'm just curious. How well do you know the inside of this house?'

'Pretty well, I suppose.'

'Upstairs?'

'Well, I've been up there a few times doing jobs for Janet. And I've been in the loft.'

'Do you remember a double-fronted mahogany wardrobe in the passageway upstairs?'

'The one that would take a rugby team to move it?'

There was a brief pause in which I struggled to regain my composure. 'Yes, that's the one. Do you happen to know if there's anything behind it? Anything important I mean. A safe? A secret passage? Priest's hole, that sort of thing?'

'No, there isn't. It's an external wall.'

'Oh.'

'There's just a window behind it.'

'Really? I don't remember seeing that from outside.'

'You wouldn't. A dirty great rowan tree has grown up in front of it. That was on my list of things to discuss with Janet, but then she had her fall. The rowan's far too close to the house. It'll be damaging the foundations.'

'I see.'

'Ruth, is something wrong? You sound worried.'

'No, it's nothing! It was just that... well, I was thinking about getting rid of that wardrobe. It's a real eyesore and it takes up so much room. If there's a window behind it, then so much the better. That area could do with more light.'

'Ah, but that's the thing, you see. That's why Janet had the wardrobe put there.'

'I don't follow.'

'It's not an ordinary window.'

'What do you mean?'

'Well, I've never actually seen it, Janet just told me about it. But surely *you* must remember it from when you stayed there as a child? It's stained glass, apparently.'

'I don't *think* I remember it. Did Janet ever say why she'd covered it up?'

'No. Just that it was gloomy. And she didn't want to be brooding about dead people all the time.'

'*Dead* people?' I asked, in a very small voice.

'Yes. It's a memorial window. There were three originally. One for each son who fell in the Great War. One of the windows was badly damaged in a storm and another got taken out when Janet had the conservatory built. But there's one left. It's behind that wardrobe.'

First of all, I tried to sell it. I rang some dealers and told them I had a Victorian double-fronted wardrobe in good condition and would they like to come and value it? Then I told them it was on the Isle of Skye. Assurances that Skye had long been connected to the mainland by a bridge made little impression. Their response remained cool. Just the one piece?... They were sorry, it wasn't worth their time and petrol... The market for Victoriana was very slow... Nobody had room for big pieces nowadays and what with the recession...

It was the same with every dealer I spoke to. After that I tried giving the wardrobe away. Tom put the word out on the Skye jungle drums that the piece was free to anyone who was prepared to take it away.

No response.

Then I rang the charity shops in Inverness and Fort William and asked if they could relieve me of my white elephant, or if they knew someone who would? I drew another blank. One enterprising soul suggested I put it on eBay, but I said I was in a hurry. I wanted the piece out of the house as soon as possible.

I didn't tell her why.

Tom obliged me by cutting down the rowan tree that was obscuring the memorial window from outside. This proved to be vastly entertaining. He chose a fine day for the job, so I had a good excuse to sit outside on a bench, swaddled in a big scarf and jumper, while I enjoyed the last of the autumn sunshine and Tom's lumberjack cabaret.

Despite his plastic goggles, he looked awesomely macho, perched in the tree like Tarzan, dealing death to the old rowan with his chainsaw. Gradually, as branches fell, the house wall and then the window itself emerged. We could now see how big it was, but, as stained glass is colourless and dark from the outside, we could discern no clear picture.

When he'd finished, we stood under the window beside the sad stump of rowan. Removing his goggles, Tom said, 'You're sure you don't remember it from when you were a kid?'

'Yes, I'm sure.'

'But then, *you* forgot Heckie,' he said reproachfully.

'No. Heckie forgot *me*.'

We contemplated the mutilated corpse of the tree, spread across the lawn. It now took up much more space than when it was upright.

Tom kicked a log. 'Shall I cut this lot up for firewood?'

'I've got a log splitter. And I know how to use it.'

'Quicker with the saw. And easier. You won't be able to use the logs this year, but we could stack them to dry. Or if you don't want them, I can take them away. I've got a wood-burner. So's my neighbour.'

I hesitated. I felt bad enough about chopping the tree down, even though Tom had convinced me it was damaging the house. For purely sentimental reasons, I was reluctant to give the wood away, but it was unlikely I'd ever use it as fuel. Even if, in my most optimistic moments, I dreamed of keeping on *Tigh-na-Linne* as a holiday home, I knew I'd never stay here in winter.

'Leave me half,' I said finally. 'Take the rest away, but leave me some for old times' sake. I'll feel less guilty about the rowan if I think I'm going to recycle some of it.'

So while I stood and watched, Tom reduced the mountain of branches and trunk to a much smaller mountain of logs. The sun was higher now and he'd removed his thick work shirt. Sweat was beginning to show through his short-sleeved

T-shirt. I sat, frankly entranced, for there was much to admire: the breeze lifting his sun-gilded curls, now darkened with sweat; the play of light and shadow on the muscles of his bare arms; the springy agility of his long limbs as he moved nimbly round tree trunk and branch. Arboricultural porn... Don't knock it till you've tried it.

Dragging myself away, I went indoors and made some coffee. Remembering the sweat Tom had worked up, I placed a glass and a carton of apple juice on the tray, then added a tin of biscuits. It wasn't really warm enough to picnic outside, but I was reluctant to sit indoors on such a fine day and Tom was clearly the hardy type.

I took the tray outside. When there was a lull in the whining of the chain saw, I called out, 'Coffee? Or there's juice if you're thirsty.'

He switched off the chain-saw and removed his goggles. When he arrived beside me, I stared at his damp face and arms.

'You're covered in sawdust!'

'Unavoidable by-product of felling trees,' he replied lifting the glass of juice.

'Do you want to have a shower here when you've finished? You must be *so* uncomfortable! And I hate to think of you getting any in your eyes.'

'I'm used to it,' he replied, helping himself to a biscuit. 'If it was a bit earlier in the year, I'd go and jump in the sea. But maybe not today.' He finished his juice, then started on his mug of coffee. 'Ruth, about that wardrobe...'

'What about it?'

'Well, don't shoot me down in flames, but I have a suggestion.'

'What's that?'

'Let me dismantle it.'

I must have flinched in horror because he laughed, then laid a hand on my shoulder. I could feel the heat of his big hand through my sweater.

'I know it seems wicked,' he continued, 'but the wood wouldn't be wasted. You could keep the mirror and hang it on a wall. It might look good in one of the bathrooms. The rest could be re-cycled. I know a good joiner who'd make you a superb bookcase out of that wood.'

'But... it's so *old*.'

'And so in the way.'

'It's a genuine antique!' I protested.

'And genuinely hideous. What's more to the point, it takes up a lot of space in front of a period window. You can't re-locate it because there's nowhere to move it to. Plus we'd need a team of men to move it. Unless you can persuade the buyer to keep it, you'll have to get rid of it when you sell.'

'I know.'

'Look, think of it this way: in terms of selling the house, that wardrobe won't do you any favours, but the window *might*. The hall will be lighter, even if the window's an eyesore. And it must have some historic value, I suppose, if it's in good condition. Perhaps you could remove it and sell it to a specialist dealer. A window's much more portable – and saleable – than that brute of a wardrobe.'

I tilted my head to one side and looked at him. 'You really don't like it, do you?'

He grinned. 'I'm just worried you're going to ask me to move it to some other part of the house.'

'No, I think you're just a wrecker at heart. I was watching you dismember that tree.'

'You were, weren't you?' Now it was his turn to treat me to an appraising look. 'Hope you enjoyed the show.' My mouth opened, then shut again, in what must have been a thoroughly unattractive fashion. Tom seemed to savour my confusion for a moment, then continued. 'Destruction can be exciting, but I prefer planting things to chopping them down. Both are necessary though. Dead wood has to be cut away, so something new can grow in its place. You know that. You're a gardener. That wardrobe is dead wood, Ruth. Let it go.'

I sighed and said, 'OK. Do your worst. But I want to keep the mirror. And be careful of the window, won't you? If we damaged that, I don't think Janet would ever forgive me.'

'She's dead, Ruth!'

'You don't need to tell *me* that!' I snapped, blinking back tears.

Tom bowed his head. 'Sorry. That was a really stupid thing to say.' Exasperated, he ran a hand through his hair, shedding sawdust. 'I'm getting out of line. We're employer/employee now, not ten-year old playmates.'

'We're *both*,' I said gently.

'Yes, we are.' That look again from those dark eyes, a look that seemed to be both invitation and warning. 'Maybe we could be more.'

'Oh, Tom - let's not complicate things!' Then, already regretting my brush-off, I laid my hand on his bare forearm, dislodging more sawdust. 'Not yet anyway.'

'Whatever you say, Ruth. You're the boss.'

Chapter Four

Dr Athelstan Blake began to nag me – in the nicest possible way – about Janet's papers. I suppose he found it hard to believe the world wasn't waiting impatiently for his book to be published. Even in his emails, his excitement and enthusiasm for his subject was palpable.

Dear Ms Travers

In your last email you were good enough to suggest we might correspond on the subject of my research into your aunt's musical output. I was wondering if you could give me any preliminary pointers regarding the great change in style that occurred some time after she returned home to Skye. (1956?) It's been assumed that the island itself proved inspirational, but in my view, her compositions don't actually show any marked change until she'd been living there for a couple of years. This development occurs some time after the final illness and death of her father (although there may, of course, be no connection between her loss and the radical change in her work.)

Although it's been assumed Skye was the source of her inspiration, the music of this period is very personal, by which I mean, it's about *people* and much of it is written for the voice. This is not at all what I would expect from a composer inspired by their rugged native *landscape.*

It's this "personal" characteristic that has, I fear, led to some critics' dismissal of Janet Gillespie's work as "domestic". This in turn has led to her being viewed primarily as a *female* composer (which we both believe has done your aunt a great disservice!) Sadly, the world of classical music is shamefully misogynist and inclined to downgrade – sometimes ignore – female composers.

When you eventually go through your aunt's papers, it would be very helpful if you could sort the manuscripts, letters, diaries, etc. into two categories:

1. Those written before her father died, i.e. pre-1958.
2. Those written afterwards.

There's a period of a year or so when Janet (I hope I may refer to your aunt as Janet?) composed nothing at all (at least, as far as I'm aware.) This coincides with the deterioration of her father's health, his death and the period in which she had to adjust to living alone at *Tigh-na-Linne*.

After this "sabbatical", there followed an outpouring of very different work, some of it brilliant, much of it pre-occupied with death and indeed with men. Yet Janet never married, nor was her name ever linked romantically with anyone else's. I have no wish to pry, Ms Travers, but if you have any information about your aunt's personal relationships, it might enable me to interpret her musical output more accurately. In particular, I've long been curious as to the identity of "Frieda", to whom the first song cycle, *In Memoriam* (1959) is dedicated. You will remember that the songs portray an ardent young man addressing his distant beloved. A familiar enough theme, but the fact that Janet dedicated the cycle to an unknown *woman* has given rise to speculation.

I fear I'm over-burdening you with my enquiries, but if you should have time to address any of these issues (particularly the stylistic

In the light of what Tom had told me about the close friendship between Janet and his mother, it seemed possible that the speculation about Janet's love life might have some foundation. But Frieda could not have been a code name for Tricia. As far as I knew, Janet hadn't met Tricia before those idyllic summer holidays in the seventies and eighties and *In Memoriam* was written many years earlier.

Athelstan's request to sort Janet's papers chronologically was a reasonable one and something within my capabilities. Given Janet's obsession with order, it seemed likely she'd have dated everything. Perhaps she'd even filed it all away in date order. Then I remembered I'd dropped a load of her work on the floor when I registered the state of her piano. I hadn't been in to the room since and those papers would still be on the floor where I'd left them.

Or I *hoped* they would.

I postponed tackling the big sort-out until a day when Tom was in the house, upstairs dismantling the wardrobe. I'd found his presence companionable and generally reassuring, except when I became aware of a certain tension between us, which I suspected was sexual on both sides, but we knew each other both too well and not nearly well enough to do anything about it. I didn't examine what I felt about Tom, I simply gave myself a variety of reasons for not getting involved.

I was too busy. It was too soon after David's death. I wasn't that attracted to him. It would complicate our working relationship.

But only the last of these was true.

Yes, I was busy during the day, tidying the garden, sorting through Janet's possessions and dealing with correspondence, but my evenings were lonely and usually entailed falling asleep over a book or in front of the TV. Naps in the evening meant I then found it hard to sleep at nights. Whenever I heard (or imagined) noises, I would lie in bed thinking of Tom and how much safer I'd feel with a big, capable man in the room. Or in the bed. Then once I'd started to think about him, it became quite hard to get him out of my mind, especially as I wasn't entirely sure I *wanted* him out of my mind. Or my bed.

It certainly wasn't too soon after David's death. Before it ended, that relationship had dwindled into a comfortable friendship. Our lovemaking was no longer passionate, nor all that frequent and I'd decided I was too young at forty-two to settle for the cosy slippers-by-the-fire scenario which seemed to suit David.

Nor was it true to say I wasn't attracted to Tom. I was. But only in a physical way. Because I'd known him as a boy, I felt as if I must know him as a man, but the fact was, I didn't. I didn't know if he'd ever been married, or why he was unattached. I didn't know much about his relationship with Janet, nor who his friends were. Tom was an unknown quantity, but also a solid, physical presence around the house and garden, capable and self-contained, all of which appealed to me in my emotionally exhausted state. But now was not the time to rush in to a new relationship with a man I hardly knew. Especially as I paid his wages.

So while Tom dismantled the wardrobe, I found three cardboard boxes and labelled them "Pre-1958", "Post-1958" and "Unknown." I entered the music room with a certain amount of trepidation, but I could hear Tom at work upstairs. (The sound of him swearing was particularly comforting.)

The grand piano was still closed and Janet's archive was still on the floor.

So far, so good.

I collected up the papers and piled them on top of the piano and began to sort. As I expected, everything was dated clearly, apart from a few odd sheets and scrappy notes that had to be consigned to the "Unknown" box. Most of it went into the "Post-1958" box. Janet had destroyed some of her early compositions, but the majority of her output dated from her years on Skye, so that box filled up quickly.

I was only examining the work for dates, but as I sorted the documents, I couldn't help noticing that the original autograph manuscripts that Janet had preserved seemed to be the product of three different hands. Intrigued, I arranged the papers in date order and made an extraordinary discovery. Uncertain of the implications, I emailed Athelstan straight away.

Dear Athelstan

You'll be pleased to know I've sorted Janet's archive as you requested. Almost everything was clearly dated and in most cases she'd also made a note of where the work was done. However, as I was sorting through, I noticed something strange. I'm not a musician and I don't really understand how musical manuscripts are produced, but I thought it rather odd that Janet's hand-written manuscripts appear to be written in three different hands. I wasn't aware she employed a copyist or amanuensis, but in any case, to my inexpert mind, the copied work doesn't add up. The earliest piece written on Skye (*In Memoriam*) exists in two versions, in two different hands:

1. Untidy, with many alterations, obviously written in a hurry, in the heat of the creative moment. This version is undated.
2. Neatly written, with almost no corrections. Dated.

Doesn't this suggest that the work was written, revised later and then copied out? But the really odd thing is, the fair copy is in Janet's hand, but the rough draft isn't. Shouldn't it be the other way round?

Later work produced on Skye is in yet another hand. The rough drafts are clearly in Janet's hand and the final versions are in another hand – but <u>not</u> the hand in which *In Memoriam* was drafted.

39

All very puzzling!

Best wishes

Ruth

P.S. I have no idea who "Frieda" was, or if my aunt was a lesbian. I think she could have been.

The speed with which Athelstan responded suggested he was under-employed at the University of Toronto.

Dear Ruth

This is extremely interesting and may have far-reaching implications! Thank you for sharing your observations.

Your assumptions are correct. If someone had copied out Janet's work, the final version might not be in her hand. It's difficult to see why an early draft wouldn't be hers. Are you convinced both scripts are different? Is it possible Janet injured her hand and this affected how she wrote? Was she arthritic?

I wonder, could I ask you to scan and email me some sample pages of manuscript? Close examination of the pages will reveal whether they're written by the same person. Composers have a very individual way of writing notes on the stave.

Many thanks!

Stan

I'd scanned some sample sheets and was emailing them when there was a light tap and Tom's head appeared round the study door.
    'Do you want to come and have a look?'
    'Have you finished?'

'Well, I haven't cleared the bits of wood away, but they're all stacked up in the hall. Apart from the mirror. I've propped that up in your bedroom. Thought that would be the safest place to put it for now. Oh – and I found this.' He handed me a small wooden casket, about half the size of a shoebox. 'It was inside the wardrobe. You must have missed it when you were clearing out.'

'Oh. Thanks.' I tried to lift the lid, but it was locked. I set the box down on the desk. 'Let's have a look at this window then.'

Tom followed me upstairs. When I got to the landing, I looked along the corridor toward the window. I stopped dead and Tom bumped into me. He apologised, but I didn't respond, I just stood there transfixed. Then I began to walk forward, approaching the window.

It took up much of the end wall. It was a bright day and the stained glass threw coloured shadows on to the walls and floor. The hall now seemed full of reds, greens and blues, a kaleidoscope of coloured light, from which a person began to emerge. A man... Or an angel.

The figure was roughly life-size, but no bigger than me. His slim, neat body was draped to the knee in folds of white fabric over which he wore a metal breastplate, so he appeared to be both angel and warrior. At his feet lay the contorted corpse of some mythical beast, half-snake, half-dragon. Its blue and turquoise scales cast sea-green shadows on to the floorboards below. Death had been dealt to the creature by a spear that the angel-warrior held aloft, as if he'd just extracted it from the beast's body and might be about to plunge it in again. The angel's pale face wore a look of solemn concentration. The battle was over, but not the war.

Where they were exposed, the angel's limbs were slim, white, and muscular, his sandaled feet beautifully formed, as were his hands: the one clutching the shaft of his spear, the other resting on the hilt of a sword hanging at his hip.

His face was thin, gaunt almost, and there were hollows under his eyes and cheekbones, as if his face had been stripped back to its essence of muscle, tendon and bone. His eyes were watchful and gazed at something above and

41

beyond me, something in the distance for which he was preparing. Danger?... Evil, perhaps.

Behind him stood trees, the same birch and alder trees to be found in the grounds of *Tigh-na-Linne*, all in exuberant green leaf, celebrating the arrival of spring and the renewal of life, while death, in the hideous form of the serpent, lay sprawled at their feet. I could almost imagine a gentle breeze rustling through those glass leaves and lifting the auburn hair of the angel warrior. Sunlight streamed through his fiery glass locks and cast a russet shadow on the wooden floor, the floor where I'd seen mud and blood.

Beneath the vanquished serpent, there was a scroll which said, "O grave, where is thy victory?" At the very foot of the window there was a small panel of glass inscribed thus: "In loving memory of James, eldest son of James and Agnes Munro, who died at Loos 25th Sept. 1915, aged 35."

I found myself quite unable to speak. Behind me, I sensed Tom shifting from one foot to the other, then he moved forward, turning to look at me as I studied the window.

'You OK, Ruthie? You're very pale. You look as if you've seen a ghost!'

'Do I?' My voice startled me, as if it had come from some other throat, not mine. 'No, I'm fine... It's just that – well, it's very moving, isn't it? He must have died in France. At Loos. Thousands of Scots died in that battle. And his poor parents tried to preserve something of him. As the archangel Michael, slaying a demon. Satan, I suppose... Or the Hun.'

'Ruth—' Tom laid a hand on my arm and I recoiled, startled by his touch. Just then the sun must have gone behind a cloud because the coloured shadows on the walls faded, then disappeared and the glass figure became dull, his flaming hair now only a deep golden brown.

'I'm fine, Tom. I just need—' I struggled to find the words. *Any* words. 'What I need is to go and make us a cup of tea. Do you think you could clear all the wood away from the walls and stack it in the garage? Anywhere you like, really. I don't care.' I turned back to the window. 'But I'd like to be able to look without distractions. And I think the hall should be cleared.' I gestured toward the glass angel. 'As a mark of respect. Would you mind?'

'I was going to clear away anyway. I just thought you'd be curious to see the window straight away.'

'Yes. I was. Thanks... *Tea*.' I replied, uttering the syllables in a robotic monotone. 'That's what we both need. I'll go and make us some tea. Won't be long.'

Without waiting for a reply, I turned and marched along the hall, down the stairs and into the kitchen where I shut the door and leaned against it, my chest heaving, my throat constricted with unshed tears.

Tears of recognition.

For I'd just come face to face with Heckie.

Chapter Five

You thought Heckie was a *boy*?

If you wanted someone to protect you from demons and dragons and things that go bump in the night, or if you wanted someone to hold your hand while you buried your face in the pillow so no one heard you cry (because you weren't supposed to know your mother was dying), would you choose a boy to do it? A kid to look after another kid? Of course not.

Looking after me was a man's job.

The kitchen door swung open and almost knocked me off my feet. Tom's bulky frame appeared in the doorway and I was momentarily confused. I realised I'd been expecting Heckie.

'Ruth, do you want me to put—' He broke off and stared. 'Hey, are you all right? You'd better sit down.' He pulled out a kitchen chair and, taking my arm, guided me toward the table. He then strode across to the sink, filled the kettle and switched it on. Just watching Tom, busy and capable, made me feel better. And a bit more sane.

He came back and crouched in front of me, so I had the unfamiliar experience of looking down at him. His untidy blond hair looked inviting and I found myself curbing an impulse to touch.

'What's up?' he asked gently. When I didn't answer straight away, he said, 'It's that bloody window, isn't it? It's really upset you. Why?'

'I don't know. It's just... well, it's so *sad*.'

'Who was he, this James Munro? Some relation?'

I looked into Tom's eyes, searching for something – I'm not sure what – and then I made my decision. I couldn't risk it. He'd never believed in Heckie anyway.

'He was Janet's uncle. I suppose that makes him my great uncle... His brothers died too. Two of them. In the war... Their poor mother! What she must have gone through, losing three sons. It's unimaginable.'

The kettle came to the boil and Tom sprang up and started to make tea. The silence was soothing, yet companionable. Setting a mug in front of me, he sat down on the opposite side of the table. He watched me for a moment, then said carefully, 'Is there anything else I can do for you?'

Why did Tom's questions always sound loaded? Was it his tone of voice, or the unblinking, direct look that accompanied them? Yet again, I was feeling that pull, something that had nothing to do with my brain, just an impulse to lean forward and touch. *Be* touched.

As if he'd read my mind, he reached across the table and took my hand. 'It all happened a very long time ago, Ruth. No use brooding about it now. The poor sod's been dead for ninety-five years.'

'Yes. I suppose he has.' I extracted my hand and picked up my mug. Sipping my tea, I decided I should keep busy. 'I think I'll carry on sorting through Janet's papers. There's an awful lot to get through. Thanks for the tea.' As I stood up, my chair scraped on the quarry tiles. The sound was harsh. Ugly. I'd noticed noise was beginning to get to me. Life on Skye was so quiet, so solitary, loud sounds had begun to seem intrusive. 'I'll be in the study,' I added. 'And while I'm in there, I'm going to see if I can find Janet's Bible.'

Tom laughed. 'You really *are* rattled, aren't you?'

I smiled and relaxed a little. The man had a real talent for making me feel better. 'It's a proper old Bible. Huge, with a family tree drawn up at the front. I think I'd like to know more about the Munro family. *My* family. When the brothers died, that sort of thing. So I'll see you later. Why don't you stay for lunch? I'll make us a sandwich. There's some soup in the fridge. Leek and potato.'

Without waiting for a response, I turned and headed for the study.

It didn't take me long to locate the Bible. It was the biggest book in the room. The dusty spine was frayed top and bottom, so, handling it with care, I took it down from the shelf and laid it on the desk. Opening it with a certain sense of foreboding, I sat and studied the end papers which had been filled with a family tree, drawn up by many different hands. As I pored over names and dates, it occurred to me, I should add the dates of my father's death and Janet's.

My spirits plummeted again. Somehow that would make it final. Janet would be gone for good. She would have become part of my history.

My eyes scanned the faded ink that recorded the lives of James and Agnes Munro's four children. The youngest, Grace Emily had produced three children: Aunt Janet, Fergus (who'd died in infancy) and my mother, Kathleen. Grace's three older brothers had all died within two years. 1914 had seen the deaths of Archibald John and Donald Alec. The following year, she'd lost her eldest brother, James Hector.

Heckie.

My first meeting with Heckie was so long ago, I couldn't remember the date or the details, but it was at *Tigh-na-Linne*. I only ever saw him there, although at the end of every holiday, I begged him to come back to Cambridge with me. When my mother became ill, I spent more time with Janet, at my father's insistence. I suppose it was meant to spare me having to witness my mother's battle with cancer, but years later, it struck me that this had been the beginning of my father palming me off on my aunt. He couldn't cope with illness or grief, or even children – all those messy, human things. He was a Classics lecturer. He dealt with dead languages, not dead people.

I don't really remember a time before Heckie. That's probably because I don't remember much about life with my mother. After she died, my father refused to talk about her. He wasn't comfortable going through the photo albums Janet had made for me as mementos, so I got used to a family life with a split personality. When I was at home in Cambridge it was just my father and me, sharing silent meals during which he usually read an academic journal while I tried hard not to scrape my cutlery on the plate. I would listen to the loud tick of the longcase clock and imagine it was trying to tell me something, word by surreptitious word, or I would stare at the pendulum as it swung back and forth, trying to hypnotise myself.

But when I was on Skye, there was music and singing, boisterous games with Tommy and long chats with Janet about what my mother got up to as a girl, chats which always ended in hugs and tears - sometimes of laughter.

And there was Heckie.

To begin with, I didn't realise he was a soldier. He wore a kilt, like a lot of men on Skye and I didn't realise the rough, khaki tunic he wore, with all its pockets and buttons, was his uniform. Heckie and I took walks together along the beach and played hide and seek in the garden. He'd sing me songs and I'd learn them; I'd recite poems I'd written at school and he would learn those. We'd sit outdoors till the light faded and whenever I wanted to talk about my mother, Heckie would listen.

What I wanted to know was, would she be happy now? She hadn't seemed very happy when she was alive, but I couldn't really remember much about the time before she was ill. I supposed you wouldn't feel very cheerful if you had cancer. I could remember a woman who was pale and very thin, with bright auburn hair – rather like Heckie, in fact – but I don't know if I was actually remembering my mother, or just the photos of her taken in happier, healthier times.

Heckie told me she was happy now. He said she really missed me, but apart from that, she was content. I asked if she could see me growing up and looking at her old photos. He hesitated and said he wasn't sure, but he thought she probably could. One day I asked him why my mother didn't come and play with me, as he did. Heckie didn't answer straight away and looked rather sad. I thought perhaps I'd offended him by implying I'd rather play with my mother than him. I apologised for sounding ungrateful, but Heckie said it wasn't that, it was just that my question was a difficult one to answer. My mother didn't come back, he said, for a good reason. A *nice* reason. She was at peace. She'd died calmly, without suffering any pain, surrounded by people who loved her. She'd just drifted off to sleep and not woken again. Heckie explained that my mother didn't need to come back because she'd said all that had to be said. It was finished.

After I'd thought about it for a long time, I decided I was happy with this explanation. I started to think of my mother as Sleeping Beauty or Snow White: very beautiful and fast asleep, only *she* would never have a Prince who would wake her with a kiss. Thinking of her like that was much better than thinking how she looked when she was ill.

I was fine until I worked out why no one else could see Heckie, why even though I got taller and fatter, he never changed. He never wore different clothes and his tufty hair, red like a fox's fur, never grew. He never got hungry or thirsty and he never had to pee (unlike Tommy, who was always nipping behind bushes when we were out walking.) I worked it all out for myself. I suppose I must have been about nine.

Heckie was dead and he'd died a long time ago.

So I asked him how he'd died.

I knew it wasn't going to be good after what he'd said about my mother's peaceful death. When he told me, I cried so hard, I thought I would choke and die myself. I threw my arms round his neck and clung to him as if he were the dearest thing in the whole world – dearer than Aunt Janet, dearer even than my father. *Much* dearer.

Heckie told me he had died in battle, a very famous battle in France, during a long and terrible and completely pointless war. (Heckie said *all* war was pointless, but he hadn't realised that when he enlisted.) He said he'd been killed by a bullet from a machine gun, but it had been quick and he'd felt no pain. His pale blue eyes didn't meet mine when he said that, so I wasn't sure if he was telling me the truth, but I didn't want to embarrass him by asking awkward questions. If Heckie was telling me a white lie, then he must have a very good reason. I trusted him and knew he'd always told me the truth before, even when it was hard for me to hear it.

He told me how he'd died and said that one day, when I

was older, I would understand these things better, but until then, I wasn't to worry. He hadn't suffered long, unlike some of the poor devils who'd survived the war, but continued to live in that hellish world, even though they'd been sent home to their families. Heckie said he'd rather be dead than trapped out there in No Man's Land for ever, listening to the crump of shells, the screams of the wounded and dying. (I didn't know where No Man's Land was, but there was something about the way Heckie said those words and the haunted look in his eyes that made me wonder if he'd known what it was to lie abandoned in this terrible place. But I didn't ask because I sensed he didn't want to talk about it.)

Heckie said he'd "come home" to *Tigh-na-Linne* because he had unfinished business. He'd died when there were still important things he needed to do. He didn't explain in any detail, but made it sound as if he was looking for something or someone. He said that, unlike my mother, he hadn't had time to put his affairs in order. He'd received a letter – a very special letter – when he was fighting in France and it had made him happy but, at the same time, very sad. He'd needed to do something about this letter, but he'd been killed shortly afterwards.

Heckie said he'd needed to put things right, but it had been impossible. He didn't know how to do it. But he hadn't given up hope. (He said you should never, ever give up hope and told me the story of Pandora's Box.) He still hoped he'd be able to make amends, after which, he said, he might be able to sleep. I think he meant sleep forever, like my mother.

That was the worst thing about the trenches, he said. The noise. Most of the men were eventually able to fall asleep anywhere, any time, even standing up, but Heckie said he couldn't sleep until he was literally falling down with tiredness. Even then he dreamed about being shelled.

In the end, he said, that was all he ever thought about. Sleep. Not food. Or warmth. Or even his special letter. Eventually, he wasn't thinking about King and country, or even his family on Skye. He just thought about sleep, craved it, as the men in the trenches craved water to drink when supplies ran out.

Heckie said there were just two things he wanted now. Sleep was one of them, I knew that. He didn't tell me what the other one was and I got the feeling he didn't want me to ask. So I didn't.

The names and dates on the page had become a blur of faded ink hieroglyphs. I lifted the cover of the worn Bible and closed it with a sigh.

I must have seen the memorial window when I was young. *Must* have. Could I have seen it before Janet decided to cover it up? (When had she done that? And why?) As an impressionable, lonely child, had I assigned the role of imaginary friend to the glass angel with the fiery hair? Very possibly.

So why had Heckie always appeared to me in uniform?

I made a mental note to find out what regiment James Hector Munro fought with, then immediately scrapped the idea. Heckie had been a figment of my imagination, the product of stories I must have heard about my ancestors. Everything could be explained quite rationally. The disturbance in Janet's study had been caused by me in a confused, emotional state. I'd simply forgotten what I'd done. As for the noises in the hall upstairs, the blood, the smell of mud, these could all be the component parts of a complex hallucination. Or just a common or garden nightmare.

And the position of my slippers? And the tucked-in bedclothes?

It *must* have been me. Who else could it be?

And the moving wardrobe?

That could hardly have been me. Not on my own. Even Tom couldn't have moved it on his own. The thought of Tom applying his considerable muscle to moving the wardrobe only increased my sense of agitation. I just wasn't myself these days. I had no idea who I'd become and I certainly didn't approve. Susceptibility to attractive men (not to mention ghosts) had never been a problem hitherto. I was the last word in practical common sense. I was a professional *gardener*, for heaven's sake! Aunt Janet, with her artistic imagination, who heard quartets in her head and composed requiems for the departed, *she* would have been the one to see a ghost, not me.

I gasped, sandbagged by a new thought.

Had Janet seen Heckie? Was *that* why she'd had the wardrobe positioned so it would obliterate the window?

No, I told myself firmly, Janet hadn't seen Heckie, because there was no Heckie to see. The wardrobe must have been in its current position all along. I'd simply been mistaken.

I lifted the Bible with both hands and carried it to the bookshelf where I slid it back into place. Everything was sorted now to my satisfaction. I was delusional and apparently well on the way to a mental breakdown, but all anomalies were accounted for. I'd finally set my mind – what was left of it – at rest.

I suppose I should have guessed Heckie would have other ideas.

It soon became clear that sorting through Janet's papers was going to take longer than I expected. Hunger eventually prompted me to stop what I was doing to go and see about lunch. As I closed the study door behind me, I felt as if I was stepping back into my present-day life – my *real* life. Childhood holidays spent with Janet and Tommy, my friendship with Heckie (is *that* what it was – friendship?), all these seemed like a lifetime ago. Yet ever since I'd seen the stained glass window dedicated to James Hector Munro, my mind had flipped back and forth between past and present in a most unsettling way. I was adrift, anchored to neither past nor present.

I resolved to spend the afternoon in the garden, cutting back and tidying, sweeping up debris, restoring order. Fresh air and exercise – and some long overdue lunch – would soon set me to rights.

When I entered the kitchen I was surprised to see Tom had made himself quite at home. He was heating the soup on the hob and had already laid the table. To my astonishment, a few Japanese anemones from the garden stood in a mug as a centrepiece. He must have picked them from the garden.

The radio was on and Tom had his back to me, preparing sandwiches, so he didn't hear or see me come into the room. I had a moment to register two conflicting emotions, both of which surprised me. My first reaction to Tom's industriousness was one of slight indignation, that he'd made himself so at home in Janet's kitchen. (No, *my* kitchen.) It felt like an invasion of sorts. The employer/employee line had been crossed again. Then, quite contrarily, my indignation ebbed away, to be replaced by pleasure mixed with relief: I was about to have lunch put in front of me and I hadn't had to lift a finger. It would be served competently and with a smile by a thoughtful and good-looking man. What on earth was I complaining about?...

Tom turned round and beamed when he saw me. 'There you are! I was just about to give you a shout. You ready to eat? The soup's been simmering for a few minutes now. Sit down and I'll serve up.' Turning away without waiting for a reply, he switched off the radio, stirred the soup and served it into bowls in what seemed like one fluid movement. 'I made ham sandwiches,' he announced over his shoulder. 'The packet said use by tomorrow. Hope that was OK? Didn't like to disturb you in there.'

He shuttled back and forth between worktop, fridge and dining table, setting out mustard, chutney, glasses and a jug of water. I just stood there, like a spare part, watching him move, as I'd done when he carved up the rowan tree. But tension was dropping from my shoulders; my face and hands were starting to relax and with that came the realisation I was really hungry.

Tom set a plate of sandwiches in the middle of the table and said, 'You start. I'll put the kettle on.'

'Thanks. This is all *wonderful*. Such a luxury to have food put in front of me.' He set down the soup, garnished with chopped chives. I hadn't even noticed we still had chives, but of course Tom knew the garden better than I did. Again, I experienced that odd mix of gratitude and resentment. It seemed like a very old feeling, something I used to experience with Tommy and I had that vertiginous sensation again, as if I were sliding about in time.

I needed to *eat*.

As I sat down, Tom joined me, helped himself to a sandwich and took a large bite. I felt a bit guilty for offering to prepare lunch, then making him wait so long for it. I wondered if his decision to do it himself had been triggered by hunger? Very likely. He'd had a hard morning, wrestling with the wardrobe.

'How did you get on?' he asked through a mouthful of sandwich. 'Did you find the Bible?'

'Yes, I did. The family tree was interesting. The memorial window depicts the eldest son.' I hesitated, then decided to censor. It was just too complicated. In any case, how do you explain something you can't explain, even to yourself? 'He was called James Munro and he was killed at the battle of Loos, the year after both his brothers died. Also in France. Their sister Grace was the Munros' youngest child. And she was my grandmother.'

'Was Janet the last of the line?'

'Yes, apart from me. And I suppose it will die out with me.'

'You don't want children, then?'

I almost choked on my sandwich. 'Left it a bit late for that!' I replied, not answering his question.

'Really? What are you? Forty-one? Forty-two? Lots of women have kids in their forties now, don't they?'

'I'm forty-two. I'd claim to be thirty-nine but, if you remember, there's less than a year between us.'

'I'd forgotten that.' He smiled and started on his soup. 'Well, you don't look a day over thirty-nine to me.'

'Thank you. For lunch and for the compliment. Today's my lucky day.' He looked up sharply - fearing sarcasm perhaps? 'No, really, Tom – *thank you*! There are days when I feel a hundred and two, not forty-two.' I picked up my spoon and began to eat my soup. 'It's been a difficult year.'

He nodded. 'You do seem a bit fragile.'

'Do I?'

'Well, changeable. Like the weather. You sort of... cloud over. But that's understandable. I mean, a double bereavement.' He shook his head. 'That would knock the stuffing out of anyone.'

'It was triple, actually.' He looked at me, his spoon suspended halfway between his bowl and his mouth, and waited. 'Three deaths. I lost my partner at the beginning of the year.'

Tom exhaled. 'Ruth, I'm really sorry. I had no idea.'

I ignored him and studied the colour and texture of my soup, both of which seemed unappetising. I picked up the pepper mill and ground a punitive amount into my bowl. 'Well, I say "partner"... He wasn't really. But I refuse to describe a man of fifty-four as my boyfriend. We'd been together for two years and known each other a lot longer.' Tom set down his spoon – as a mark of respect, I suppose. 'No! Eat up before it gets cold! I'm going to.' We resumed eating and after a mouthful of soup, which still seemed tasteless, I continued. 'It wasn't quite as bad as it sounds. I mean it *was*, it was awful. He dropped down dead in front of me and I was on my own and I didn't know what to do... But David wasn't— well, he wasn't the love of my life, is what I'm trying to say. And I suppose I feel rather guilty about that. That he died unloved. By me, anyway... Don't get me wrong – he meant a lot to me. He was a very good friend. The best. That was the problem really... Anyway, I'd told him I wanted to call it a day. End the relationship. I'd told him that very day. And then... well, then he went and *died*!'

I remember dropping my spoon into my soup bowl and the splash it made, but I couldn't work out how Tom's arm was suddenly round my shoulders, his hand threading through my hair, sweeping it back from my face. Then I realised he was doing that because I was crying. He pulled me toward him, but he was still standing, so my head was pressed against his stomach, which, even through his thick work shirt, felt so flat and hard, a great kick of desire shuddered through my body. I was shocked by the strength and sheer mindlessness of my response, but I made no attempt to pull away.

Tom cradled my head and made soothing noises. He didn't try to say anything, which was a relief and gradually I was able to compose myself. I lifted my head slowly, reluctant to let him see the wreck of my face, but as I looked up, he bent and, taking my wet face in both hands, kissed me. It was a long kiss but he didn't try to force my lips apart. He didn't have to.

Eventually he let me go and stepped away, his breathing heavy. He wiped his mouth on the back of his hand and, avoiding my eyes, murmured, 'Sorry for jumping you like that. But... Well, I've been wanting to do that for a while.'

I turned and pushed my soup plate away. 'No need to apologise. I didn't exactly put up a fight, did I?'

When I dared to look at him again, his chest was still rising and falling and I was in no doubt as to what was on his mind. With pupils dilated, his eyes looked dark and purposeful. I wondered if he was about to sweep the lunch things on to the floor and take me on the kitchen table. I was asking myself if I wanted him to – I fear the answer might have been in the affirmative – when sanity reasserted itself and I heard the voice of reason say, very politely, 'I've been meaning to ask you... Would you like to come and have dinner? *Supper,* I mean.'

He frowned. 'Is there a difference?'

'You'll have lower expectations if I say supper.'

He gave me that reckless look again, the one that made me fear for the crockery. 'My interest in food is pretty limited.'

'Well, that's probably just as well, because I'm not a very good cook.' I stood up and tucked my chair under the table, careful to maintain my distance. 'Are you free on Friday?'

'Yes. And if I weren't, I'd cancel.'

I shot him a look, then said, 'Good. That's settled then.'

'Time?'

'Seven o'clock?'

He nodded, then there was an awkward pause while we both stood and looked at each other, waiting for the other to speak. I cracked first. 'Tom, do you think perhaps you'd better... go?' I indicated the table. 'But do take some sandwiches. It would be a shame to waste them. After you went to all that trouble.'

He stared at me for a moment, then threw back his head

and laughed. The sound was loud and male and glorious. Unable to help myself, I started to giggle. He made a move toward me and I stepped back, still laughing.

'No! Go, Tom. *Now.*'

'OK, I'm leaving! You're the boss, Ruthie.' He picked up his jacket and shrugged it on. 'See you Friday. For *supper*. I'll bring a bottle. And low expectations.'

He headed for the back door and I watched him go, Tom's back view being almost as appealing as his front. As the back door closed, I sat again, poured myself a large glass of water and drank it straight down. Then, ravenous, I devoured all the remaining sandwiches.

Chapter Six

Still feeling a little flustered, I left the dishes on the table and went in to the sitting room where I sat by the French windows, checking email on my laptop. The activity was mindless and soothing and soon lowered my pulse rate to normal – that is, until I read Stan's latest. I had to read it twice before the full implications sank in.

Dear Ruth

I have examined carefully the sample pages of Janet's work you were kind enough to scan for me. My comments are of course tentative at this stage, but I think we can be reasonably certain there are three hands at work here.

If you have no reason to suppose your aunt employed some kind of *amanuensis*, then the existence of these three hands has, I'm afraid, serious implications. I repeat: I'm not offering judgements at this stage, merely my first thoughts on the matter, so I hope you won't take offence at what I now wish to set before you.

It's difficult to avoid coming to the unhappy conclusion that Janet plagiarised someone else's work and passed it off as her own. I sincerely hope to find another explanation, but if these three pages are representative of what you have on Skye, it looks suspiciously as if Janet produced her own early work (which enjoyed only limited success), then gained access to a superior piece of work by composer unknown, which she then transcribed and published as her own (perhaps with that composer's approval, even co-operation?)

The sample page from Janet's later, successful period is a fair copy executed in yet another person's hand, but as it's clearly a final version, we have no reason to suspect plagiarism here. Janet could simply have employed someone to transcribe for her. (She was very busy professionally at this stage of her career.)

But this doesn't resolve the question of why the draft of *In Memoriam* is not in Janet's hand.

All these conjectures have serious implications for my projected study and I can make no further progress until I'm able to examine the autograph scores. If you would be kind enough to allow me to do this, I'll make arrangements to travel to Skye at your earliest convenience. (I would stay at a hotel and work there, assuming you'd let me remove the papers from *Tigh-na-Linne*.)

Once I have access to the documents, I really wouldn't expect to bother you (unless, of course, you wished to be involved.) Apart from a close examination of the autograph scores, I shall have to sift through Janet's letters and journals looking for clues to the identity of a potential collaborator. (At this stage I prefer to think of Janet collaborating with persons unknown than to think there was any deliberate plagiarism.)

Alternatively, if you prefer, the papers could be packed up and sent to Toronto at my expense, though this might actually entail more work for you than having me on site. There's also an element of risk in shipping a historic archive across the Atlantic.

I'm aware my views will come as a shock. The implications are potentially serious and professionally embarrassing for your aunt's reputation. All I can suggest is that you allow me to examine the papers as soon as possible so we can set our minds at rest, or, if our worst fears are realised, embark on some sort of damage limitation exercise.

Of course, if you wish to protect your aunt's reputation, you can prevent anyone from examining her archive. It might even strike you that the best way to forestall further speculation would be to destroy the autograph manuscripts. I would beg you not to do such a thing. Assuming you haven't discussed these anomalies with anyone else, you and I are probably the only people who know about them. (Unless of course Janet's collaborator is still alive. An interesting thought!) You can rely on my discretion. Much as I'd relish the opportunity to investigate this musical mystery, I would – with much regret – abandon my researches. It wouldn't be possible to make a proper study of Janet's work without access to her original scores.

When you've had time to consider, perhaps you'd be good enough to let me know if you'll allow me to pursue my investigations, which were, and still are intended to enhance your aunt's professional standing. Until someone proves otherwise, Janet Gillespie was the composer of *In Memoriam* and many other pieces that I consider to be some of the finest and least appreciated in the twentieth century classical repertoire.

I look forward to hearing from you soon.

With very best wishes,

Stan

P.S. Please don't hesitate to call me and don't concern yourself with time zones. I'm a very poor sleeper and, in any case, would regard the opportunity to discuss Janet's work with her niece a privilege, not a disturbance.

I sat staring at the screen, stunned, until the screensaver kicked in and started the horticultural slide-show which, on my laptop, passed for a family album. My mother died long before the digital age and my father always refused to pose for photos, or spoiled them by moving, so the laptop shuffled shots of me with David, friends or film crews at the Chelsea Show, Hidcote, Sissinghurst and other famous gardens. These were interspersed with pictures of Janet at *Tigh-na-Linne*. One of my favourites showed her looking oddly sinister in Wellingtons and midge hood, dealing death to invertebrates with a spray gun. Always kind, if undemonstrative, Janet gave no quarter on the garden battlefield.

But Aunt Janet, a plagiarist? *Never.*

The woman I knew, who epitomised the Highland virtues of honesty, courtesy and self-effacement, would never take the credit for someone else's work. But what other explanation was there? And what did I know anyway? I thought I knew Janet well, but it turned out I didn't know a thing about her love life and, knowing nothing, I'd arrogantly assumed there was nothing to know. I could be just as wrong about her professional life. The classical music world was ruthlessly competitive and the dice had always been loaded against women. I knew how much her music had meant to Janet and how broken-hearted she'd been when she had to give up performing and resort to teaching for a living. So why assume she wouldn't have used any means possible to further her career?

The whole business made me feel uneasy: the idea that there was a side to Janet – more than one, in fact – that I hadn't known. I didn't want to deal with it. And I certainly didn't want Athelstan at *Tigh-na-Linne*. Tactful and courteous as he seemed, I didn't want to be landed with entertaining an eccentric academic whose enthusiasm for little-known composers might encourage him to outstay his welcome. The best plan was surely to send the whole archive to Toronto, well-packed and well-insured, and let Athelstan do his detective work there. If, that is, I wanted him looking into the Gillespie cupboards and finding skeletons.

That unsettling thought reminded me of the box Tom had

found inside the wardrobe. Consumed with curiosity, I shut down my laptop and headed for the study, consoling myself with the thought that, if the box contained a skeleton, it would be a very small one.

As soon as I picked up the box, I remembered it was locked. I shook it gently, but couldn't hear or feel anything moving inside. Why would anyone lock an empty box? I studied the exterior which was delicately inlaid with mother-of-pearl flowers and insects. It had probably belonged to a woman. Too small for a jewel casket, it had perhaps held trinkets or letters. Did it now hold letters from Tricia? I couldn't remember where Tom and his mother had lived, but it was somewhere in England. They'd had a long journey to Skye for their holiday, so Tricia and Janet can't have met often – certainly not while Tom lived at home. They probably did write to each other.

Again, I experienced a queasy feeling. I wasn't comfortable with my eager curiosity to know about the life Janet had wished to keep private, but a locked box is a temptation few could resist. I knew I was likely to succumb.

Examining the fastening, I could see it wouldn't be difficult to force with a knife, but I didn't want to risk damaging the box. In any case, as Tom had pointed out, Janet was extremely organised. If the box was locked, there would be a key. But where?

The box had been stored in a corner of the wardrobe so she can't have needed ready access to its contents. The more I thought about it, the more I thought the box must contain love letters.

I did a deal with myself: I would look for the key and, if I found it, I would open the box. If it contained letters, I wouldn't read them, not unless it looked as if they'd help Stan with his research. It would be no invasion of Janet's privacy to just open the box, would it? Unbidden, a memory swam into my mind of Heckie telling me the story of Pandora...

I would simply look for the key. That surely could do no harm?

61

I spent the rest of the day looking for the key in drawers and boxes and working my way methodically through key rings, but to no avail. I should have just let it go, but failure only made me all the more determined to find the key.

My moral scruples were dwindling by the minute.

I tried to put the box and its contents out of my mind, but the following day it occurred to me that the key might have been in the lock originally or stored near the box. It must be very small, so perhaps Tom had missed it. It could have fallen to the floor when he was dismantling the wardrobe.

I took the box upstairs. As I turned the corner on the landing, I faltered, remembering the shock of recognition when I'd first seen the figure in the memorial window. I approached cautiously, eyes down, scanning the floor for a key, but I saw nothing, just dust and a few splinters of wood where Tom hadn't cleared up thoroughly.

The hall was gloomy. The light of a dreary winter's afternoon was further dimmed by the coloured glass through which it had to pass. I reached for the switch on the table lamp, then hesitated. The last time I'd done this, I'd seen mud and blood on the floor. But *that*, I chided myself, had just been a bad dream.

I switched on the lamp. As I examined the floorboards in front of the window, the light bulb flickered for a moment, then settled down. Variations in current were common on Skye, as were power cuts. Perhaps the bulb was about to go. I thought nothing of it. *Almost* nothing.

I finally spotted the key, wedged in a gap between floorboards, barely visible. I pounced on it, extracting it carefully, then, holding my breath, I inserted it into the lock. It turned easily and so – just call me Pandora – I lifted the lid.

The box was crammed with letters, but these weren't written by Tricia. They looked far too old. Peering at the envelopes, I saw they were addressed to *Tigh-na-Linne*, but to a *Mr and Mrs J F Munro*.

James Hector's parents.

I put my hand into the box to gather up the letters and

found there was something solid underneath. A notebook or journal of some kind – old, battered and very dirty. I set the letters down on the side table and extracted the little book. As I handled it, my fingers dislodged powdery grains of dirt and, as in my dream, I thought I could smell damp earth and decay.

I put the empty box down beside the letters and opened the soiled notebook. As I turned them, its closely-written pages crackled with age. Some were stuck together, caked and stained with what looked like dried mud. And something else: a dull, reddish-brown substance.

Blood.

As if my fingers had been burned, I dropped the book and clapped a hand to my mouth, stifling a cry. My nostrils filled with the stench of death and it was then the table lamp went out.

I wasn't plunged into darkness, but it took my eyes a second or two to adjust to the altered light. It took my body longer to adjust to the sudden change in temperature, as if every door and window in the house had been flung open to the dank November air.

As I stared at the notebook lying open on the floor, its blistered and blood-stained pages were turned by a breeze from nowhere. Then from behind me, a long, pale hand reached down, picked up the book and placed it carefully beside the letters.

A voice said, 'D'you remember what lay at the bottom of Pandora's box, Ruth?'

That voice. That beloved Highland voice: calm, low and musical; a voice I hadn't heard since childhood.

Unable to move, unable even to tear my eyes from the notebook, I whispered, 'Hope'.

'Aye... There's always hope. You didn't forget *that*, even if you forgot me.'

I wheeled round, inflamed by childish anger. 'You forgot *me*, Heckie!'

He stood before me, dressed, as always, in kilted uniform, his creamy skin of a pallor so unearthly, it seemed to glow in the twilight. His sad, blue eyes regarded me kindly and a half-smile played about his lips, twisting a mouth that my child's eyes had never noticed was generous. He was shorter than I remembered and his eyes were now almost level with mine. Trembling, I beheld a slender young man of medium height, perhaps in his mid-thirties, but all these characteristics would strike an observer long after he'd noticed the man's hair: a dark, vivid auburn, almost shocking against his ivory skin.

Heckie sighed and the air grew colder still. 'I didn't forget you, Ruth. You stopped believing in me. So you couldn't see me any more. I couldn't make you see me. I can't make anyone see me, unless they believe. D'you not remember your William Blake? *If the sun and moon should doubt, they'd immediately go out.*'

'But he said he'd—' I broke off, absurdly reluctant to tell tales, even thirty years after the event. 'Someone told me you were dead.'

A slow, lopsided smile spread across Heckie's face. He tilted his head and said, 'I *am* dead, Ruth.'

'I mean, he said he'd *killed* you.'

The pale eyes narrowed. 'Tommy?' I nodded. The sad smile again. 'No, Tommy didn't kill me. A German bullet did that. Don't you remember?'

'I remember what you told me.' My eyes travelled to the bloody notebook. 'But *was* it that clean, Heckie? Was it quick? You said so, but I was never sure I believed you.'

'Och, you were just a wee girl. You didn't need to know any more.'

Silence hung between us while, for a few seconds, I tried to imagine how Heckie might have died; how long it might have taken. Nausea was rising, so I said quickly, 'After Tommy and I had that fight... I mean, after he said what he said, you never came again. So I believed him.'

'I can't come to you unless you need me, Ruth. You have to be willing. You thought it possible for Tommy to kill me, so I knew you were ready to move on. I think you knew it too. You broke away, from me and from Tommy. You started to fend for yourself. And you started to grow up.' He paused and studied my face, then nodded, as if satisfied. 'I always knew you'd grow up bonny. I never dreamed you'd turn into a beauty.'

Astonished, I gaped at him, my mouth trying to form words. 'So why... why have you come back?'

He spread long-fingered, elegant hands, hands that must have done so much killing. 'You need me. And I need you.'

The telephone's shrill summons made me jump so high, I put my hand out to clutch at Heckie for support. My fingers met little resistance, as if they were displacing water and his body felt just as cold, but he steadied me with chilly hands. The table lamp flickered back to life and lit his extraordinary gaunt face with its skeletal hollows, the double of the figure in the window behind. As he turned his head, his blue eyes glittered. I thought of hoar frost and shivered.

Heckie released me. As he did so, he became paler still, then transparent. As his body appeared to evaporate, I clutched at him again, but there was nothing there. Nothing solid. Just the smell of damp earth.

Chapter Seven

The phone stopped ringing and I began to breathe. It started up again immediately, shredding my nerves. I strode into the bedroom, snatched the phone off its cradle and snapped, "Hello?" in a voice guaranteed to put the fear of God into cold-callers.

'Ruth, it's me. Is something wrong?'

'*Tommy?*' I said, thrown by a voice I hadn't been expecting.

He laughed softly. 'Funny to hear you call me that after all these years... Look, I was just ringing to say, I forgot to lock up yesterday. The garage door, I mean. Sorry about that. I was a bit... well, fazed when I left. My mind was on other things.'

'Oh... Right. I'll lock up. Thanks.'

I suppose I must have sounded like the Speaking Clock because Tom said, 'Ruthie, are you all right?'

'Yes, of course!" I exclaimed, my voice just this side of hysteria.

'Is someone there?'

'No! There's no one here. No one at all. Just me. Why? Who *should* be here?'

'Calm down! I was only asking. You just sounded a bit strange, that's all.'

'Strange?'

'As if a masked man was holding a gun to your head, or something.'

'I'm fine!' I announced. 'But I'm rather busy. Was there anything else you wanted?'

'Well, no...' Tom replied, sounding mystified, as well he might. The man's tongue had been down my throat the day before. 'Just thanks for lunch, I guess.'

'You're welcome!' I said brightly. 'Bye!'

I rammed the phone back on its cradle and sank on to the

bed. I closed my eyes, put my head in my hands and wished the world – *my* world – would simply go away.

You can prepare yourself for a lot of things in life. A wedding. A baby. A death. (Even your own.) You can see some things coming. A road accident. Divorce. Bankruptcy. But you can't – you simply *can't* – prepare yourself for an encounter with a ghost.

For a start, they don't exist. *Obviously.* And even if they did, *you* aren't the kind of sad weirdo who'd see one. Ghosts only happen to attention-seeking fantasists with over-active imaginations and a shaky grip on reality.

And that certainly wasn't me.

So meeting a ghost wasn't a matter to which I'd ever given any thought. Not like, say, meeting Johnny Depp. Or the Queen. (Some TV personalities get invited to those big garden parties at Buck House where the Queen gets to network. Me hooking up with HRH wasn't as unlikely as it sounds. Not nearly as unlikely as seeing a ghost.)

I decided it was time to leave. Go home. (But wasn't *Tigh-na-Linne* my home? A second home that Janet had made for me, then given to me?) I should go back to my nice, sane London flat where I only got burgled once a year, on average. Doubtless I would soon become inured again to the noise, dirt, expense and aggression of metropolitan life. At least London didn't have ghosts. Or if it did, they'd never bothered *me.*

So I would pack up and go home.

I pulled open the bedside drawer and took out a notepad and pencil. I wrote TO DO at the top of the page and began to draw up a list.

1. Send Janet's archive to Toronto.

There was no other way I could resolve the matter of her plagiarism. If I took Stan at his word and asked him to abandon his book, there would be other academics knocking at my door, asking the same awkward questions and they might not be as charitable as Stan. The potential story wasn't quite "Musical high jinks in lesbian love nest", but it was close.

If Janet had done anything underhand, the music establishment would crucify her and her professional reputation would never recover.

I didn't believe she was guilty, but the matter couldn't be settled without further investigation and, for some reason, I trusted Athelstan. What can you learn about a man from a few emails? Not a lot, but more than you might think. My instincts said Stan was sound and I always trusted my instincts. They spoke to me loud and clear, even if they sometimes told me things I didn't really want to know. Like the fact that David and I had just been going through the motions of a sexual relationship. Or that some of the time I'd spent with Tom, I'd been thinking about going through those motions with him.

I wasn't exactly proud of my instincts, but so far, they'd told me no lies. And now they said, 'Run'. So that's what I was going to do.

I wrote down

2. Pack up my stuff

3. Shut up house

and then froze as a thought struck me. I wouldn't be able to get away without spending another night at *Tigh-na-Linne*. There was just too much to do. Apart from Janet's papers, which would have to be parcelled up and sent to Canada, I had to make the house secure for the winter. That meant draining the water system to avoid burst pipes. Or alternatively, I needed to leave some back-up heating on. At least that way the house wouldn't become damp and the contents deteriorate. The last thing I wanted to have to deal with in the spring was a house full of mouldy furnishings and mildewed books, especially if it was going on the market.

Was I going to put *Tigh-na-Linne* on the market?...

Common sense said yes, especially as I was currently unemployed, but my heart baulked at the idea, at making any decision apart from the decision to run. I hadn't thought it through, I'd just panicked. (So would you if you'd seen a ghost.)

I tossed the notepad aside and lay down on the bed. Was I cracking up? Should I ring Dr Mackenzie, who'd been so understanding when Janet died? But what could I say?... 'I've seen a ghost. Well, not a ghost exactly, more of an imaginary friend. A distant relative, in fact. My great uncle Hector who died in 1915. On the Western Front, at the Battle of Loos.' What could I say, who could I talk to, without being dismissed as off my head? (And surely I *was* off my head if I thought Heckie was talking to me?)

The person I needed to talk to wasn't David, or Tom, or even Dr Mackenzie, it was Janet. I wanted Aunt Janet to tell me what I should do. I wanted her to make me laugh, make me see how completely absurd I was being.

But Janet was gone.

Grief twisted my innards again and I felt that lurch toward emptiness and despair, as if I was tumbling into an abyss. Drawing my knees up into a foetal position, I lay still on the bed, trying to decide what to do.

There was someone else I could turn to... Someone who'd helped me before, many times. When my mother was ill. And when she'd died. Someone who'd kept me company when Tommy locked me in the attic for hours because I wouldn't let him use my new roller skates. Someone who'd never let me down, *ever*, not until I believed him to be dead. And now? If I needed him? If I *believed* he existed? What then?

I sat bolt upright, all my senses alert, my nerve ends jangling. Wanting to dispel the late afternoon gloom, I switched on the bedside light and surveyed the room. I saw nothing untoward, but unless I was imagining it, the temperature was falling rapidly. I gathered up the thick folds of the bed's faded patchwork quilt, wrapped it round me and, scarcely breathing, I waited.

Silence. Even the wind outside seemed to have dropped. The only sound was the distant, rhythmic grinding of the waves clawing at the shore.

Then, there was a light tap at the door.

My heart rose up into my mouth and I ordered it back down to its proper place. Willing lungs and vocal cords to function, I said, quite superfluously, 'Who is it?'

I heard my blood pounding in my ears, then a low voice, a gentle growl, like the noise my teddy bear used to make when his tummy was squeezed, said, 'Hector.'

Flooded with a mixture of terror and elation, I buried my face in the quilt until I thought I'd suffocate, then looked up and said, with more composure than I felt, 'Come in.'

The bedroom door swung open to reveal Heckie in the doorway. He appeared to be waiting for permission to enter. Unable to speak, I simply nodded.

He came in, closed the door behind him and stood still. There was a long silence. Eventually he said, 'You were wanting me?'

'Yes. Thank you for coming back.' My voice sounded much too loud. Was it always this loud?

Hector bent his auburn head in a little bow. 'I'm at your service.'

'Yes, I know. Even if I don't know *why*,' I added faintly. 'Heckie— oh, I feel such an idiot calling you that! It's so childish. You do realise I'm older than you now?'

'Aye. The thought had occurred to me.'

'From now on, I want to call you "Hector". Is that all right?'

He bowed his head again. 'Whatever suits.'

'Good.' I fell silent, at a complete loss as to where or how to begin. The being I now called Hector still stood waiting by the door, so I indicated the stool in front of the dressing table. 'Would you like to sit down? Oh— I don't suppose ghosts get tired, do they?'

'Oh, aye. We get *awfu'* tired,' he replied, sitting on the stool. 'There's a deal of hanging about in draughty corridors, cellars, graveyards and the like. So we try to take the weight off our feet whenever we can.' He regarded me, that half-smile hovering round his mouth again.

'You're mocking me.'

The smile vanished. 'Not for the world. But I was born a hundred and thirty years ago. I wouldn't know how to convey to you just how bone-weary I am.'

'I'm sorry. It wasn't meant to be a frivolous question. I'm just... nervous. And confused.'

'Aye, I know. If there's anything I can do—'

Panic came flooding back and I interrupted. 'Hector, you don't mean me any harm, do you?'

He looked astonished, almost angry. 'If I'd another life to lay down, Ruth, I'd lay it down for you.'

That took my breath away and it was a moment or two before I could continue. 'You said before that you needed me.'

'Aye. In a way, I do.'

'What way?'

'In the days when I still believed in an almighty God, I might have claimed, "He works in a mysterious way, His wonders to perform". But now... Well, I don't know how it will happen, or when, or why, but I think there will be wonders, Ruth. If we let things take their course and don't interfere.'

'*Wonders*?'

'Aye.'

'For you or me?'

'Both, maybe.'

I contemplated this vague but exciting prospect, then said, 'When did you stop believing, Hector?'

'In God?' His shoulders sagged and he studied his long fingers as he wove them together. 'At Loos. When the order was given for us to advance into clouds of our own chlorine gas. I decided that either God did not exist or, if he did, he should no longer be *allowed* to exist. But as you see, it was I who ceased to exist. Man proposes,' he added with an ironic smile. 'And God disposes.'

'Was that how you—?'

'No. I was lucky that time.'

'Did you—'

'Not now, Ruth,' he said gently. 'I'll tell you one day. I promise.'

I exhaled, relieved to be spared the details. 'So what is it you want of me, Hector?'

'It's hard to explain, but... I need you to not get in the way.'

'In the way? Of what?'

'Of what's meant to be.'

'Which is?'

He paused, then said, 'I don't know.'

'That's not terribly helpful. If you don't know, how can I keep out of the way?'

'I don't know that either. I apologise for being so lamentably ill-informed. Wisdom doesn't always come with age, not even *my* age. But I believe *you'll* know, Ruth. You'll know what needs to be done. And I can help you do it. We can help each other.' Hector's eyes were wide and bright now, as if his spirits had revived. 'D'you believe me?'

I thought for a moment and it seemed to me there was a little hopeful fluttering in my heart too. 'Oddly enough, I think I do. When I don't think I'm completely deranged, I *do* think we can help each other. Why on earth should that be?'

'Blood, perhaps. The same blood runs in your veins as ran in mine. Or because we've both seen more death than we know how to bear.' He lowered his voice and I sensed he was losing ground again. 'Perhaps because we're both lonely.'

I looked down at the quilt and studied its intricate pattern of hexagons. I tried to remember who'd made it. Janet had told me years ago, but I'd forgotten. Hector would probably know. It might have been his sister. Or perhaps his mother.

I raised my head from contemplation of the quilt. 'I'm not just lonely, Hector. I'm bloody *alone*.'

He regarded me with those cool, clear eyes, as if weighing me up, re-assessing something. My age, probably. He hadn't seen me for thirty years. Was he looking for the child he'd once known?

'You're alone, Ruth, but you're alive. You're very alive. And where there's life—'

'Oh, I know, you don't have to tell me. But what about *you*, Hector?'

'Me?'

'What if there's... no life?'

'Och, well, I hope anyway.' He shrugged. 'Where's the harm?' His smile had nothing of contentment about it. It was merely a re-arrangement of facial muscles, leaving the sadness in his eyes untouched.

My head was beginning to ache. I closed my eyes and told myself that when I opened them again, Hector would be gone, the temperature of the room would be back to normal and the air would no longer be tainted with the smell of decay – a smell to which I was already becoming accustomed. Willing

Hector to be gone, I opened my eyes again.

He was still there, sitting patiently in front of the dressing table, the many folds of his kilt spread over the stool, his hands clasped loosely in his lap. As I looked at him, my eyes must have widened. He frowned and said, 'Is something wrong?'

'I've just noticed... The *mirror*.' Hector didn't turn round, but gave the slightest of nods. 'There's no reflection!'

'There's nothing to reflect.'

'So I *am* imagining you!'

He fixed me with a look of such weary despair, I felt I should apologise. 'Ruth, you didn't imagine the wardrobe moving. Or Janet's fountain pen. Or the lid of the piano. I *think*,' he said with exaggerated patience, 'I made my presence felt.'

'Yes. You did. I'm sorry. You are real.'

'Aye.'

'A real ghost.'

'Aye, if such a thing is not a contradiction in terms and your mind can comprehend it.'

'I'm not sure it can.'

'I'd sympathise, but I find myself unable. You see, I experienced the sea of mud and blood that was Loos. The chaos and carnage of No Man's Land. I received – and, more remarkably, I *obeyed* – an order to lead my men into a thirty-foot-high bank of deadly fog. So I have no very great difficulty in believing I'm a ghost. I've seen things – and *done* things, Ruth – that have given me greater pause and would sooner tempt me to question my sanity. Or yours.'

As Hector delivered this speech – all of it to the floor, as if he didn't trust himself to make eye contact – I studied his appearance. The thing was, he *looked* perfectly normal. He appeared solid enough: slight physically, but with a suggestion of wiry strength. His pallor was extreme and there was something rather odd about his eyes, but for all I knew, this is what James Hector Munro had looked like when he was alive. His spectral form certainly didn't look any different from his glass counterpart in the memorial window and that had presumably been based on photographs. Looking at

Hector was just like looking at a real man.

Except that he had no reflection.

And the air in the centrally-heated bedroom was cold and smelled of newly dug earth - black and damp. A smell that hitherto I'd always associated with new life, a new growing season, fruitfulness. Not death.

Despite Hector's explanations, my confusion was growing with every minute that passed. I felt a great longing for sleep, but at the same time, I knew I didn't want to dismiss him. (*Could* I? Would Hector do as he was told?)

'You need to sleep,' he murmured.

I was so startled by this act of telepathy that I became instantly alert again. 'No, I'm fine. I'm just struggling to take it all in, that's all. I feel as if my brain has been asked to accept the existence of another dimension.'

'I believe it has.'

'Then I suppose it will take time for me to adjust.' I stared at Hector again, then realised what had been bothering me. 'I'm not seeing you as you were, am I? As you were... *then*,' I added tactfully.

'You see me as I present myself to you. I can choose. Up to a point.'

'How do you mean?'

'What you see is an act of will. My will. I can't sustain it indefinitely. It was easier when you were a child, when you believed I was alive. And whole. It's harder for me now. Now that you know. I'm beset by doubts, Ruth. Yours.'

'So how I think of you affects how I see you?'

'You see what you want to see. Which is why I was never frank with you when you were a wee girl.'

'You're saying it would be easier for you if I thought about you as – as you were at the end?'

'Aye, it would. But I wouldn't want to look at your face and see horror. And revulsion. I want us to be able to look each other in the eye. With trust. And affection. As we once did.'

'So do I... So I should carry on thinking of you as you were when you were alive?'

'Aye. I think it best.'

'I'm sorry if that makes things harder for you.' He raised a pale hand in an eloquent, wordless gesture. 'I think I'll get my head round it all, eventually. But I need time. Time to think.'

'Of course.' He stood up. 'I'll leave you now.'

Before I knew what I was doing, I leaned forward on the bed, extending a hand toward him. '*Must* you?'

He regarded me with surprise. 'No. I can stay, if you wish.' He sat down again.

Since I could think of nothing else to say, I sat feeling rather foolish, while Hector waited a few feet away, quite still, as if he'd sat there for a hundred years and was prepared to sit for a hundred more.

'You know, I think perhaps I *would* like to sleep. But—' I gazed at him, suddenly and unaccountably close to tears.

'You'd like me to sit by the door.' It was a statement, not a question. 'As I used to, in the old days.'

I struggled for a moment to remember what he was referring to and then I saw my younger self, enveloped in bedclothes, peeping out and fixing my anxious gaze on the man seated on the floor by my bedroom door, relaxed but watchful, like a dog. Satisfied Heckie was on sentry duty, I would close my troubled eyes and fall asleep, knowing he would be gone when I woke.

'I think I'd like that. If you don't mind.'

Hector rose and walked over to the door, then turned back. 'Will I wait outside, Ruth?' he asked uncertainly. 'You used to want me to watch *this* side of the door, where you could see me. But now you're older...'

Was it possible for a ghost to look *embarrassed*? It must surely have been a trick of the light. Hector stood, eyes cast down, waiting for instructions. I don't know if my adult self spoke, or the child I used to be. (I was beginning to wonder where one ended and the other began.) The Ruth who couldn't bear to be alone said, 'Stay. As you used to. Please.'

Hector went and sat down in front of the door. 'I'll be here until you wake. But when you wake, I'll be gone.'

'I remember... Thank you, Hector.'

He raised his hand again, dismissing my thanks, as if such things were unnecessary between us. As he settled his back against the door, I turned off the bedside light, wrapped myself in the quilt and lay down. I peered into the darkness, trying to see if Hector was still there. The curtains were undrawn, but there was no moonlight to illuminate his pale features.

Once again, as if he'd read my mind, Hector announced, in that soft, comforting growl. 'I'm here. You can sleep now, Ruth. Good night.'

'Goodnight, Heckie.'

When I woke, an hour or so later, I sat up immediately and switched on the bedside light.

Hector was gone.

I felt completely bereft.

Chapter Eight

Waking to find Hector no longer on sentry duty at my door, I told myself he'd never been there. I got off the bed and went downstairs, switching on every light as I descended, until the whole house was cheerfully ablaze. Only once did I look over my shoulder.

As I surveyed the uninspiring contents of the fridge, I decided there was something very wrong with me. The way my thoughts were running gave new meaning to the phrase, "in two minds". My brain seemed to have divided itself into two distinct and contradictory halves. Let's call them Sane Mind and, for the sake of argument, Insane Mind.

Sane Mind registered that I'd woken from a fitful doze in which I'd dreamed I'd had an amiable and wide-ranging chat with the ghost-angel pictured in the memorial window. Insane Mind, meanwhile, was bracing itself for the unspecified "wonders" of which Hector had spoken. By the time I'd rustled up some cheese on toast, Insane Mind was curbing an impulse to summon Hector's ghost for a bit of congenial company, while Sane Mind pointed out politely that if I wanted to avoid further unsettling dreams, I should lay off the cheese.

I carried my frugal supper over to the kitchen table and saw that Insane Mind had won. I'd laid two places. I'd even set out two wine glasses. All appetite gone, I sank on to a chair. *This* was what I used to do when I was eight. I'd insist that a place for Heckie be laid at Aunt Janet's table, and, without demur, she would oblige.

As my Welsh rarebit congealed, I poured myself a glass of red wine. Then I poured one for Hector.

Sane Mind now advised me, as a matter of urgency, to email Dr Athelstan Blake to inform him I would shortly be returning to London to revive my flagging career. Not to be outdone, Insane Mind countered with the suggestion that I invite Dr Blake to come and pursue his musical research at *Tigh-na-Linne*.

Perhaps this wasn't such a terrible idea. Something told me (Insane Mind, probably) that Stan would be thrilled to discover Janet's house was haunted. Doubtless his curiosity and Canadian courtesy would extend toward paranormal manifestations. For a few moments, I allowed myself to fantasise about Stan and Hector meeting, maybe sinking a few drams of Talisker. Then I (or rather Sane Mind) remembered there was no such thing as ghosts. And that included Hector.

It was getting late but I suddenly felt the need to be outdoors, smelling the scents of the night, my feet planted firmly on the earth, grounded. Kicking off my slippers, I grabbed my coat from the back of the door and pulled it on. I stepped into my Wellingtons and went outside.

The cold November air was a shock to my system after the toasty, Aga-fuelled fug of the kitchen, but it was refreshing. Fallen leaves crackled underfoot as I strode across the lawn, spongy now with autumn rain. As I inhaled the smell of decaying vegetation, I began to feel better. Then I realised one of the reasons I felt better was because I was thinking about Hector again. I couldn't fathom how thinking about him made me feel better *and* worse, but it was a familiar enough sensation. It was how I used to feel when I was with David: comforted, companionable, whilst knowing there was no future in the relationship.

Tigh-na-Linne's tall, illuminated windows cast lozenges of light onto the wet grass. As I approached the shrubbery, I glanced back and thought how warm and welcoming the house looked, how inhabited, as if a big family lived there. Instead, there was only me.

And Hector. *Possibly*.

Again, I felt that panicky lurch toward something irrational, which was also something familiar. Hector and I had played Hide and Seek in this very shrubbery. I'd climbed these trees and he'd stood below, ready to catch me if I fell. (I never did, perhaps because I knew he was there.)

Wishing I'd brought a torch out with me, I turned away

from the forbidding darkness of the shrubbery and walked back, past the big lily pond spanned by a dilapidated wooden bridge – Janet's homage to Monet's Giverny. My spine jolted as my boots hit the path again and I set off to patrol the perimeter of the house. *My* house.

Despite my proprietorial pride, things were not looking good for me. "Asset-rich, cash-poor" summed up my situation. I'd paid too much for my London flat, assuming it would appreciate, then the recession bit deep. The flat was actually too small, but I couldn't afford to move. My contract with the BBC hadn't been renewed and I was unlikely to get another now. I was getting on in television terms. (TV is much kinder to men than women when it comes to matters of age.) I was unemployed and currently living on my savings. Those were no longer substantial since David and I had blown thousands on our holiday-of-a-lifetime last year, spending a month in Australia, seeing the sights and catching up with his son, daughter-in-law and their new baby. (As I was finally meeting the folks, I'd half hoped David would propose while we were away. When he didn't, I told myself I was relieved. Then I realised I *was*.)

I didn't regret the trip, especially in the light of what happened to poor David, but now I was short of funds, short of space and short of a job. Or I needed to sell *Tigh-na-Linne*.

Setting aside my sentimental attachment to the place, would it sell? It needed refurbishment, but appeared to be basically sound. It was expensive to run and unless you were a keen gardener or employed one, the size of the plot was daunting, but the view was one of the best on Skye and would command a high price. The house itself was really too big for a family home, but too small to convert into a hotel. It would make a splendid guesthouse, but I didn't see myself as a landlady.

Could I run it as a horticultural study centre? Or a nursery? Janet had a polythene tunnel and propagated her own plants, giving away the surplus. I could turn the vegetable garden over to seed beds and the site could be developed in a variety of ways. Despite the prevailing inclement weather and the curse of midges, there were a lot of keen gardeners on Skye. But a nursery wouldn't make much money. Enough to run the house perhaps, but not enough to pay the wages of the staff I'd have to employ.

My ruminations were shattered by an eerie, not quite human shriek from the shrubbery. I spun round, peered into the darkness and, without thinking, called out, 'Hector?'

There was no reply. After a few moments, the bloodcurdling shriek came again. This time my startled brain made the connection. A vixen. Janet used to tell me about fox cubs playing on the lawn and the unearthly cry of their mother. So that was it. Just a fox. Nothing to worry about. A fox, with fur the colour of Hector's hair…

Damn. Why did everything make me think of Hector?

I walked on, trying to think like an estate agent. *Tigh-na-Linne* had a lot going for it, including a history. It had been the home of a reclusive composer of some standing. The story of her forebears was also interesting, if tragic: three sons lost in the Great War, wiping out the male line in two years. I wondered what those poor men had been before they enlisted? Hector had died at thirty-five. He must have been established in a profession.

Hector again. *Stop it.*

I looked up at the house's impressive façade and stood listening to the distant sound of waves scraping the shingle. It struck me there was TV potential in the story of *Tigh-na-Linne* and the making of its beautiful garden, especially if Janet had had to live a lie, concealing her love for another woman. A vision of Tom Howard being interviewed about his mother swam into my mind. At once my hypothetical documentary seemed more commercial. Tom was charming, articulate and easy on the eye. I knew two female producers (and one male) who'd salivate at the thought of Tom in front of the TV cameras.

I was warming to my idea when I heard another noise. Not animal this time and not human. Metallic, as if something had been banged or dropped. Was someone breaking in to *Tigh-na-Linne*?

I cursed myself for coming out with neither my torch nor my phone. I stood still and listened out for the noise again.

Then I remembered that despite Tom having rung me to explain, I hadn't gone out and locked the garage door. And that was the direction the noise was coming from. Perhaps that's what I'd heard: the door being opened or closed. The garage contained various tools and pieces of gardening equipment, but not my car, which I left parked on the drive. Was someone stealing tools? Crime was almost unknown on Skye and what little there was, was largely drink-related, but Tom had said he made a habit of locking the garage door as a preventive measure.

It didn't seem a good idea to approach the garage on my own, especially as my intruder might be making off with some heavy object, like hedge-trimmers. But if there was no sign of a break-in – and there wouldn't be as I'd obligingly left the garage unlocked – I'd find it hard to make an insurance claim stick.

Resolving to keep my distance from the intruder, I decided I would approach the garage and shout out something formidable, like "Oi, you!", at which (I told myself) the terrified intruder would literally down tools and run. But as I set off in the direction of the garage, someone grabbed my shoulder and pulled me back, so that I stumbled and would have fallen, had I not met with something soft and yielding, like a huge cushion, that kept me upright, but prevented me from running away.

Veteran of two London muggings, I didn't even bother to scream before fighting back. Who was there to hear me apart from my intruder? I stamped hard where I thought my assailant's foot would be, while simultaneously jabbing with my free elbow in the direction of his kidneys. Then for good measure, I jerked my head backwards, hoping to hit his nose or, if he was tall, his jaw.

Might as well try to wrestle with marshmallows. There was nothing there. Or rather, there *was*, but it wasn't a man.

The cold night air now seemed significantly colder, especially in the region of my face. A voice close to my ear said, 'It's me. I'll let you go if you promise you'll not try anything foolhardy.'

'Someone's stealing my property!' I hissed.

'That's a matter for the police, not a defenceless lassie.'

'Hector, for God's sake, I'm not a *lassie*, I'm forty-two! I grew up! Or didn't you notice?'

'Oh, aye – I noticed!'

'Well, will you please let me go?'

He released me and, caught off-balance, I promptly fell against him again. As he set me upright, I heard distant running footsteps, then a vehicle driving away.

'There! If you hadn't stopped me, I could have got a look at him.'

'It wasn't worth the risk to you.'

'That was for me to decide!'

I rubbed my arms, more because I was cold than because they hurt, but Hector saw and misinterpreted.

'I'm sorry I hurt you.'

'Oh, you didn't really. You frightened me, that's all. The sensation was really creepy.'

'*Creepy?*'

'Yes. You don't feel like a – well, a *mortal*, I suppose.'

Hector's face was hard to read in the darkness, but I thought he looked hurt. 'That's because I'm not.'

'No, I know.' I blundered on. 'It was just that, you holding on to me like that – well, it reminded me of the time I nearly drowned. Here. In the pond. I got caught up in a load of weed and water lily roots and I panicked. Tommy had to wade in and drag me out.'

'No, he didn't. That was me.'

'What do you mean, it was you?' I asked indignantly.

'Did you see who dragged you out?'

'No. I was half-conscious. I'd swallowed a lot of water. And mud. It was *disgusting*. I was sick for the rest of the day.'

Hector said nothing and wouldn't meet my eyes.

'I don't understand... Tommy was there when I opened my eyes. And he *said* he'd saved me from drowning,' I added, uncertain now.

Hector still didn't reply.

'It was *you*?'

He nodded.

'Did Tommy *see* you?'

'No. He wasn't there. He must have run away. By the time he re-appeared, you were lying on the grass, recovering.'

'Oh... I see. Well, thank you. I didn't realise.'

After a moment Hector said, 'Is it really that unpleasant?'

'What?'

'Being held by me?'

I blinked in astonishment. Not known for my social skills, I'd managed to hurt the feelings of a *ghost*. 'No. But it does feel cold. And very odd. As if there's nothing actually there. Yet you can feel something. It's a bit like being underwater.'

'Sounds bad to me.' Hector turned away and muttered, 'Like drowning in a shell-hole full of mud.'

'Oh, no! Nothing like as bad as *that*!' I stopped dead, wondering if I was addressing someone who *had* drowned in a shell-hole full of mud. I started to shiver. It wasn't just the cold.

'I'm very sorry if I frightened you,' Hector said. 'Or if my behaviour was... intrusive.'

'No, it's just that I wasn't expecting you.' I shivered again.

'Away inside with you now. Lock your doors, then ring the police. When they arrive you can go and check if anything's missing. But make sure someone accompanies you.'

'Hector, will you please stop bossing me about!'

He looked taken aback. 'Forgive me. I was used to giving orders. And having them obeyed.'

'And it shows! You were an officer, I take it?'

'Aye, at the end of my life, I was.'

The words hit me like a slap in the face. 'I'm sorry. I didn't mean to sound disrespectful. I just don't know how to talk to a dead person.'

'Please don't concern yourself. I've never wanted anyone's pity! Understanding, perhaps...' He sighed and went on. 'When I was alive, home on leave, I found myself wishing there was a way to convey exactly what it was like at the Front, but—' He broke off and, clasping his hands behind his back, bowed his head. 'There isn't. The desolation was... indescribable. Either you were there, or you were not.'

'Could you *try* to tell me something about it? Something that you'd like me to understand.'

83

Hector gazed at me, as if assessing what I could handle, or possibly what *he* could handle, then he said, 'Let's walk back. You'll be getting cold. Would you like to take my arm? Such as it is,' he added, with a wry smile.

I hooked my arm through his and we began to walk along the path. As we passed in front of the lighted windows, Hector's thin face was illuminated and I could see the pale, electric blue of his eyes and the extraordinary length of his curling, sandy lashes. Then as we passed the window, we'd be plunged into darkness again so that, as he spoke, he seemed to appear and disappear.

'What was soul-destroying about life in the trenches was never seeing, never hearing anything natural. Anything *alive*. Apart from the men. Though many of them were dead or dying. There were the infernal lice, of course. And rats... But no bird sang. No dog barked. There wasn't a leaf on a tree. Eventually there wasn't even a tree. Just rain. And rats. That was all that was left of God's creation. It was the Book of Genesis in reverse. Chaos.'

I could think of nothing to say that wouldn't sound trite, so I stopped walking and turned to face Hector. I was close enough to see a glint in his eyes, which in a mortal might have heralded tears. (Could ghosts weep?) To save his feelings, I began to walk again, asking conversationally, 'What did you do before the war?'

'I was a schoolmaster.'

'Oh, *well*. That explains a *lot*.'

He turned his head and grinned at me. With a rush of affection, I remembered my childhood playmate. I also noticed how much more attractive Hector was when he smiled, in so far as one could feel attracted to a ghost (which surely wasn't very far?)

We arrived at the back door and I stood, completely non-plussed, fighting an urge to invite Hector in to drink the glass of wine I'd poured for him some time ago. At a loss, I said, 'What will you do now?'

'I'll wait out here a wee while. Make sure there's no one else prowling around.'

'And then?' He didn't reply but his expression clouded and

84

I saw his mouth tense. 'Hector, can I ask you something?...
Where *are* you when you're not with me?'

As I waited for him to answer, he seemed to age. His eyes
became dull and the muscles of his face went slack. He shook
his head and said, 'I wouldn't know how to describe it to you.
No words of mine could ever be adequate.'

'Try. Please. When you're not with me, I think about you
and – well, I wonder where you *are*. I'd really like to know.'

I watched as his chest rose and fell in a great sigh, then,
with what appeared to be an effort, he said, 'I suppose you'd
call it... limbo. Another kind of No Man's Land.'

Silence hung between us but I knew Hector was still
thinking, struggling once again to share his world with me.
Eventually, he said, 'There are some lines of Milton's that
perhaps—' He faltered, then said, 'We read a lot of poetry in
the trenches. There was a *craving* for beauty. For... *sense*.'

'Can you remember the Milton?' I asked softly.

'Oh, aye. It's memorable, right enough.' He gazed at some
distant point over my shoulder, and began to intone in his
deep, gravelly voice.

> '*A dark*
> *Illimitable ocean without bound,*
> *Without dimension; where length, breadth and height*
> *And time and place are lost; where eldest Night*
> *And Chaos, ancestors of Nature, hold*
> *Eternal anarchy, amidst the noise*
> *Of endless wars, and by confusion stand.*'

My hand flew to my mouth. 'Oh, Hector...'

'It's from *Paradise Lost*. A description of Hell.'

I swallowed and tried to steady my voice. 'I can't bear to
think of you being in such a place! After all you've suffered.'

He shook his head. 'I'm beyond such things now. Beyond
everything.'

'*Everything?*'

He stared at me for a moment, as if he wanted to say
more, then he turned to go. 'I must away.'

'Stay!' I clutched at his arm and was startled yet again by

the insubstantiality of his body.

'Och, you don't need me now.'

'I know, but I don't want you to have to return to – to that place.'

'Very well. I'll wait at your door then. While you sleep. But Ruth—'

'Yes?'

His eyes avoided mine. 'I think I'd better wait outside.'

'The house?'

'Your door.'

'Why?'

He shrugged. 'I'd prefer it. As you pointed out, you're no longer a wee lassie. And I feel... awkward, being in a lady's bedroom. It's not something I made a habit of when I was alive.'

I smiled. 'So you do still have some feelings then? Embarrassment, at least?'

'Aye. When I'm in my human form, I appear to have a full complement of feelings. Things are... much as I remember. But you're not, Ruth.' His eyes searched my face. 'You're not at all as I remember.'

I took his hand, bracing myself for the strange sensation, but my own fingers were so cold, I barely registered the chill of Hector's. He looked down at our joined hands and a little laugh seemed to die, half-strangled at the back of his throat. 'Dear God, I haven't held a woman for almost a hundred years!' He raised his other hand to my face and lifted my chin. 'And you remind me of the last woman I held, Ruth. She was as fair as you're dark, but she was strong like you.' He smiled. 'And wilful.' He let go my hand and stepped back. 'Away inside with you now. It's cold and it's late.'

'You'll wait outside my door tonight?'

'Aye, I will.'

'But you won't be there when I wake.'

He shook his head, then turned and began to walk slowly back along the path.

I'd opened the back door and was about to enter when a thought struck me. I turned and called out.

'Hector!'

He spun round, his kilt swinging.

'Aye?'

'Did Tommy *push* me into the pond?'

Hector spread his hands. 'I didn't see the accident happen. I just knew you were in trouble. Your need called out to me.'

'I can remember Tommy being there before it happened... He must have run off to get help.'

'Did it come?' Hector asked as he approached again. 'Did Janet appear?'

'I think so... Well, she must have. I can remember her shouting at Tommy, sounding hysterical. We weren't allowed to play on the bridge, you see. The wood was often slippery and that pond's deep in the middle. But Tommy had dared me. He said Janet would never know... I don't really remember what happened after that. But I got into big trouble later. Tommy told Janet playing on the bridge was *my* idea. I didn't really mind because I thought he'd saved me from drowning. I thought he was a hero.'

'Don't distress yourself. It was a long time ago. You were both – what? Eight? Nine?'

'But it was horrible! And now it seems even more horrible than I remember.'

Hector laid his hands on my shoulders and looked into my eyes. 'I wouldn't have let anything happen to you, Ruth. And I won't. Not if it's within my power to prevent it. And that power is considerable. *Believe* it.'

'I think I do. Thank you.'

I knew if I didn't walk away right now, I might put my head down on Hector's insubstantial chest and howl, so I said a curt, 'Good night', then opened the door and went inside, with a sob lodged in my throat like a giant fish bone.

Sitting on a kitchen chair by the Aga, cold and exhausted, I tried to summon up the energy to ring the police and failed. It was late. The crime (if crime there were) wasn't serious. It was probably just kids looking for stuff they could sell on eBay. If they'd found it, I only had myself to blame. What would I say when asked if the garage was locked? I could

87

hardly lie, nor could I face a police constable's withering look if I told the truth. Not tonight anyway. In any case, I might not even know what had been stolen. It was not as if I had an inventory. I would probably need to ask Tom if he thought anything was missing.

Tom.

Was *that* what had upset me so much? Discovering that my childhood friend had a mean and dangerous streak? Well, I already knew about the mean streak. What young child isn't occasionally cruel? But what Hector had implied seemed to go beyond that. Malice and deceit were hard for me to swallow, even years after the event.

But what on earth was I doing, taking the word of a *ghost* against Tommy's? Hadn't I already concluded I must be on the verge of a nervous breakdown?

The fact remained, when I'd tried to run to the garage to see off my intruder, something had prevented me. My neck was still sore where I'd pulled a muscle, throwing back my head to hit my assailant. That struggle had definitely happened. And the conversation that followed?...

Something Hector had said came to mind. Words he'd quoted. (He was right, they *were* memorable.)

'*A dark, illimitable ocean without bound...*' Or something like that.

Were those words by Milton? If they were, did that prove Hector existed? Or had I subconsciously memorised some lines of poetry?

I dragged myself away from the warmth of the Aga and went in search of my laptop. I carried it back to the kitchen, switched on and stared at the screen, waiting. I'd barely scraped English O-Level and had only vague memories of studying Shakespeare and *Lord of the Flies*. I'd done science A-levels, then trained at horticultural college. How would I know any Milton?

The Google home page appeared. I typed in the phrase I remembered, plus "Milton" and hit return. A page of results came up quoting those very words. I clicked on one and learned that the quotation came from *Paradise Lost* and was indeed a description of Hell. That still didn't prove Hector existed, nor that I was sane. I had no idea how the subconscious worked. Perhaps I'd seen these words in Hector's journal.

I was clutching at straws and I knew it. I hadn't opened that book since I'd found it. I hadn't dared. So I couldn't believe I'd scanned Milton's lines and subconsciously committed them to memory, not when my mind was already freaked out by handling a book stained with blood – possibly the owner's.

But still my scientist's mind craved *proof*.

I shut down the laptop, checked the back door was locked and went up to bed. There was no sign of Hector apart from his glass incarnation. I got ready for bed, but before turning out the light, I opened the bedside drawer and took out his journal. The earthy smell was faint, but distinct. Overcoming my sense of revulsion, I opened the little book and forced myself to read some of the words beneath the stains.

There were dates, descriptions of weather, records of letters received, of deaths and other casualties. Every so often there were titles of books (or possibly poems) and a few lines in quotation marks. Hector seemed to collect other people's words and, as he'd told me, it seemed he'd read a lot of poetry. But he didn't appear to have written any. All the poetry was carefully attributed. Not only was the author recorded, but also the title of the poem, often the name of the anthology.

And then I found it.

Milton's description of Hell. It was the last quotation in the journal, transcribed not long before Hector died.

I'd never seen this page before. This I knew for a fact because the page had been stuck to the next, glued together with dried mud. I had to peel the two pages apart to read them. Did this prove Hector existed? I still didn't know for sure, but one thing I *was* sure of: I'd had enough of trying to believe he *didn't*.

I put the little book back in the drawer, switched off the light and got into bed. For a few moments, I lay still, listening to the silence of the night, then I whispered, 'Goodnight, Hector.'

There was a slight movement of cool air around my face and then the bedroom door (which I'd left slightly ajar) closed with a gentle click. Silence descended once again, like a blessing.

I was still thinking about Hector in the trenches, writing in his journal, when belatedly, I registered a word I'd seen on one of those filthy pages. Galvanised, I sat up in bed and switched on the light. I got the journal out again and quickly leafed through, searching for a name. I was about to give up, almost convinced I'd imagined it, when there it was, right at the end of the journal: a short entry, dated only days before Hector was killed. It said, "Received letter from Frieda. This is a very bad business. I am in Hell."

Frieda.

The woman to whom Janet had dedicated her song cycle, *In Memoriam.*

Intrigued, excited even, I turned back to the beginning of the journal and started to skim the first page, looking for more references to Frieda. As I read, it suddenly struck me that I was sitting in bed, devouring the very private journal of a man who sat patiently outside my bedroom door. I hadn't asked his permission to read the journal and I had no reason to believe if I'd asked, he'd have given it.

Reluctantly, I closed the book.

Received letter from Frieda. This is a very bad business. I am in Hell.

It didn't sound like a subject I could bring up casually in conversation. Given the delicacy Hector had already shown, insisting on waiting outside my door; given that he'd been born in 1880, I couldn't imagine he'd relish the thought of a woman reading the unconsidered words he'd scribbled while facing death on a daily basis. This was not a journal written with any hope of publication or even any intention of sharing. It was a private record of the occasionally desperate thoughts ("I am in Hell") of a man who'd lost his faith, his two brothers and many of his friends and who ultimately gave everything for what he himself described as a pointless war. It was not my place to read this journal, however curious I was to know the identity of Frieda. I would never dream of reading, without permission, the diary of a *living* person. Hector might not be alive, but he wasn't exactly dead either. Not to me.

With a sigh of disappointment, I put the journal back in the bedside drawer and turned out the light again. I lay in bed, staring into the darkness, cursing my moral scruples. If only I could bring myself to think of Hector as dead, there would be no obstacle to further investigation.

And then it hit me. The solution.

Dr Athelstan Blake.

As far as Stan was concerned, Hector was dead. Stan could – *should* – read the journal as part of his research into Janet's music since he was keen to know more about Frieda, the dedicatee of *In Memoriam*. So I could send the journal to Canada...

Never. I couldn't bear to part with it.

I didn't care to examine the reasons why I felt so strongly, but I wasn't prepared to entrust a precious family heirloom to the vagaries of transatlantic post. So if I wouldn't post the journal, Stan would have to come to Scotland to read it.

I fell asleep wondering whether Christmas on Skye would make a refreshing change from the inane round of London media parties. Would Dr Blake appreciate an invitation to celebrate the holiday, Highland-style? Something told me – Sane Mind, for once – that he'd jump at the chance.

Chapter Nine

When I woke the following morning it still seemed a sane idea to invite Stan to Skye. It also seemed to be the only way I could actually move forward. I wasn't ready to put *Tigh-na-Linne* on the market yet. I couldn't bring myself to read Hector's journal, nor did I feel able to ask him directly about "the bad business" with Frieda. And how could I advance Janet's musical reputation (or protect it) if I refused to let Stan investigate? In addition, his research might unearth a story I could use in some way to revive my own career. There had to be a TV programme in there somewhere, perhaps even a book. A different one from the musical study Stan was planning. A book about *Tigh-na-Linne*, its garden and the history of the Munro family.

A ghost story.

Running on, my mind suddenly tripped over itself. *What the hell was I doing?*

Finding excuses to stay at *Tigh-na-Linne*, that's what I was doing, when I should be back in London, schmoozing producers in wine bars, and lunching with useful people, giving them my feeble impersonation of a media tart.

I'd hated all the fatuous celebrity nonsense that went with being a gardening guru. "Delia of the Delphiniums" just about summed it up. It wasn't what I had in mind when I trained at horticultural college, but I'd somehow drifted into it. Telegenic, a good communicator and enthusiastic about my work, I was a natural apparently. TV gardening programmes are built on such personalities.

David had had a better life/work balance with his gardening column in a Sunday paper, a modest income from writing book reviews, plus the royalties from his own old-fashioned, but ever popular gardening manuals. He'd always found time to "stand and stare", whereas I'd never had enough – not enough time to spend with my father, Aunt Janet or my ever-decreasing circle of friends. I certainly hadn't had time to meet other men. When I wasn't filming, I was writing scripts or travelling for programme research. I had a career, but I didn't feel I was *living*. Losing my job had been something of a wake-up call.

The trouble was, I'd woken up in limbo. No job, no man, a big old house I ought to sell, an address book full of friends and contacts I hadn't seen in months, in some cases years. It meant starting all over again.

What was it Hector had said about me?... That I would know what to do? What a joke.

Yet I did feel a strong impulse to invite Stan to Skye. It felt like the right thing to do. I wondered whether I should ask Hector's advice, but I could hardly be straight with him about wanting Stan to do my dirty work for me. (*Was* it dirty work? Wasn't it simply researching my family history? Yes, if I could just remember that Hector was dead.)

Sick of indecision, I gave in to my impulse and emailed Stan with an invitation to come and stay in December. Madness of course, but if I hadn't sent it, I would have had to deal with the fact that I'd be spending Christmas on my own, without David, without my father, without Janet. I didn't have any other family I could impose on, nor any single friends who could be relied upon to be around over the holiday period. They very sensibly went ski-ing or sunbathing and with my uncertain finances, I didn't feel inclined to join them.

For all I knew, Stan might be fully booked, spending Christmas with children and grandchildren, but there was no harm in asking. To tell the truth, I rather liked the idea of spending Christmas on Skye with an eccentric academic.

And a ghost.

As I finished my breakfast, I remembered I needed to check the contents of the garage and lock up again, so I wrapped up well and went out to investigate the scene of the crime.

I couldn't tell if anything was missing. The lawn mower and strimmer were still there and so was the rotavator. There was a pair of hedge trimmers, but I had a feeling there should have been two. All the smaller tools were hanging in rows on the wall (Janet's obsessive tidiness extended to garage, greenhouse and potting shed) and I couldn't see any gaps. Perhaps the intruder had heard me talking to Hector and bolted.

I locked up, pocketed the key and walked on through the garden, heading down to the beach. I stopped when I got to the pond and watched a grey heron. It stood hunched and motionless, like a stone ornament, staring dolefully into the water's murky depths. There must still be some fish then. Janet had said the pond had been a bathing pool originally, fed from a spring, so it was several degrees warmer than the freezing sea and not subject to treacherous currents. The four Munro children had no doubt played and swum in it in summer and perhaps skated on it in winter. Now the pond was in sad need of attention. It was choked with pondweed and the rotting wooden bridge needed replacing. I added the jobs to my mental *To Do* list and walked on, trying not to feel despondent. There was no denying, if I kept *Tigh-na-Linne*, it could turn out to be a money pit. I mustn't be blinded by sentiment. The house would have to earn its keep.

Despite the brightness of the November day, it was bitterly cold once you moved away from the shelter of the garden. I pulled my fleece hat down over my ears and strode along the shingle beach, wishing I had a dog for company. Or even Hector.

I hadn't gone far when a vibration in my coat pocket told me my mobile was ringing. (My tasteful ring tone couldn't compete with the roar of the breakers on the shore and the crunch of my boots on the shingle.) I looked at the screen, but it was a new number, someone ringing from abroad. As I answered, I walked away from the water's edge, toward the shelter of some rocks.

'Hello?'

'Ms Travers? Ruth? I hope I'm not disturbing you. This is Athelstan Blake.'

For a moment I was thrown by the transatlantic lilt and then my brain, numbed with cold, finally stirred. 'Dr. Blake?' I glanced at my watch and made a quick calculation. 'But surely it must be 4.00am in Toronto?'

'4.10 to be precise, but I couldn't sleep and I was checking email when your invitation arrived. I was so excited, I had to tell someone and I thought it might as well be you. I'm not interrupting your breakfast, I hope? Or work?'

'No, not at all. I'm out for a walk on the beach. And shortly about to expire from hypothermia, I fear.'

Stan laughed, then said, 'Tell me what you can see! Are you looking out at the islands?'

'Yes. Visibility's good today. It isn't usually in November.'

'Do you have snow yet?'

'No. We don't ever get much – though they say this is going to be a hard winter. I imagine you have some already?'

'Plenty. But we're used to it. The Canadian gene pool supplied us with a useful mix of English phlegm, Scottish ingenuity and Inuit stoicism, so we get by.'

'Do *you* have any Scottish blood?'

'If you go back far enough. I was told my grandmother emigrated from Scotland. I've always wanted to come over to research my family history. You can do a certain amount online, but I imagine it's no substitute for actually being in the land of your forefathers.'

'You've never been to Scotland then?'

'Why, no, that's why I was so excited about your invitation! I managed a short stay in Europe in my youth, but I never made it as far north as Scotland. *Yet still the blood is strong, the heart is Highland and we, in dreams, behold the Hebrides...* That's from *The Canadian Boat Song*, first recorded in 1829. Ex-pat Gaels used to sing it – in Gaelic, of course – as they rowed down the St Lawrence River. I heartily concur with the sentiment.'

'So I take it you'd like to come and stay?'

'Ms Travers – Ruth – I can't tell you how thrilled I am with your invitation. But are you sure? You know, you really don't have to offer me hospitality.'

'Oh, but I do!' I heard myself and wondered why I'd said that. The impulse was genuine. It wasn't just courtesy. I felt I had to invite Stan because there was so much I wanted to talk to him about. But I took refuge in good manners. 'Highland hospitality is both legendary and mandatory. I may only be half-Scots on my mother's side, but I don't propose to do things by half-measures. You're very welcome, Dr Blake.'

'Please, call me Stan.'

'Your first name is very unusual. It must be Anglo-Saxon.'

'My father was a historian with a passion for the Anglo-Saxons, for which I've never quite been able to forgive him. "Hereward" would at least have had a glamorous ring to it.'

It was my turn to laugh. 'My father was an academic too. Classics. He despaired of me because I rejected books and history and went into horticulture.'

'Well, we obviously both bear the scars and will have much to talk about – if you're really sure it won't be too much trouble?'

'It won't, I assure you. It will just be you and me for Christmas – I have no family – so I'll be glad of the company. I'm finding it's a big house to rattle around in on my own.'

'Is it haunted?'

Stunned, I didn't reply for a few moments, then said cautiously, 'Why do you ask?'

'Wishful thinking, I guess.'

'Have you ever seen a ghost?' I asked as I plodded up the beach and back through the gate into the garden.

'I regret to say, I haven't. But I maintain an open mind on the subject. On most subjects, in fact. So do you have a ghost in residence?'

'Well, I – I'm not sure. But I think there may be *something* strange going on. There's a... a definite presence.'

'I knew it!'

'Knew what?'

'That Janet knew more than she was letting on. For fear of ridicule, I guess. Well, you can hardly blame her. She spent her life struggling to be taken seriously. Declaring a belief in the paranormal would hardly have strengthened her cause.'

'What makes you think Janet might have seen something?'

'An interview she gave on radio. She was asked about *In Memoriam* and her interest in World War I and her female take on that. Well, *that* was a red rag to bull, of course.'

'What did she say?'

'She said, although she'd never known the men in her family who'd died – it was three brothers, I gather?'

'Yes, Janet's uncles. My great-uncles.'

'Is that so? Well, Janet said she'd felt the presence of the past at *Tigh-na-Linne*. The *legacy* – I believe that was the word she used. Living there had made her conscious of how the past reverberates down the years and on into the present, even into the future. It was a fascinating interview. I'll email you a transcript. Janet was ahead of her time in her thinking – I mean, when you consider this was only the 1950s. DNA was a very new discovery then. But Janet believed we carried some sort of *imprint* of the past in our mental and spiritual make-up, that some people could sense the presence of the past in objects, buildings, geographical areas. She even thought some could sense the presence of the dead – somehow connect with their lives – and that the resonance of those lives could influence the living. From what you say, I think Janet was talking about herself and that maybe she'd seen a ghost.'

'Yes, I think perhaps she had.' I was now standing outside the house, beneath Hector's memorial window. I looked up at the dark patchwork of glass which, seen from inside, would bring his form brilliantly to life.

'Do you sense the past at *Tigh-na-Linne*?' Stan asked.

I hesitated, then said, 'Yes, I do. Quite strongly.'

'Oh, this is thrilling!' he chuckled. 'Have *you* seen the ghost?'

'Will you think I'm raving mad if I say... I have?'

'Not at all! I'm completely sympathetic to such aberrations. Perhaps I should explain. In my own small way, I'm a composer. My academic work buys me time to indulge that passion. Now, I couldn't begin to explain to you the process of composing, or where my music comes from. But what is the nature of inspiration, if not a sense of the past, of artistic tradition, combined with a feel for the future and the *potential* of the future? Did you know Beethoven composed for a type of piano that didn't yet exist? He imagined the kind of music that could be played if it did. Now *that* is vision.'

I walked on briskly, heading for the back door and the warmth of the kitchen. 'So you really don't know where your music comes from?'

'No idea. To me it feels as if the melodies are out there, inaudible, but *detectable*, like something you can just see out of the corner of your eye. They're vibrating silently, waiting for someone to receive them. Channel them, if you like. If there's music out there that only some people can hear, I see no reason why there shouldn't be beings out there that only some people can see. In other words, ghosts.' Stan sighed and added, 'Does that make any sense at *all*?'

'Yes, it does, actually. It makes a lot of sense to me.'

'I'm delighted you think so! You know, the so-called "music of the spheres" was supposed to be silent, but Buddhists believe you can develop a third ear through meditation and so attune to this silent music. Fascinating, isn't it? The way all these strange ideas connect.'

'That's really interesting! And heartening, in a way. I was beginning to think I was losing my mind.'

'Janet once said, "A creative artist needs to keep sanity in check".'

'*Did* she? Oh, bless her!'

'I used to be more sceptical myself, when I was young and not easily impressed, but I have a clever little sister who's a particle physicist. Believe me, by the time you've had String Theory explained to you, ghosts seem really quite mundane and the existence of time travel only a matter of – well, *time*.'

I unlocked the back door and stepped inside. 'You've given me such a lot to think about.'

'Likewise, I'm sure. It's been a real pleasure to talk to you, Ruth.'

'So you think you'll come over then? In December?'

'I certainly shall. Term ends on December 7th so I'll fly over some time after that. The following week probably, if I can get a flight.'

'I'm home now, so if you like, I can ring you back on the landline. This call will have cost you a small fortune.'

'And worth every cent. No, I won't prattle on, much as I'd love to spend more time talking to you. I'll email later when

I've checked available flights. Thank you again for your kind invitation. To spend Christmas on the Isle of Skye with Janet Gillespie's niece – and a ghost! Well, you know, for a sentimental Canadian musicologist who dreams of the Old Country, it doesn't get much better than that. Goodbye, Ruth. I'll be in touch. Take good care now.'

'You too. Bye, Stan.'

He hung up and I put my phone down on the kitchen table, feeling strangely exhilarated. It wasn't just the sea air and exercise. I'd finally *done* something. Wheels had been set in motion, though Heaven knew in what direction they were travelling. But I had plans. I even had a guest for Christmas. Two, if you counted Hector.

Absurdly cheerful, I made a large pot of coffee and sat down with my laptop by the Aga to thaw out. I decided I would spend the day drawing up a draft outline for a documentary about the history of *Tigh-na-Linne* and its occupants, including a composer and gardener – no, *two* gardeners – who had sensed the presence of the past.

I must have sat at the laptop for hours, recording my ideas and memories of Janet, things she'd told me over the years about my dead relatives. I made notes on Post-its of all the things I needed to research. Who had built *Tigh-na-Linne*? Had anything stood on the site previously? Who'd designed the three memorial windows? There might be photos of the other two somewhere, so I made a note to sort through the family albums and shoeboxes of photos Janet had hoarded. I made another note to contact the Local History Society.

I also wanted to know what and where Hector had taught before he enlisted and, much as it might distress me to know, I needed to find out how he'd died, so I noted queries about his regiment and the battle of Loos. Janet's study was lined with books, not all of them related to music and gardening. There might be some military history. Or there was always Google.

As I surrounded myself with sheets of paper and Post-its, it seemed clear there was enough material for a programme of some sort, possibly a book, depending on the quality of the pictorial material I could find. Fortunately Janet had recorded the development of the garden over the years and in all seasons, but none of her shots had been taken on a digital camera. I made a mental note to start taking photos myself in the spring.

But would I be here in the spring?...

Pushing this troubling thought to the back of my mind, I got up to switch on the light and realised I'd missed lunch. It was already mid-afternoon. Suddenly hungry, I made some toast and spread it with peanut butter. I didn't want to stop, even to make myself a hot drink, so I poured a glass of milk, sat down at the table again and began to sort through my notes.

I really needed to know about Frieda. She was the link between Hector and Janet. Hector had been distraught about the "bad business" and Janet had dedicated a major work to her, so Frieda had to be important. When had Janet begun work on *In Memoriam*? The autograph score was undated, but it had been published in the late 1950s. Was Frieda still alive when Janet dedicated *In Memoriam* to her? If she'd been an adult when Hector knew her, (a reasonable assumption if she'd sent a disturbing letter to a soldier at the Front), then she would have been in her sixties at least, possibly even seventies. Did *In Memoriam* refer to Janet's dead uncles (including Hector) or was it written for Frieda, who by then was also dead? Clearly, there was still a lot of research to be done before I could tell the story of *Tigh-na-Linne*.

I carried on Googling and making notes until, stiff and tired, I forced myself to stand up and stretch. The table was now covered with bits of paper and some had drifted on to the floor. As I bent to retrieve them, I realised I was getting hungry again and had nothing prepared for dinner. Yet another supper of tinned soup and cheese on toast, I supposed. My spirits plummeted at this dismal thought, so I headed for the larder and withdrew the remains of last night's red wine and a packet of crisps.

I poured a glass, ripped open the crisps and sat down again, feeling rather sorry for myself. Self-pity was superseded by irritation when I realised I was sitting there, like some damn medium at a séance, trying to conjure up Hector.

Because I was lonely. Because I enjoyed his company. Because – paradoxically – I felt safe when he was around. Because - oh, just *because*.

When the music started, I assumed it must be the radio. A neighbour's radio. Then I remembered I didn't have any neighbours. So I concluded it must be a CD player that had somehow switched itself on. Except that the sound seemed to be coming from the direction of the music room, where there was no CD player.

I stood up and made my way to the music room. When I turned on the light, I found Hector seated at the Bechstein, playing a piece I recognised as one of Janet's compositions. There was no sheet music open on the piano and I wondered in passing when Hector had learned to play it, let alone so well. But playing complex music from memory, in the dark, was presumably no great feat for a ghost.

Hector didn't stop, nor did he acknowledge my presence, so I sat in an armchair where I could observe. Looking at him in profile, I was aware of the military straightness of his spine, the angle of his tilted head and the ease with which his white hands seemed to drift over the keys, as if he barely touched them.

The music came to an end, but only when the last chord had died away completely did I allow myself to speak.

'You play.'

'Aye. In a manner of speaking.' Hector didn't turn to face me, but continued to stare at the keyboard.

'Did you play when you were alive?'

He nodded, but still didn't look at me.

'You said you were a teacher. What did you teach?'

'Music. I also taught piano privately.' He laid a hand tenderly on the polished rosewood. 'This was my piano. My parents bought it for me. For my sixteenth birthday. After I left home, I never had a room big enough to house it, so it was always a great joy to come home and play. Especially when I was on leave... There wasn't a great deal of music in the

101

trenches. The lads sang, of course – some of them very well. And we had pipers. But there was no piano. My fingers used to ache for the touch of the keys. They'd yearn for the feel of the ivory, the way you might long to touch a woman's skin...' He laid a hand high on the keyboard and depressed a few keys, making a pretty tinkling sound, like water trickling from a fountain.

'What was it you were playing just now?'

'*In Memoriam.*'

'Yes, of course. I didn't recognise it without the words.'

'There was a wordless version first. The lyric came later.'

'Do you know who wrote the words?'

'The ones that weren't taken from the Requiem Mass were from a poem by Andrew Marvell. *The Definition of Love.*'

Hector finally swivelled round on the piano stool and looked at me for the first time since I'd entered the room. He fixed his sad gaze on me and began to recite.

> '*My love is of a birth as rare*
> *As 'tis, for object, strange and high;*
> *It was begotten by Despair,*
> *Upon Impossibility.*'

His mouth curved then, twisting into a mirthless smile. He shook his head and said, 'I was surely born under an unlucky star. I loved but once in my life and it was—' He shrugged. 'An *impossibility*. Then once again. In death.'

For some reason, my heart began to pound, almost as if I were afraid. 'Hector, what do you mean?'

Ignoring me, he turned back to the piano again, spread his hands over the keys and played an eerie discord. 'And still... an impossibility.'

'Hector, who was Frieda?'

He didn't move, but his hands froze above the keyboard. Without looking up, he announced, casually, 'You have a visitor.'

As he finished speaking, there was a loud knock at the back door. Despite the warning, I jumped, then glanced nervously at my watch. It was only seven o'clock. There was no excuse to ignore the caller. I stared helplessly at Hector's expressionless face, unsure what to do. Then there was another knock, louder this time. I got up and hurried from the room, closing the music room door behind me in a futile gesture, as if it would somehow ensure Hector would be there when I returned.

Chapter Ten

I wasn't dressed for visitors.

When I'd got up, I'd thrown on an old pair of tracksuit bottoms and an Aran sweater, originally David's, which was two sizes too big for me. I wore no make-up and my hair (due for a wash) was scraped back into an elastic band. On my feet I wore what I referred to as my "Himalayan Wellingtons". As soon as I'd set eyes on these slipper-boots, I knew they must be really warm. Why else would anyone wear anything so ugly?

It was this vision of loveliness that opened the back door to my unexpected caller. Or rather, Tom.

Not just Tom, but Tom clutching a bottle of wine and a bunch of chrysanthemums. Tom in a *suit*. Not just a suit, but a smart blue-grey number that fitted in all the right places. Tom, with newly-washed hair that formed a cloud of fluffy blond curls that settled on his forehead and into which his perfectly arched brows shot when he took one look at me.

I put my hand up automatically to smooth my hair, then remembered it was scraped back into a high and unflattering ponytail, the kind Scots call "a Gorbals facelift."

'Hi...' Tom said, with a kind of sighing, downward inflection, like a punctured tyre. He looked me up and down. Clearly unimpressed, he said, 'You weren't expecting me, were you?'

'You're right. I wasn't. Should I have been?'

He stared at me, his expression stony. 'Well, it's Friday. It's seven o'clock. You said come for supper. With low expectations,' he added. 'I think maybe I didn't pitch mine low enough.'

Squealing, I clapped a hand over my mouth and bent double, pole-axed by embarrassment.

'Oh, *Tom*! I am so sorry! God, I'm such an *idiot*! Is it really

Friday? *Already?* I had no idea... Oh, God, come in. Really, I am so, so sorry!' As I closed the door behind him, the full extent of my incompetence hit me. 'Oh, *bugger...* I haven't got any food in either.'

Tom thrust the flowers into my arms, set the bottle down on the kitchen table and strode over to the fridge. He opened the door and examined the meagre contents. After a moment, he said, *'Jesus...'* in a really depressed voice, then, 'Have you got any spaghetti?'

'Only dried.'

'Eggs?'

'Two. I *think.*'

'Right, you've got three rashers of bacon. Some longlife cream. And what looks like an antique lump of Parmesan.' He withdrew his head from the fridge and said, 'I assume you've got white wine?'

'Oh, yes!'

'No problem then. It's *spaghetti carbonara* and I'm cooking. Now get upstairs and put some decent clothes on.'

I approached and looking up into his unhappy face said, 'I'm so sorry. I've had a really weird week. And I lost track of time. I had no idea it was Friday.'

He was looming over me, his face close to mine and I could smell something delicious. His aftershave, I suppose. Pointing to the tissue-wrapped bottle on the table, he said slowly, as if addressing a not very bright child, 'I'm opening that in fifteen minutes.'

'*No!*' I was aghast. 'Twenty! You *have* to give me twenty. *Please!*'

'All right, twenty. But the champagne gets opened in twenty minutes, whether you're down or not.'

'Champagne? Oh, Tom, you shouldn't have!'

'No, clearly, I shouldn't,' he replied with a withering look. 'I don't suppose there's a fire lit in the sitting room?'

'No,' I replied in a small voice.

'I'll see to it,' was his terse reply.

He removed his jacket and slung it on the back of a chair, then started to roll up his shirtsleeves. Fixing me with a look, he said, 'Go on. Get a move on. My shattered male ego is unlikely ever to recover, but you can at least *try* to make it up to me.'

'I will. I'll try very hard. Back in twenty minutes.'

'Nineteen now.'

'I really am sorry!'

'Up. Stairs. Now.'

I padded over to the door, then turned back and said, '*You* look terrific, by the way.'

'You don't,' he replied, filling the kettle. 'So scram. Go and do that transformation thing women do. I've seen the *Before*. Now I want to see the *After*.'

'Oh... So no pressure, then?' I called out cheerfully as I left the kitchen.

I'd just set my yak-booted foot on the first stair when I heard a roar of laughter from the kitchen. Relieved beyond measure, I took the stairs two at a time.

Nineteen minutes to dress, apply make-up and rescue my hair. It was not unknown for me to spend nineteen minutes choosing what to wear. Which *shoes* to wear. In those nineteen minutes I also had to come up with a really good reason for my absent-mindedness that didn't include ghosts. I hadn't just forgotten my invitation, I'd forgotten *Tom*, adult Tom anyway, who, only a few days ago, had occupied my thoughts to an embarrassing extent, even invading my dreams.

Eighteen minutes. My clothes lay discarded on the floor and I stood naked in front of my open wardrobe, surveying its contents. Something that didn't need ironing was required, so I reached for a red jersey wrap dress that would cover my arms and legs and keep off the *Tigh-na-Linne* chill. Yet it still looked glamorous, revealing a certain amount of cleavage and, depending on how you sat, a certain amount of leg.

My choice of dress reflected my confusion about dinner with Tom. I certainly wasn't out to seduce him (though to judge from the champagne, he might be out to seduce me) but I did want to look seduction-worthy. As a matter of principle. I also felt I owed it to the poor guy to make an effort.

Seventeen minutes. I'd put on my prettiest underwear (as a morale boost, not because I thought it would be making a public appearance) but, as I tied the belt of the dress, I decided I wouldn't bother with tights. I'd already put my thumbs through one pair in my haste to dress and, in any case, my legs were still a bit brown from the summer. So that just left shoes. Strappy sandals? My nude toenails looked dispiriting, so I opted for shiny red killer heels, the ones I'd bought to wear to a TV award ceremony, to demonstrate that my feet and ankles weren't actually shaped like Wellington boots. They'd made me taller than David, but I wouldn't have that problem with Tom. (And *that* thought, I noted, caused just a little flutter in my tummy.)

I sat down at the dressing table, cursing the dingy light and tried to remember the last time I'd applied makeup. Janet's funeral? Dear God, was it really that long ago?... I brushed my hair and stared critically at my reflection, then I remembered Hector and how he had none. Did he know what he looked like? Could he actually remember after nearly a hundred years?... Hector couldn't ever have been considered handsome, but he was striking. Rather beautiful in a peculiar, vivid way. I certainly couldn't imagine forgetting what he looked like.

As I tipped the contents of my make-up bag on to the dressing table, I realised with something akin to shame that I was thinking about Hector while Tom was downstairs preparing the dinner I'd offered to cook for him. And Hector wasn't even *real*. Or if he was, he wasn't a man, so I should stop thinking about him as a man. With twelve minutes to go, I should stop thinking about him altogether.

I put the finishing touches to my make-up, applied mousse to my hair and blow-dried it, then I selected silver earrings and a matching necklace David had bought me in Orkney. I sprayed myself with perfume and – *voilà!* – I was ready. With two minutes in hand, I considered my reflection in the full-length mirror.

Not bad.

Grief had caused me to lose weight this year and the heels meant I was now super-model tall. I hadn't thought of getting my hair cut in months, so it now hung long and heavy around my face, lending me a certain shampoo-commercial allure. The red dress was good with my dark hair and showed I still had a waist, despite my tendency to live on toasted cheese and red wine.

I had no idea what Tom would think and told myself I didn't really care. He would have to admit I'd made an effort and there's only so much you can achieve in nineteen minutes.

I blotted my lipstick and turned away from the mirror. David's old sweater lay discarded on the floor and I had a sudden vision of him lying in a heap in the snow, looking like a bundle of old clothes. The memory knocked the wind right out of me. I badly wanted to sit down and compose myself, but I feared if I did, I might cry, then I'd have to re-do my make-up.

Ignoring the heap of clothes on the floor, I sailed out of the bedroom, slightly unsteady on my heels. There was a smell of wood smoke in the hall and I could hear the comforting sounds of a log fire crackling in the sitting room below. Tom had been busy. Just before I turned to go downstairs, punctual to the minute, I looked back along the corridor at the memorial window. It was dark of course, so I couldn't see Hector's figure clearly, only a collection of glass shapes separated by meandering strips of leading.

An aroma of frying bacon began to dominate the wood smoke and reminded me I was hungry. I set off down the stairs feeling a slight pang of disappointment, which I couldn't really fathom. As I placed my hand on the kitchen door handle, I realised I was disappointed Hector wouldn't see me in my glad rags, wouldn't know I'd scrubbed up rather well. Not that I imagined he'd care. If Hector had ever been a red-blooded male, he certainly wasn't now.

So with Hector – and Hector's blood – on my mind, I made my entrance.

I opened the door to find the air cloudy with steam and throbbing with Classic FM. Candles were lit on the table (where had Tom found those?) and the top lights were out. Unaware of my presence, he was holding the bottle of champagne in both hands and was easing out the cork.

'I made it then,' I said brightly, feeling suddenly awkward in my finery. Tom spun round and as he did so, the cork popped and foam began to bubble upwards slowly. He stood transfixed, staring at me with his mouth slightly open, the champagne apparently forgotten.

I grabbed two glasses from the dresser and stepped forward, holding one out for him to fill. As I stood close, I could smell whisky on his breath. Glancing across at the worktop, I saw an empty tumbler and assumed he'd helped himself while cooking. He certainly knew his way around the kitchen.

Without speaking, he carefully filled both glasses, then set the bottle down on the table. He looked me up and down, smiling, raised his glass and said, 'Here's to you. You look... *amazing*! Cheers!'

'You're very kind. *Slàinte!*' I sipped my champagne but Tom downed half a glass, as if it were lemonade.

'Was the "Before" fancy dress just a cunning ploy to make me appreciate the Cinderella transformation scene?'

'No. Poor Cinderella is completely incompetent and forgot the Prince was expected.' I swallowed another mouthful of champagne. 'I'm just not used to socialising here. I've become a hermit, obsessed with my family history! Do you know, I seem to have actually invited a crusty old Canadian academic to stay for Christmas, just so we can discuss Janet's music and my family tree. I must be out of my mind.'

Tom went over to the hob, set down his glass and pushed spaghetti into a pan of simmering water. 'Janet and Tricia used to spend Christmas together. When Tricia moved to Skye, I mean. And I was out of the way. They used to have musical *soirées*.'

'Was Tricia musical then?'

'Oh, yes. She sang and played the piano. When I was young she used to play the flute, but then she had to sell it. We needed the money. She always wanted me to learn the piano, but we couldn't afford lessons, let alone a piano. And I wasn't interested anyway. You couldn't keep me indoors on a sunny day.'

'I hadn't realised Tricia was musical.'

'That was what brought them together, I reckon. A love of music. And gardens. Which reminds me,' he said, turning back to face me. 'You haven't put my chainsaw somewhere, have you?'

'Oh, God...'

'What's the matter?'

'I forgot about the break-in. I meant to tell you.'

'Break-in?'

'I don't even know if it *was* a break-in. Well, I know it *wasn't* because the garage wasn't even locked.'

'Hang on a minute, you're not making sense. Start again at the beginning.'

'I didn't lock the garage. After you rang me. I didn't go out and lock up. I got... distracted.'

Tom looked annoyed, but all he said was, 'And stuff's been taken?'

'I don't know. I couldn't see anything missing.'

'But you didn't see my chainsaw? I left it in the garage after I finished work that day. Didn't mean to, I just forgot. I was a bit distracted too if you remember. In a nice way.' He smiled at me and I remembered our kiss and my confusion. 'That's why I rang you,' Tom went on. 'To tell you to lock up. So someone's nicked it then?'

'I don't know. I wasn't looking for a chainsaw.'

'You'd have seen it. I left it just inside the door because I meant to take it home with me. If it was still there you'd have fallen over it.'

'Oh, Tom, I'm sorry. It wasn't there!'

'Shit!' He ran a hand through his hair, clearly exasperated with me. 'I have to have one for work. I've got another, but it's a bit temperamental.'

'Get a replacement and give me the bill. It's my fault entirely.'

'You're talking £350 to replace that one.'

'Oh... Well, that's OK.'

'You'll get some of that back on the insurance, won't you?

I mean, this was theft.' I didn't reply and Tom said, 'You did call the police?'

'No, I didn't.'

'Bloody hell, Ruth – what's got into you?'

'I didn't know if it was a break-in, I just heard noises... and it was very late... But I expect I'll be able to claim. I'm sorry, Tom, but I've just been so pre-occupied! Things have been really... *strange* lately.'

He could see I was close to tears. He put his glass down on the table and took my face in both hands. 'Hey, don't get upset! It's just a bloody chainsaw.'

'I'll replace it.'

'It's only money, Ruth, not life and death! Any problem that can be sorted by throwing money at it is not a real problem. *Having* money – that's the problem. Though luckily, not for *you*,' he added, then he leaned forward, still holding my face and placed his lips on mine in a lingering kiss that smelled too strongly of whisky for me to enjoy. Still holding my face, he said, 'Has it ever occurred to you, that if Tricia had been a man – or Janet had – and they'd married, *Tigh-na-Linne* would now be *my* home? Now there's a thought.'

The kitchen timer started bleeping and Tom released my face, caressed my hair, then went over to the hob to drain the pasta.

'Sit yourself down. Just a few last minute things now.' He reached for his champagne glass, drained it, then said, 'You do the refills. Where will I find a colander?'

'In the cupboard to your left. Top shelf.'

I refilled Tom's glass and topped up mine. The bottle was already half-empty and I was beginning to feel light-headed, so I sat down at the table. Tom set a plate in front of me with a flourish, then set another on the other side of the table. He removed his tie, rolled it up and pushed it into a pocket of the jacket he'd hung over another chair. He sat down looking happy and relaxed, but I felt like a guest in my own home.

The pasta was delicious and conversation was easy, apart from the fact that I was distracted by the speed with which Tom drank and the absence of any effect on him. When the champagne was gone, he leaped up and went to the fridge and brought out a bottle of wine he must have chilled earlier. He obviously wasn't intending to drive home, but I couldn't see him walking in November. It would take about forty minutes to get to *Larachbeag* on foot. I began to wonder if, in fact, he wasn't intending to go home. I had a spare room made up, so staying over wouldn't be a problem. I did wonder if getting Tom to *occupy* the spare room might be.

After we'd finished eating, I stood up to clear away and, forgetting the hazard of my wrap-over dress, I leaned over to pick up Tom's plate. It must have looked deliberately provocative, I suppose, so I didn't really blame him for getting the wrong idea. It was my own stupid fault. His hand went up to the base of my throat and slid down over my necklace. His hand was still descending when I tipped a plate so that cutlery slid off and landed noisily on the table. At the same time, I stepped backwards, out of his reach.

It must have looked accidental and he cleared up the dirty cutlery without a word. As I loaded the dishwasher he went back to the table, topped up my glass and refilled his.

It was ridiculous for me to feel nervous. Tom was an old friend. I found him attractive and he knew it, but it made absolutely no sense that I should feel threatened by him. I should feel flattered, surely? What was it that was making me feel trapped? The weight of his expectations? Perhaps the fact that I couldn't just walk away if I wanted.

As I switched on the dishwasher, I told myself I was just woefully out of practice, playing the dating game. Two rather sedate years with David had protected me from the rough and tumble of predatory males.

(Predatory? Is that what I thought Tom was?)

'By the way,' he called out. 'While I think of it – that bridge. The one across the pond. It's completely rotten. Do you want me to remove it? I know it's picturesque, but it's dangerous. Someone could fall in and drown. That pond's pretty deep in the middle.'

I turned round and searched his face, looking for some clue to the past, some hint that he remembered, but I saw nothing. In the flickering candlelight his dark eyes were fathomless, his expression inscrutable.

'Yes, I would like you to get rid of it, please.' I hesitated, then said, 'Do you remember?'

'Remember what?'

'That time when I... fell in. Fell into the pond.'

He frowned. 'When you were a kid, you mean?'

'Yes. We were both playing on the bridge.'

'And you fell in?'

'I— yes, I suppose I must have.'

'No, I don't remember.'

'I nearly drowned.'

'*Really?* How come I don't remember?'

'You said you'd pulled me out. Saved my life.'

'*Did* I? Well, if that's what I said, I suppose that's what I did. I'd forgotten all about it. Quite the little hero, wasn't I?'

'You really don't remember?'

'Don't think so. Though now you come to mention it, I do vaguely remember you getting very wet and muddy once... Yes, you were lying on the grass, covered in pondweed. But I don't remember pulling you out.'

It was on the tip of my tongue to ask if he remembered pushing me in, but my nerve failed and I turned away to fill the kettle and set it on the Aga. Feeling shivery, I leaned against the rail, drawing comfort from the warmth radiating from the stove's metal shell. I told myself I just wasn't wearing enough clothes. It had nothing to do with the conversation with Tom.

A chilly draught seemed to come from nowhere and blew a lock of hair across my face. I put my hand up to push it back, but then the draught blew in the opposite direction, lifting my hair before I could touch it.

Hector.

No sooner had I registered a sense of profound relief, than it was replaced by a wave of irritation. How long had Hector been here? Why hadn't he made himself visible to me? It was bad enough being creeped out by one man. Was I now to be spooked by another? Or rather, a ghost?

I resented Hector intruding on my evening with Tom almost as much as I resented feeling relieved he was around to keep an eye on me. As the kettle came to the boil, I felt cross and tired and, to tell the truth, a little drunk, which must have been why I said something so very silly.

'Coffee and brandy by the fire?'

Tom's face lit up and I was rewarded with one of his film star smiles, which I have to say, went some way toward cheering me up.

'That sounds great.'

I didn't bother to tell him where the brandy was and, sure enough, he laid a hand on it in seconds. While I made coffee, Tom put two glasses and a bottle of Courvoisier on a tray and set off for the sitting room. I loaded the coffee things on to another tray and started to follow, then stopped. I looked round the room, waiting. After a few seconds, I said, very softly, 'Hector?'

There was no reply.

'Hector, I know you're there,' I whispered. 'Go away. *Please*. You aren't needed. And I can't bear to be *spied* on. It's hard enough for me to cope when you're visible. So please, leave me alone. I'm entitled to my privacy.'

There was still no reply, but Tom put his head round the door. 'Come and see my wonderful fire. It's really cosy in there now. Here, let me take that.'

He relieved me of the tray and went on ahead. At the kitchen door I turned, looked round the room a final time and whispered, 'Hector, *go away*. Or if you won't go, at least stay in here.'

There was no answer, but a paper napkin suddenly blew across the table and floated down on to the floor.

Chapter Eleven

The sitting room was warm and inviting. Janet's shabby chintz décor was definitely improved by the low level lighting Tom had organised: a table lamp and a couple of candles were the only sources of light apart from the log fire. He'd removed the fireguard and was sitting on the sofa facing the blaze. I thought it would look odd if I didn't sit next to him, but I knew what would happen if I did. I was hovering over the coffee tray, trying to decide what to do, when I felt a chill breeze again. I suspected Tom had felt it too because he got up, poked the fire, and put another log on.

The draught could have come from the ill-fitting French windows, long in need of replacement, but I had a sinking feeling Hector had joined us. First one candle flickered and then the other. Hector on the move?... As I stirred the coffee, I didn't know who was irritating me most – Tom or Hector. Right now, Hector possibly had the edge.

Despite Tom's ministrations to the fire, the temperature in the room had dropped. As I turned to hand Tom his coffee, I saw something I'd never seen before. In a dimly lit corner of the room, Hector was gradually materialising – an even more alarming sight than Hector materialised. At first he seemed to be just a pair of piercing blue eyes, then his pale face assembled itself around the eyes. His white hands emerged from the semi-darkness, then the light from the fire caught his red hair. The colours became brighter, his form clearer and more solid-looking, until finally, I could see Hector in detail. His eyes were fixed on me, his expression stern, as if he were trying to tell me something.

'Well,' Tom said. 'Are you going to give me that coffee, or not?'

'Oh, sorry. Yes, here you are. Do you take sugar?' I asked absently, looking over Tom's head to where Hector stood, motionless, but watchful.

'No, thanks. Come and sit down. I poured you a brandy.' Tom indicated the lamp table at the side of the sofa.

I glared at Hector in a futile gesture of dismissal, but he folded his arms and looked as if he was prepared to make a night of it.

I was furious. It was bad enough having to decide how to deal with Tom, but to have to do it with Hector *watching*? Silently outraged, I sat down next to Tom on the sofa – mainly to ensure Hector wouldn't be in my field of vision. I stared into the fire and tried to relax.

'This is the life, eh?' Tom said, savouring his coffee. 'I love firewood. It warms you twice.'

'Twice?'

'Once when you cut it, then again when you burn it.'

'Oh, yes. I see.'

He rested his head on the back of the sofa and extended his long legs toward the fire. It was all very pleasant (apart from being observed by Hector), but I found myself hoping Tom would fall asleep, so I could leave him dozing on the sofa and go to bed. My hopes were dashed when he laid a hand very gently on my thigh. Had he made a grab, I think I'd have moved or said something discouraging, but he just laid his hand on my thigh and spread his fingers.

The sensation was far from unpleasant as the heat from his big hand penetrated the fabric of my dress and warmed my bare skin underneath. If Hector hadn't been standing in the corner, sulking like a disgraced child, I might even have enjoyed it.

When Tom's hand began to slide up and down, it was almost soothing. The rhythm of his strokes, the warmth of the room, plus the brandy made it hard for me to keep my eyes open, so I too lay back and closed my eyes. I might even have dozed off for a few seconds. If so, I was woken by the pressure of Tom's hand on my naked thigh and his mouth on my neck as he planted delicate but insistent kisses that were moving downward in the direction of my breasts. I sat up quickly and shifted away.

'What's wrong?' Tom asked, his eyes unfocused, his

mouth slack and sensuous. 'I was enjoying that. Weren't you?'

'I think I was nodding off, actually. I shouldn't have had that brandy. It's made me feel very sleepy.'

'Perhaps you need a bit more stimulation,' Tom replied. Leaning across, he flipped the skirt of my dress open and slid his hand between my thighs, then his mouth came down on mine, hard. I laid my hands on his chest and, with an effort, pushed him away.

'Tom, I don't think we're ready for this.'

'Don't worry – I brought the necessary.'

'That's not what I meant!'

'Am I rushing you? Sorry. But you looked so gorgeous lying there. Sort of abandoned. And I thought maybe that's what you wanted. So what *do* you want, Ruth? What do you like? Tell me...' His hands were on me again, one of them fondling my breast. I pushed him away, shouting, 'Tom! This is *not* what I want!'

He let me go and sat back, looking confused. A movement of air behind me announced Hector's approach and, out of the corner of my eye, I could see him moving round the room. I braced myself for Tom's shock as Hector came into view, but he didn't react. Evidently he couldn't see him. I looked from one man to the other, unable to believe I was the only person who could see Hector, who'd now taken up a position by the French windows and was staring intently at the phone.

'What's the matter?' Tom asked, frowning. 'Jesus, you're not *frightened* of me are you? Hey, Ruthie, it's only me! Tommy! Come here and let me give you a hug.'

As he made another grab for me, the phone rang. Never was I more grateful to hear that strident sound. I stood up, straightening my dress and said, 'I'd better get that.' I walked over to where Hector was standing, turned my back on him pointedly and picked up the phone. 'Hello?'

'It's me. Don't hang up. I need to talk to you.'

I spun round to face Hector, speechless with surprise. It was unmistakably his voice on the other end of the phone, but he was standing right beside me, not speaking, not even looking at me. His expression was baleful and his eyes were fixed on Tom.

Unable to catch Hector's eye, I spoke into the phone. 'I'm afraid this really isn't a convenient time. I'm rather busy at the moment.'

'Aye, and that's what I was wanting to talk to you about.'

'Well, in that case, I think you'd better ring back tomorrow.'

'Get rid of him, Ruth. The miscreant child has matured into a blackguard.'

'Look, I appreciate your interest, Mr Munro, but I really don't wish to discuss this *now*. I'm entertaining a guest.'

'This one expects to stay the night.'

'That's no concern of yours!'

'It is if you expect me to sit outside your bedroom door all night.'

My jaw dropped, but I made a quick recovery. 'Thanks all the same, but I don't think I'll be requiring that service.'

Hector looked at me then, his eyes wide, his expression pleading. The voice at the other end of the phone said, 'You need my protection, Ruth!'

'I do not! Nor do I need your advice.'

'He locked you in the attic. He pushed you into the pond and left you to drown!'

'That's a matter of conjecture. I think we should stick to the facts, don't you?'

'When you turn your back, he looks at you as if – as if you're something on a butcher's slab!'

'Times have changed, Mr Munro! This is the twenty-first century. I have no complaint about the service you've provided in the past, but if I wish to engage a new contractor, that's my business.'

'Och, you're drunk, woman!'

'I certainly am not.'

'You're making a mistake, Ruth!'

'Possibly. But if I am, it's *my* responsibility, not yours. Goodbye, Mr Munro. Oh, and please don't ring back. I shan't answer the phone.'

Shaking, I replaced the phone on its cradle.

'Who the hell was *that*?' Tom asked, laughing. He'd refilled his brandy glass and was drinking again.

'Oh, just some building contractor. He'd given me an outrageous quote for building an extension,' I said randomly.

'Stupid time to ring.'

'Oh, the man has absolutely no concept of time!' I heard myself, then looked round guiltily, searching for Hector. There was no sign of him and I felt relieved. To avoid joining Tom on the sofa, I kneeled down in front of the fire and poked at the burning logs. Maybe Hector was right. Perhaps I *was* drunk. Tom had been topping up my glass all evening and I'd lost track of how much I'd had.

I didn't hear Tom move, so the next thing I knew was his arms going round my waist and his face nuzzling my neck. I tried to wriggle free. 'Tom, I'm sorry, I'm really not in the mood for this. Not after giving Mr Munro a piece of my mind.'

He didn't answer. He gave no sign of even having heard. His hands were busy at my waist, but it was a moment or two before I realised he'd undone the belt of my dress. As he pulled it open, I yelled, 'Tom, *no!*'

'You don't mean that,' he murmured in my ear, then slid his hand inside my dress and began to fondle my breast.

I twisted away from him and tried to stand up, but he was kneeling on my dress and I heard it rip. He grabbed my shoulders and pulled me back so hard, I toppled over on to the hearthrug. He rolled me on to my back as if I were a doll, then lay on top of me, pinning me to the ground.

'Get off!' I bellowed in his face, but he was completely gone. His eyes looked dark and dead, as if he was on some sort of automatic pilot. I tried to bring a knee up to his groin, but he was so big and heavy, I just lay there helpless. He held me by my wrists and looked down at me, smiling lazily, as if savouring the moment. I started to feel frightened.

If Tom tried to kiss me, I decided I would bite his tongue or even head-butt him, which might daze him long enough for me to get out from underneath. I was watching his face, waiting for it to come into range, when behind him, I saw Hector materialise. He stood over us, looking down, his expression murderous.

I looked up at Hector over Tom's shoulder and whimpered, 'I'm sorry, I didn't mean it! Please—'

119

Tom grinned and said, '*That's* more like it! You just like a bit of rough house, don't you? Well, that's OK. Happy to oblige.'

As I struggled, he kissed me, forcing his tongue into my mouth. I thought I would choke. Behind Tom's golden head, I saw Hector move quickly to the fire. He bent down and, to my utter astonishment, plunged his white hand into the fire, displacing a log so the coals shifted and then settled again. Tom, who was now fumbling with the catch of my bra, took no notice, but I threw my head to one side, craning to see what the hell Hector was playing at.

As Tom lay on top of me, crushing my ribcage so I could hardly breathe, I watched, appalled, as Hector put his hand into the depths of the fire again. His fingers emerged holding a glowing red coal, which grew duller as he held it. Grim-faced, he moved toward Tom.

'No! You mustn't! I shrieked.

'Just watch me, lassie,' Hector whispered.

To my horror, he extended his arm, touched Tom's cheek with the hot coal, then dropped it on the hearthrug where it lay, burning a hole.

Tom screamed and rolled off me, clutching his face and swearing profusely. Scrambling to my knees, I clutched at the folds of my dress, pulling it round me. I got up, staggering, then bent down to pick up the fire tongs. I took the hot coal and threw it back on to the fire. I was about to replace the tongs when I thought better of it. Sinking into an armchair at a safe distance from Tom, I decided to hang on to them in case his ardour still wasn't quenched.

'Are you all right?' I asked, my voice hoarse with shouting.

'No, I'm bloody not! I've got a burned face!'

'Should you see a doctor?'

He shook his head. 'No point. It's superficial. Just bloody painful!'

'I've got some Savlon. Is that what you put on burns? Or do you need a dressing of some sort? I could have a look in Janet's First Aid box if you like. But I'm afraid I'm not much of a nurse.'

'Don't bother. I'll live.' Touching his cheek gingerly, he

glared at the fire. 'I've never known that happen.'

'What?'

'A fire spit out a big lump of coal like that.'

Hector was still standing over Tom and his lips curled into a smile. I looked up at him and, without thinking, snapped, 'You'd better leave, before you do any more damage.'

'Yes, of course,' Tom replied. 'I'm sorry,' He looked at me and winced, but something told me it wasn't the burn that was causing him most pain. Both men were staring at me now, though Hector was beginning to fade. God knows what I must have looked like, sitting there. Certainly not Florence Nightingale, with my tangled hair, smudged make-up and my torn dress wrapped tight around me.

Tom shook his head. 'I don't know what got in to me.'

'Booze. Far too much.'

'You do know, don't you, that I wouldn't have—'

'I don't want to discuss it, Tom! I just want you to leave. *Now*. Please call a taxi. Or start walking. I'm going to bed. Good night.'

I left him sitting on the singed hearthrug and went up to the bathroom where I locked the door and kicked off my shoes. Removing my make-up, I tried not to think about how the evening might have ended. Then I told myself I was being ridiculous. Tom would never have hurt me. He was my *friend*. But the fact was, I didn't know the man at all, I only knew the boy. And according to Hector, the boy had left me to drown.

I stared at my naked face and watched as big fat tears slid down my blotchy cheeks. I didn't recognise myself. How did I ever get to be this lonely? This vulnerable? This *crazy*?...

Wiping my eyes, I told my reflection I was going back to London. Stan would just have to be cancelled. Inviting him had been yet more evidence of my lunacy. Tom could look after the house and garden till I put *Tigh-na-Linne* on the market. He owed me now. Exhausted and emotional, I picked up my shoes and padded across the hall to my bedroom.

Where I found Hector waiting.

~

121

As I switched on the light, I saw Hector seated at my dressing table, facing the mirror. He had his back to me, so I looked at the glass expecting to see his face, but of course there was nothing there. He was staring at blankness.

He rose as soon as I came into the room, turned and stood almost to attention, his hands behind his back, his face as blank as the mirror. I dropped my shoes and quickly tied the belt of my dress to make myself decent. Furious with Hector, Tom and especially myself, I said, 'You had no business to be there tonight! You weren't invited and I specifically asked you to keep away!' Hector didn't reply and just stood there like a post, so I bent down to pick up the clothes I'd discarded earlier and tossed them on to a chair. 'You really didn't need to hurt him that much.'

'I *wanted* to hurt him that much.'

'*Why*?' Hector didn't reply. I stared at his impassive face and slowly, light began to dawn. 'Oh, my God – I do believe you're *jealous*!'

He looked startled then and said, 'He wasn't listening to you. Or looking at you in a way that befitted a gentleman. He simply wanted to... *possess* you. Had you not been willing, he would have forced—'

'Of course he wouldn't!'

'Are you *sure*, Ruth? Quite sure? This is the lad who pushed a wee girl into a pond and left her to drown!'

'You don't know he did that.'

'I think *you* do.'

'Tom was just trying it on this evening. Some men are like that. They get drunk and boorish. Surely men haven't have changed *that* much in a hundred years?'

'No gentleman would have treated a lady the way that scoundrel treated you.'

'Well, Tom isn't a gentleman. And I'm not a lady.'

'Are you saying you *enjoyed* being treated like that?'

'Of course not! Tom was very drunk and he went too far. He'd misread the signs. But that was partly my fault. The other day I'd given him the impression— But this is none of your business, Hector! I don't have to explain myself to – to a *ghost*!'

'So you'd make excuses for his behaviour then?'

'No! But it wasn't as simple as you seem to think. Things got very... *confused*. So did I. And Tom picked up on that confusion.'

'What do you mean?'

I sighed. 'You were born in 1880. I'm not sure you'll understand. Tom's a very attractive man. And he knows it. And... well, women like to feel desirable.'

'Och, hell!' Hector snarled. 'D'you need to be treated like a *streetwalker* to feel desired?'

'Oh, come *on*! How else is a guy to make his feelings known? Morse code? Telepathy?'

Hector blinked at me, his eyes wide. 'By declaring them, of course.'

'*Declaring* them? What do you mean?'

It was Hector's turn to be confused. He bowed his head and was silent again. After a while, I assumed he'd conceded the argument, but then he looked up and, standing very straight, addressed me, saying, 'Until now, I'd loved only one woman. A woman whom I admired and respected beyond all others. A woman whose beauty, kindness and intelligence I believed to be unsurpassed. It was my intention to make her my wife. For reasons I don't propose to go into, she would not accept my marriage proposal, even though she loved me and... gave me proofs of that love. Unfortunately, my life was cut short before I was able to persuade her to change her mind...

'I never expected to feel love – feel *anything* – ever again. I certainly never expected to feel... desire. Of any kind. After my experiences as a soldier, I was convinced I'd never feel the desire to harm a human being ever again. In all this, I was much mistaken. I've found in you, Ruth, a woman whose character and beauty I admire... and whose body I wish to possess. You've also shown me a man I find I wish to kill, simply because he's capable of giving you what I cannot. Capable of *taking* from you what I cannot.

'I'm proud of none of this, but I wish to demonstrate to you, with the very limited means at my disposal, that you're not only desired by me, you are *loved*. Until now, I'd never thought much of the loss of my body. I was resigned to being just a spirit. A soul. The essence – I hoped, the *best* – of my human self. Until now.' Hector drew himself up to his full height and looked at me, his blue eyes blazing. 'Had I the opportunity, I would choose to die again – and in the same terrible manner – if I could be made whole for just an hour. An hour in which I would wish to do nothing more than offer myself, body and soul, to you, Ruth.'

I stared at him, scarcely able to take in what I'd heard. 'Hector... I – I don't know what to say.'

'There's nothing to say. I simply wished you to know, that's all. I may seem – and from what you've said, I may *feel* to you like a cold fish, but in what passes for my heart, there burns a desire for you as real, as painful and as hopeless as any I knew when I was a man... And now I think I'd better leave.'

Speechless with shock, I watched him as he turned away. When he reached the bedroom door, I cried out, 'Please don't go!'

He wheeled round, his eyes glittering. 'Och, don't ask me to stand outside your door *tonight*, Ruth! I'm by no means certain I'd be able to resist the temptation to open your door and gaze on you while you sleep, allowing myself in my imagination the liberties of which I'm no longer capable!' The derision in his voice was more than I could bear, though I knew his scorn was directed at himself and his spectral form.

I swallowed and, my voice not entirely steady, said, 'How do you know?'

'I beg your pardon?'

'Have you tried? I mean, how do you know what you're capable of? Have you actually ever tried to make love to a mortal woman?'

'Of course not!'

'Then how do you know you can't?'

His eyes searched mine for what seemed like a long time. I saw confusion. Fear. Then a kind of wild hope.

'But... you say I feel *cold*. Insubstantial. You surely wouldn't want to touch me... Would you?'

'Right now, I do. I want to touch you. *Hold* you. I don't

think I really care what you feel like, Hector. Whatever it's like, I want it. Because no one's ever spoken to me the way you have tonight. No one's ever put his hand into a fire to protect me. A ghost has never been in love with me before. And I – well, I've never fallen in love with a ghost.'

'Ruth—'

'So whatever's available, whatever you're offering, that's what I want. Do I make myself clear? This is *my* declaration, Hector. I don't want you sitting outside that door, or even standing at the end of the bed, lusting. I want you *in* the bed. And, if it's at all possible, in *me*.'

He took a step toward me, then hesitated, uncertain. I turned and switched on the bedside lamp, then folded back the patchwork quilt and bedclothes, my hands shaking. When I straightened up, Hector still stood as if dazed, so I walked over to him, reached past his shoulder and switched off the top light. As I drew my arm back, he grabbed my hand, pressed the palm to his cold face and closed his eyes. His flesh yielded, but my hand didn't penetrate his form. There was an uncanny resistance. Had he felt more solid, I suppose I might have thought of a corpse, but Hector was no more corporeal than a waterfall, or a river in spate. I could sense that energy, that force in him.

I took his chill, long-fingered hand and slid it inside my dress so that his palm lay on the curve of my breast. I didn't need to ask what he could feel. The expression on his face and the noise that escaped his lips suggested he might be close to collapse, but he spread his fingers and they slipped easily beneath the lace of my bra. The sensation was one of cold, silky water trickling over my body. His fingertips found my nipple, which hardened under his touch, then he pulled me toward him and pressed his mouth on mine.

For a second I panicked. Inundated by the cool liquidity of Hector's form, I felt as if I was drowning, until I realised I didn't need to hold my breath or prevent him from entering my mouth. I was quite safe. Relaxing, I gave myself up to that sensual, generous mouth, enjoying the movement of his cool tongue against the heat of mine.

He let me go and I opened my eyes, to see him

unbuttoning his tunic, revealing a lean and muscled torso, pale as a marble statue. I ran eager palms over his chest and shoulders, which felt cold and smooth to my hot touch.

'Hector!' I exclaimed, gasping with pleasure and surprise. 'To think all this has been going to waste for a hundred years. It's simply *tragic*.'

He laughed, bent down and lifted me. It was as if I'd been knocked off my feet by a powerful wave and was now being carried out to sea. I felt powerless, but the sensation was far from unpleasant. Hector put me down on the bed and I lay back on the pillows while, with trembling fingers, he undid the belt of my dress and slipped it off me. I assumed he wouldn't have any idea how or where a bra fastened, so I spared him the awkwardness and removed it myself while he took off his boots and socks. At the sight of my naked breasts, he seemed almost overcome and clasped the bed head, as if he needed to support himself. I sat up, wriggled out of my knickers and, naked now, I set about unfastening the buckles of his kilt, steeling myself for potential disappointment.

I needn't have worried. When we first met, Hector had said he presented himself to me as I would wish to see him. As his kilt slid to the floor, I saw him *exactly* as I would wish to see him. I shivered with excitement, which he misinterpreted.

'Och, you're freezing, lassie!' He turned his head and gave a nod in the direction of the fireplace. Immediately, a blazing fire appeared in the Victorian grate where some ancestor of mine had set a hideous two-bar electric fire. I shrieked in alarm, thinking the bedroom was on fire. Hector laughed again, caught hold of my hand and kissed my fingers. 'You'll not catch cold now.'

I lay back again, watching the firelight play on his white limbs as he climbed on to the bed and lowered himself to lie between my parted thighs. He cradled my head with one of his hands and said, 'You're sure now? I wouldn't want to take anything you don't want to give.'

'Take it all, Hector,' I murmured, threading my fingers through the tendrils of his hair, as fiery as the flames in the grate. 'Whatever I have is yours. And I want *all* of you.'

He slid an arm under my waist and, pulling me toward him, showered my face, neck and breasts with soft, cool kisses that caressed my skin like summer rain. Then with an impatience I couldn't begrudge – that I welcomed – Hector pushed his way inside me, easily, tenderly.

The sensation of something cold and hard at the centre of my being disturbed me for only a second, then I embraced it. Aware now of every movement Hector made, his body so chill and separate from mine, I couldn't recall when I'd felt so aroused. Whether this was because of the physical oddity, or because I was excited by the idea of a ghost lover, I couldn't say. I knew the man in my arms was long dead, yet I'd never felt so alive. My mind couldn't encompass the paradox, but my body could. I abandoned all thought and surrendered to the driving rhythm of Hector moving inside me.

My excitement built quickly, till I cried out, clutching Hector's back, pulling him down, deeper inside me. Then he pulled back and thrust hard, his pale eyes fixed on mine. I stared into the depths of a bottomless pool of icy water and wanted to drown there.

As he reared up over me in the flickering firelight, Hector's expression changed. I pressed my palms against his chest and with a surge of irrational joy, I felt the beat of a pounding heart beneath the yielding, white flesh. He closed his eyes, cried out, then I felt him shudder inside me. For one alarming moment, he seemed to fade and I was aware I could see the bedroom *through* him. Then as he sank down on top of me, it was as if gentle waves had begun to lap around and over me.

I clutched at what was left of his body. 'Hector, please! Don't leave me! Not yet. Stay!'

The liquid that seemed to flow over me began to solidify and Hector's form took shape again in my arms. Eventually he opened his eyes and, propping himself up on his elbows, looked down at me.

'I lost concentration. For a moment only. I'm sorry.' His pale forehead creased with anxiety. 'But you, Ruth? You're... content? You weren't disappointed?' he asked, his voice low and frayed with emotion. 'You felt something?'

'Felt something?' I took his beloved face in my hands. 'Good God, Hector, it was *extraordinary*. I've never experienced anything like it!' His sudden grin was a disarming mix of vulnerability and triumph. I felt strangely moved.

Something else was starting to move. Thus it was I made the startling and very gratifying discovery that ghosts require no recovery period. Hector looked surprised, then, as he realised what was happening, he smiled and moved his hips against me experimentally. I moaned with pleasure.

'Well, that does it,' I murmured, running my hands up over his chest. 'I'm through with mere mortals...'

When I woke the following morning, Hector was gone. As usual. There was no trace of him on my body or in the bed, no sign of any fire in the grate. Nothing. I was heartbroken. Could he not have left me *something* to prove I hadn't dreamed our encounter? If a ghost can conjure spontaneous combustion, surely he could manage to leave a note on the pillow?

Depressed, I got out of bed and pulled on my dressing gown. As I did so, my eye was caught by a pile of clothes stacked on the dressing table stool. All the garments I'd shed the night before, from my pretty lace bra to my baggy tracksuit bottoms, had been folded neatly. Beneath them, my shoes had been placed side by side, under the stool, as if ready for inspection.

My lover might be a ghost, but first and foremost, he was a soldier.

Chapter Twelve

Now I was upright, I realised how hung over I was. Craving caffeine, I stumbled downstairs and found the kitchen in a chaotic state. The work surfaces were littered with dirty pans and empty wine bottles and the air reeked of stale booze and bacon fat. A bunch of wilted chrysanthemums, still in their paper wrapping, sat on the worktop. (Tom's exhaustive knowledge of *Tigh-na-Linne* didn't appear to extend to the storage of vases.) I picked up the flowers and, scattering petals like confetti, dumped them in the bin.

I put the kettle on and went to the fridge for milk. There wasn't any. Furious at my domestic incompetence, unable to face black coffee or the clear up, I switched off the kettle, drank a glass of water and fled to the sitting room, which was just as depressing and smelled worse - of spilled brandy and burned wool.

I kneeled down to examine the damaged Persian rug. Admittedly, it wasn't in the first flush of youth and showed signs of wear, but a black hole was another matter. I wouldn't be able to forget how the hole got there, so I rolled up the rug and put it out in the hall, registering as I did so that Tom had at least had the sense to put the fireguard in front of the fire before leaving. Or perhaps that had been Hector?...

I'd managed not to think about Hector for several minutes, but now memories came crowding in, one after another in relentless succession. My response to each one was the same. A single word. *Impossible.* Whatever I thought about and in whatever way, my response was simply, "Impossible".

A ghost had saved me from a nasty assault.

Tom had been injured by a jealous and vengeful ghost.

I'd had a sexual encounter (of a lengthy and most enjoyable kind) with a ghost.

A ghost appeared to have fallen in love with me.
I appeared to have fallen in love with a ghost.

I didn't know whether to laugh or cry. I was slightly inclined toward the latter because even if the extraordinary events of last night had actually happened, there could, of course, be no future in a romantic relationship with a ghost. *Any* kind of relationship with a ghost. What was it the poet had said?...

'It was begotten by Despair,
Upon Impossibility.'

The memory of Hector sitting at the piano, quoting those words from Janet's song cycle brought me to the brink of tears, but still I held out. Drawing curtains, opening windows, plumping cushions, pulling dead leaves off houseplants, I kept busy and didn't dissolve until I found myself sitting by the phone, hoping it would ring, hoping it would be Hector.

When the phone *did* ring I jumped off my chair and my pathetic snivelling became a wail. I clapped my hands over my ears and ran to the sofa where I curled up in a ball and waited for the noise to stop. When it didn't, I started to think perhaps it *was* Hector, though there was no reason he'd ring when he could show up in person and talk to me (unless of course this was to be the supernatural equivalent of dumping by text.)

Pulling myself together, I approached the phone, willing it to stop ringing before I got there. Then I lost my nerve and pounced before Hector could hang up.

'Hello?'

'Ruth? Good morning. It's Stan.'

'*Stan?*' As my eyes welled up again, I considered two courses of action: slamming down the phone or unburdening myself to an insomniac professor, three thousand miles away.

'I hope I'm not disturbing you?'

I'd already soaked the tissues I had in my pockets, so I dabbed at my eyes with the belt of my dressing gown and said, 'No. I – I was just thinking about making some breakfast.' My voice was tremulous and a certain amount of sniffing was unavoidable. 'I had a late night last night.' The memory of *why* I'd got to sleep so late last night nearly set me off again, but I dug my nails into my palm to distract myself with pain. 'It must be the middle of the night for you. Can't you sleep?'

'Oh, I had a couple of hours. That's enough for me. I was lying there thinking about my visit and realised I was too excited to sleep.'

'Oh... I see.' This was clearly not the moment to tell Stan I was going to withdraw my invitation.

'Ruth, forgive me, but are you *sure* I'm not disturbing you?'

'No, this is fine. Really.'

Evidently unconvinced, Stan persisted. 'You sound upset. Has something happened?' I was considering how best to reply, when he said, 'Have you seen the ghost again?'

I laughed. That seemed a more socially acceptable response than howling. 'Yes, I've seen the ghost. I've seen rather a lot of him lately.' And that was enough to bring to mind a vision of Hector's pale, naked body, gilded by firelight. As a consequence, I missed Stan's next remark. 'I'm sorry – what was that you said? The line isn't too good at this end,' I lied.

'I was asking if you'd managed to establish the identity of your ghost?'

'Oh, yes. I know who he is. Or rather was. He was actually very easy to identify. There's a memorial window at *Tigh-na-Linne*. Made of stained glass. It's strange and very beautiful. There used to be three. The one that remains was installed in memory of Hector Munro who died in 1915 at the battle of Loos. The window is a representation of him as an archangel. Michael, I think.'

'The Glass Guardian.'

'I beg your pardon?'

'This window sounds as if it could have been the inspiration for Janet's piece, *The Glass Guardian*. She wrote a chamber opera for children with that title. It was an early work of hers and she later withdrew it. Critics dismissed it as immature, even naïve, failing to realise she'd written the piece to be performed by talented amateurs and children. It's a quaint little story about a young girl who has an imaginary friend. But the friend isn't a child—'

'He's a dead soldier who befriends the girl and protects her from harm.'

'Why, yes! Of course, you must know the piece.'

'No, I've never heard it. But I think I know why Janet wrote it.'

There was silence at the other end of the line, apart from a long whistling sound. Then Stan said eagerly, 'The friend was *Hector*? The man in the window? Your ghost?'

'Maybe he was Janet's ghost as well.'

'So the Glass Guardian actually *exists*!' Stan exclaimed, delighted.

'Oh, yes, he exists all right. Do you know any more about the opera?' I swallowed and said, 'I mean, do you know how it ends?'

'I'm afraid it's not a piece I'm familiar with. I've never seen it performed. But I remember reading a contemporary review. The soldier is searching for his lost love—'

I groaned. 'Oh, no...'

'Yes, I know it sounds a little corny,' Stan explained, misunderstanding. 'But the plot is no sillier than most opera. The young girl tries to help him find the woman, but it takes years and eventually they discover that she's dead, by which time the girl has grown up. The Glass Guardian realises that, in fact, the love of his life is under his nose.'

'But... he's a *ghost*. There can't be a happy ending. Not unless she dies.'

'Or he comes back to life, I guess. I don't remember the details. I know the piece wasn't successful, partly because Janet refused to tag on a happy ending. She said she didn't see the need to compromise, just because her intended audience was young. She believed children were made of sterner stuff. Of course, in that respect, she was way ahead of her time. Janet was contemporary with Enid Blyton, but artistically, she related more to the psychological complexity – the *darkness* – of Lewis Carroll's *Alice*, of *Peter Pan* and *The Water Babies*. She believed children could get to grips with concepts of death and immortality just as well as adults. *Better* than adults, in some cases... Janet's younger brother died in infancy, didn't he?'

'Yes. He died of scarlet fever. When he was four, I think.'

'So she would have had to come to terms with the darker aspects of life at an early age.'

Even earlier, it suddenly occurred to me, than *I* did, with my mother dying when I was eight. Had Hector comforted Janet when she lost her brother? When, as an adult, Janet had laid a place at table for "Heckie", had she known my imaginary friend wasn't imaginary?...

'Ruth, are you still there?'

'What? Oh, yes. Sorry, I was thinking about Janet losing her little brother. And all the sadness this family has known.'

'Ah, but so much *love* too.'

'Love?'

'Well, that's the other side of the coin, isn't it? Your great-grandparents lost three beloved sons and they installed those memorial windows. Janet wrote *In Memoriam* as an act of love and remembrance for the fallen, who included her three uncles. She took on the role of mother to you after her sister died. Now that can't have been easy for a single, professional woman, who by all accounts was pretty reserved. Janet must surely have loved her sister – and *you* – very much. There's been a great deal of sadness in this family, but there's also been a great deal of love.'

'Stan, you have such a wonderfully positive take on life! Is it to do with being Canadian?'

He chuckled and said, 'Well, I'm sure I don't know! I'd have to think about that. But it's always seemed to me that shadows can only be cast – in life, as well as in art – where a strong light exists to throw them. I suppose I've always been inclined to look for the light. And I usually find it. It's just that, when darkness descends, we don't always remember to look for the light.'

'Do you think it's loss that conjures up... this ghost?'

'Our Hector? Maybe. I suppose it's possible Janet saw him when she was a child, grieving for her brother. Perhaps she saw him again after her father died.'

'What makes you say that?'

'Because that's when the watershed in her work occurs. She found a new musical voice. It's almost as if *In Memoriam* was written by someone else.'

Someone else.

There was a wordless version first. The lyric came later.

With the phone clamped to my ear, I stalked across the room and sank down on to the sofa. My mind racing, I struggled to frame a coherent sentence. 'Stan – the music... Is it really *that* different?'

'Why, yes! That's why I was so interested to hear that the autograph scores varied so much. But Janet wouldn't be the first composer to have undergone a life-changing experience that fed back radically into her work. The death of her father might have been a crushing blow. Janet could have gone under or she could have re-invented herself. I think the key to what actually happened could well be Frieda – about whom we know nothing at all. But I'm prattling on and keeping you from your breakfast. You must be famished.'

'No, I seem to have lost my appetite.'

'Well, I won't detain you a minute longer. I just wanted to tell you that I've looked at flights and they're filling up rapidly, so I was wondering if it would suit you if I flew out to Glasgow on December 10th? I might spend a couple of days seeing Edinburgh and Glasgow and then I'd come over to Skye. Would that fit in with your plans?'

'Oh, yes, I'm sure that'll be fine. I hadn't really thought – I mean, I don't actually *have* any plans. I find myself rather at a loose end here. The sooner you get here the better really.'

That wasn't *at all* what I'd meant to say. Recovering, I added quickly, 'I mean, the long-range weather forecast is bad. Well, bad by *our* standards. The UK grinds to a halt if we have anything more than a moderate snow fall. It's quite pathetic.'

'Oh, don't worry. Being snowed in on the Isle of Skye would be the icing on the Christmas cake for me. I'd feel like something out of Agatha Christie. And I'd stand a better chance of meeting this Hector.'

'Doesn't the prospect alarm you?'

'Oh, certainly! I'm a devout coward. But it would be a

privilege to be terrorised by a real Scottish ghost. So don't go hiring any exorcists now, will you? Not until after my visit anyway. I know it's selfish of me, but I trust you'll bear up under the strain.'

I laughed and said, 'Stan, you've achieved the impossible. I didn't think anything would make me laugh today.'

'Well, when those shadows encroach, just remember to look for the light.'

'I will. Thank you.'

'I'll be in touch with more travel details nearer the time.'

'OK.'

'Once again, it's been a pleasure to talk to you, Ruth.'

'You too, Stan. Take care.'

And he was gone.

I sat on the sofa, dazed, staring out the French windows, dreading Hector might appear. *Longing* for Hector to appear. It was very cold with no fire in the grate and then I remembered the window I'd opened earlier to air the room. I got to my feet and closed it, then stood and looked out at the garden. It was bleak and almost devoid of colour now the wind had stripped the autumn leaves from the trees. Autumn never lasted long on Skye. It was winter already.

As I continued to stare out the window, the garden gradually became a blur. I thought my eyes must have filled with tears again. Blinking several times, I found I still couldn't see the trees. Then I realised it was snowing. My heart leaped, as it always did, at the sight of the first snow of winter. It wasn't just a flurry either. This was serious snow, large flakes that were settling so that the grass was beginning to disappear.

As snow erased the garden, I tried to face up to my future, which to me looked as bleak and blank as the garden outside. I knew what I ought to do. I ought to cancel Stan and walk away from *Tigh-na-Linne*, away from Hector and Tom. I needed to go back to London, get a job and look up my old friends. Date some mortals, that's what I ought to do. No question.

I stood and watched the snow fall until the lawn had completely disappeared. A robin came and posed on the stone birdbath, completing the Christmas card effect. I wondered why Christmas cards with robins in the snow always looked so naff, when a real robin in real snow made you stand and stare and feel grateful.

Hey, look at me, Stan – I'm looking for the light. And finding it.

Christmas on Skye... Log fires. The cosy fug of the Aga. Freezing walks by the sea. Mugs of cocoa. Stars hanging like brilliant jewels in the blackest of night skies. The majestic Cuillin mountains covered in snow. Drams of Talisker raised to the memory of Aunt Janet, my father and David. Absent friends.

So it was all settled. With Stan for dubious company, I would embrace the dark, while looking for the light.

And Tom could go to Hell.

And Hector?...

Hector was already there.

As I showered, dressed and prepared a sketchy breakfast, Sane Mind and Insane Mind resumed their bickering.

Hector surely couldn't have composed music that purported to be Janet's?

Well, he played the piano and taught music. He might have composed as well.

But even if he had, Janet would never have passed off Hector's work as hers.

He'd quoted the lyric from *In Memoriam* and knew its source. How did he know?

No doubt he and Janet discussed her compositions when they had their ghostly musical soirées.

But that still doesn't account for why the original manuscript wasn't in Janet's hand.

Perhaps Hector acted as her scribe and took dictation – giving a whole new meaning to the expression "ghost-written"...

I cleared up the kitchen, unloaded and re-loaded the dishwasher, then went to the music room where I spread out sample pages of Janet's scores, including *In Memoriam*. As I studied the title page, I noticed some words I'd missed before, written in faint pencil underneath the dedication "To Frieda". They were in German and attributed to Goethe.

Meine Ruh' ist hin,
Mein Herz ist schwer.

I didn't speak any German, but Google would no doubt furnish me with a translation. Why would Janet preface her score with a quotation from a German poet? Because the composition was inspired by the Great War? But Janet hadn't written this quotation. It was not her hand. If it was Hector's, why would he quote a *German*? He'd been killed by Germans. So had his two brothers and many of his friends.

Perhaps the meaning of the words would shed some light. I went and fetched my laptop, switched on and, after a few moments, typed the German words into a Google search, then looked for a translation.

My peace is gone,
My heart is heavy.

The lines were apparently from Goethe's *Faust* and described the consternation of young Gretchen who has fallen for Faust in a big way. Sitting at her spinning wheel, she's close to losing her mind. All of a piece with the last entry in Hector's journal. ("Letter from Frieda. This is a bad business. I am in Hell.") But *was* it Hector who'd chosen this quotation?

Then Sane Mind felled me with a hammer blow of common sense. I was a complete idiot. All I needed to do was compare the writing on the score with Hector's journal.

I ran up the stairs, clutching the sheet of manuscript, set it down on the bed and pulled open the bedside drawer where I kept Hector's journal. I took out the little book and opened it randomly. I didn't even need to compare. I'd been studying this handwriting for the last half hour.

So Hector had composed *In Memoriam*. A song cycle about an impossible love, in which the lovers are separated not only by distance, but ultimately by death. He'd dedicated it to

"Frieda" and prefaced it (in the language of the enemy) with words that meant

My peace is gone,
My heart is heavy.

And my aunt had passed off Hector's composition as her own.
But why?

Chapter Thirteen

It had stopped snowing. The garden was cloaked in a thick white mantle and the leafless trees looked black in comparison. I stood at the window and admired the stark beauty of their shapes, something I hadn't even noticed before the snowfall.

I hardly ever saw snow like this. In London, no matter how early you got out, there would be dirty footprints in the snow and brown slush piled at the side of the road. In a matter of hours, snow in the city became an ugly, depressing inconvenience. Here on Skye it was an agent of transformation.

As I looked out at the white expanse, I was dazzled by the sunlight reflected off the snow, by the brightness of the blue sky, the clarity of the air. The garden was unfamiliar, almost unrecognisable now, a brave new world. The prospect of exploration was irresistible, so I turned my back on Janet's dusty manuscripts and Hector's muddy journal to venture outdoors, where everything was clear, bright and utterly simple.

I plodded across the snow in my Wellingtons, delighted. It was already a couple of inches deep and as my feet sank into the immaculate white carpet, I felt a remnant of the thrill I'd known as a child, running across virgin snow, leaving my mark, spoiling the pristine surface in an impulse that had nothing to do with destruction, everything to do with exhilaration.

I walked round to the pond and stood at the water's edge where it had already begun to freeze, then, shivering, I set off on a brisk circuit, keeping my eyes averted from the bridge from which I'd fallen all those years ago. A heron took off in a huff, but a pair of mallards, made of sterner stuff, merely glared at me. I pondered the circulatory system of ducks. How could they stand the temperature of the almost-freezing water? What ran in their veins instead of blood? Anti-freeze?... I sensed my thoughts turning in a direction that would lead to Hector and our (cool) night of passion, so I increased my pace and concentrated on putting one foot in front of the other.

As I came full circle round the pond, I glanced up at the house and was surprised to see Tom walking toward me. I stood still, struggling with the confused feelings that had arisen at the sight of him: pleasure that I had someone to share the garden with; irritation that I was probably in for an embarrassing apology.

He raised a hand in greeting, then strode across the snow to meet me. As he approached, I could see his face looked haggard, as if he hadn't slept. Or perhaps he was nursing a hangover. He came to a halt in front of me, but didn't speak or smile. His mouth was bracketed by deep lines that I didn't remember seeing before and his eyes were dull with exhaustion. He hadn't shaved, possibly on account of the livid, red weal on his cheek, the size of a thumbnail, where Hector had burned him with the hot coal.

As the awkward silence became prolonged, I said, 'How did you know I was out here?'

'I knocked. When you didn't answer, I thought you'd probably be in the garden. I followed your footprints.'

'Oh. Of course.'

Tom plunged his hands deep in his jacket pockets, cleared his throat and said, 'I've come to crawl.'

'That's not necessary, Tom. We'll take apologies as read, shall we? I think we both suffered enough embarrassment last night.'

'No. I have to apologise. About a lot of things. It's a long list. What you might call an inventory.'

'What do you mean?'

'Shall we walk? To keep warm? This could take a while.'

'Do you want to go indoors? I could make some coffee.'

'No, if you don't mind, Ruth, I'd like to stay outdoors. I

think it brings out the best in me. And I like the snow.' He looked round at the garden, squinting in the sunlight. 'It's *clean.*'

'OK,' I said doubtfully. 'Let's walk then.'

We set off, walking side by side. It occurred to me, even before Tom started speaking, that by choosing to talk like this, he wouldn't have to look me in the eye. I could understand his reluctance. In fact, I shared it.

After a few moments he said, 'I owe you a lot of money.'

I stopped walking and turned to him in surprise. 'What on earth are you talking about?'

'Can we keep walking, please? I'll explain.'

We walked on, then after a few paces, he blurted out, 'You're paying me too much. My wages, I mean. I'm charging you more than I charged Janet.'

I stopped again and turned to stare at him. To his credit, he met my eyes, though clearly it wasn't a pleasant experience.

'*Why?*'

'Because I need the money.'

'Are you in trouble?'

'Oh, yes. I'm in deep shit.'

'I see. Do you want to talk about it?'

'That's why I'm here. Can we keep walking? It's just... *easier* somehow.'

We set off again and after a moment, he announced, 'I'm a compulsive gambler. No, please, keep walking.... I'm addicted to gambling. I don't know if you realise, but compulsive gambling is as much an illness as alcoholism.'

'Yes, I did know. But I've never known a compulsive gambler.'

'Well, you do now.'

We walked on in silence while I tried to absorb the new information.

'How do you manage to gamble on *Skye*?'

'I don't any more. But my debts go *way* back. So do me and gambling. I had poker-playing chums. We used to go to casinos. Clubs. In the end, the only friends I had were gamblers. So I came here. To Skye. Out of harm's way, I thought. Where I discovered you can gamble with things other than cash.'

'But Tom, I don't understand. When you came round to tell me about working for Janet, you were offering to pay money *back*.'

'That's right.'

'And I could easily have found out you were overcharging me, simply by checking Janet's accounts.'

'Yes, I know. That's the rush, you see! That's how it works. I *could* have been found out. But I wasn't. I took a gamble that you wouldn't check the accounts. You're not that kind of girl. And you didn't think I was that kind of guy. *Especially* since I was offering to return the money Janet had been paying me for doing nothing.'

'Are you saying you *knew* I'd let you keep it?'

'Let's just say it was a calculated risk. Quite a big one, given the state of my finances. But I figured someone who worked in TV and owned a smart car, a flat in London and a big pile like this would feel too embarrassed to ask for the money back. You'd look mean. So I could afford to look honest. A man of integrity. I thought that could be... useful. And I thought it might persuade you to give me my job back.'

'Tom, I just can't believe you'd—' The power of speech suddenly deserted me and I swallowed hard.

'That I'd treat anyone so badly, especially an old childhood friend? You're too trusting, Ruth. You think everyone is as honest and kind as Janet. As *you*. I could see that when I met you again. You seemed much the same as when you were young. Sensitive. Caring. And gullible. The kind of girl who believes in fairies... You didn't check Janet's accounts, did you?'

'No.'

'You see? That gamble paid off. But I also took a chance on you wanting sex with me.' He shrugged. 'You win some, you lose some. It usually evens out. Until you get a run of real bad luck. And eventually *all* gamblers get a run of real bad luck. That's what sends us into the Programme. Losing it all. Having nothing left to gamble with.'

'Have you lost everything?'

'Pretty much. Wife. Kid. Friends. Money, obviously. I don't have money any more, only debts. I've lost count of the jobs I've had. The Forestry Commission sacked me for nicking equipment. I was lucky they didn't prosecute.'

'Why on earth would you—'

'Sold it for cash. By the way, you don't owe me for a chainsaw. *I* took it.'

I stopped walking and bowed my head. 'Oh, *Tom!*'

'Another gamble. I didn't think you'd remember to lock the garage. You sounded pre-occupied when I rang. Something had rattled you.'

I looked up at him. 'You could tell that on the phone? I barely spoke!'

'If you play poker, you get used to reading people. It becomes a habit. So I came back to see if you'd locked up. And I was right. You see, I even bet against myself! So then I thought it would be a blast to steal my own chainsaw. I figured you wouldn't miss a couple of hundred quid. And I squared it with myself that, since you hadn't locked the garage, anyone could have come along and stolen my chainsaw. It just so happened that the someone was me.'

I shook my head from side to side. 'This is just... *horrible!*'

'It is, isn't it? You can see why my wife left me... But your chainsaw money would have been just a drop in the ocean. I've got to sell *Larachbeag* now. To pay off debts. I won't get much for it, but it's all I've got left to sell apart from my van and my tools. I can't work without those.'

'But where will you live?'

'Don't know. I had a plan that I'd get shacked up here with you, all nice and cosy for Christmas, then maybe you'd bugger off back to London and leave me here with a cushy caretaking job. But I blew it, didn't I? Should've known. Gambling and booze don't mix. Booze screws your judgement. One drug at a time, that's the rule. But I forget. "Too much is never enough" - that's always been my motto.'

'Tom, I still don't understand. Why are you *telling* me all this? Humiliating yourself. And me.'

'It's what I have to do. Part of the Recovery Programme. Step Five: *We admitted to ourselves and to another human being the exact nature of our wrongs.* You're another human being. And you're on my list.'

'List?'

'Step Eight: *We made a list of all persons we had harmed and became willing to make amends to them all.* So that's why I'm here. To make amends. And to say sorry for being a Class A bastard. To tell you, I'm sick and I need help.'

'Are you getting any help?'

'Oh, yes. Help's available, but mostly I choose to ignore it. Because I'm a *stupid* Class A bastard. You offered me friendship, but I took advantage of you. In every single bloody way I could.'

I looked down again, unable to think of anything to say. Steeling myself, I looked up into his face again. I could no longer see the man I'd thought handsome; the man I might have ended up sleeping with. This one looked bone-weary. Miserable. Broken.

'Do you know where your wife and child are?

He flinched slightly at the question, then said, '*Ex*-wife. No, I've no idea. She doesn't want me to know. I haven't seen or heard from them in years.'

'I'm sorry.'

'No, it's the best thing. Definitely. Well, best for *them*.'

There was another long silence in which I felt the cold creep up through my Wellingtons. I wriggled my toes to keep my circulation moving, then said, 'Is there anything I can do to *help*?'

Tom blinked at me, then threw back his head and laughed, making the booming sound that had cheered me up on previous occasions. It sounded hollow now. The startled mallard and his mate took off, affronted.

'*Help?* Jesus, Ruth!' Tom ran a hand through his tangled hair and when he spoke there was an odd catch in his voice. 'I've lied to you, stolen from you, cheated you, practically *raped* you! And you ask me if you can *help*?'

'I'd like to, if I can. I've known what it is to be hard up. And down on my luck. At the moment I don't have a job or even the prospect of a job. So I can sympathise. In a way.'

'It's more than I deserve.'

'Probably, but that's not really the point, is it? It's about friendship. I think of you – well, I *thought* of you as a friend. An old friend. And I do understand that what's wrong with you is an illness. So... I'd like to help. If I can.' He stared at me, his lips parted. In disbelief, I suppose. 'Maybe if I help you, you'll stop stealing from me.' A flicker passed across his face that might have been amusement, but I fixed him with a look and said, 'We were drinking Janet's champagne last night, weren't we?'

He winced and closed his eyes. 'Sorry. Forgot about that one. I took it from the wine rack ages ago.'

'And moved another bottle into the gap so I wouldn't notice?'

'That's right. All part of the fun,' he muttered grimly. 'If there's *any* way I can do it, I want to make reparation, Ruth. I can't pay you back, but I'll happily add you to my long list of creditors. And if you want to continue employing me, I'll work for nothing until we're square.'

'Reparation is all part of it, isn't it? The Programme.'

'An essential part.'

'Would you *want* to carry on working for me?'

'Yes. And I promise I won't steal anything else.'

I stared into Tom's face. He managed to meet my eyes and hold my gaze, but I could see it cost him an effort. I suddenly recalled Hector telling me I would know what to do. So I silenced Sane Mind and said, 'Well, I still need a gardener and handyman. But I'd insist on paying you. Though I'm not prepared to pay you any more than Janet did.'

'No, of course. That's... that's very good of you.'

I had a horrible feeling he might be about to put his arms round me, so I turned and pointed to the pond. 'You can dismantle that rotten bridge for a start. I know the weather's not ideal, but that bridge is bothering me. Take it down before the weight of snow makes it fall into the pond.'

'Consider it done.'

'The other thing you can do, Tom, is be my friend. I don't want to sleep with you, but I could use a friend. A *reliable* friend. Sounds like you could too.' He said nothing, but just stared down at the snow-covered ground. To spare his feelings, I rambled on. 'There could possibly be long-term prospects here. For the right person. I've been thinking about opening a plant nursery.'

'At *Tigh-na-Linne*?'

'Yes. It's just a mad idea at the moment. I'm not sure what to do with the place, but I don't really want to sell it, not unless I have to. So I'm trying to think of some sort of business venture. I'd be interested to know what you think, if you had any ideas. But whatever I decide to do here, there could be building work. Landscaping. Planting. Some of these trees are old and dangerous. They need to come down and new ones should be planted. If I did go ahead with the nursery idea, I'd need staff. Possibly a manager. But it would have to be someone reliable. One hundred per cent.'

'I understand.'

'And if I decide to put *Tigh-na-Linne* on the market, I'll need someone to keep an eye on the place for me until it's sold, especially during the winter. So we could possibly come to an arrangement that would suit us both.' Tight-lipped now, Tom simply nodded, apparently unable to speak. 'But it would all depend on whether I felt I could trust you. Trust you *completely*.'

'Yes, of course. I'm really grateful that you're— well, that you're not giving up on me.' He passed a hand over his eyes, dragging at the skin. 'Because I'd just about given up on myself.'

I laid a hand on his arm. 'Let's just take it a day at a time, shall we?'

He nodded. 'It's the only way. With people like me, I mean. We *have* to take it one day at a time.'

'Well, that's what I propose to do too. Now, I don't know about you, but after all this soul-searching, I'm in desperate need of caffeine. Would you care to join me?'

'I'd like nothing better.'

'Come on then. Let's get the kettle on.'

I hooked my arm through Tom's and together we plodded through the snow, back up to the house.

~

Hector behaved himself. I'd worried he might throw a supernatural tantrum if Tom crossed the threshold again, but I wasn't even aware of his presence and after a stilted, but fairly amiable coffee-drinking session, Tom departed unscathed.

For the rest of the day, I braced myself for Hector's appearance. The slightest draft or noise made me imagine I sensed his presence. As the afternoon wore on and evening approached, I found myself wondering if he would appear at night, in my bedroom. And if I would be sleeping alone.

Anticipation became tension, then tension turned to annoyance as Hector failed to show, even though, as I understood it, he could be summoned by my need for him. Perhaps sexual need didn't count. Or (and this was not a flattering thought) perhaps Hector knew I was waiting for him, but chose not to appear.

Why would a ghost play hard to get?

I spent the evening looking over the notes I'd made about the history of *Tigh-na-Linne* and the Munro family. When that subject palled, I started drafting a vague business plan for turning *Tigh-na-Linne* into a horticultural centre of some sort. But neither subject distracted me for very long from my real preoccupation: Hector's non-appearance. So I abandoned my notes, shut down my laptop and settled for an early night.

As I climbed the stairs, I became aware of a strange sensation: a prickly feeling at the back of my neck, so uncanny that eventually I stopped and looked round. I hadn't heard any noise and I'd checked the house was locked before retiring, so I wasn't worried about intruders. No, this was more a sensation of being watched, or rather *followed*, because I continued to experience it as I turned off at the top of the stairs and walked along the passage to the bathroom.

I knew it had to be Hector watching me, but I couldn't imagine why he wasn't materialising. Did he think I couldn't sense his presence? As I entered the bathroom, the prickly sensation ceased, which to my mind only confirmed it was Hector stalking me. His sense of propriety would never allow him to observe a lady at her ablutions. Convinced I was no longer being spied on, I decided to take a shower in an attempt to dispel the tension that had built up during the day.

When I emerged from the bathroom some time later, wrapped in a towel, I wasn't at all surprised I felt observed again. Hector had evidently waited for me outside the door and was now accompanying me, unseen, to my bedroom.

I entered and left the door open, but already I could tell he hadn't followed me into the room. I walked out again, sensed his presence, then walked back in, unaccompanied. I sank down on the bed, still wrapped in my towel, annoyed, disappointed and perplexed in equal measure.

'For Heaven's sake, Hector! *Come in*. Do you think I don't know you're out there? Why won't you show yourself?'

There was no response of any kind, except that the bedroom door began to move slowly. As it swung, my spirits rose and I stood up, wondering if I was about to be embraced by my invisible lover, but by the time the door was shut, I knew Hector was on the other side of it.

'Hector?' I called. 'What's all this about? Why are you ignoring me?'

No response.

'Aren't you supposed to come when I call you? Don't you have to respond to my need? Or have the rules changed?'

Still no response.

Fed up with game-playing, I tucked my towel in firmly, tossed back my damp hair and headed for the door. I flung it open and stepped into the passage and stood there, hands on hips, too angry to feel the idiot I must have looked, talking to the air.

'Hector, you've seen it all before, so why the coy performance? I know you're there, so why won't you let me *see* you?'

My nostrils twitched as I detected the mix of mud and blood I'd originally found so disturbing, but which now had a more stimulating effect on my heart rate than the most expensive male cologne. I turned toward the memorial window, the direction from which the smell emanated. Hector began to appear as a pale shape, or rather, bits of him appeared and then disappeared, as if he was only partly materialising. When I was finally able to see his face, it came as a shock. He seemed to be suffering, perhaps suffering greatly. His eyes were unfocused, sunk in dark hollows and his lips were compressed in a grim, determined line.

'Hector, what's wrong? Are you in pain? Why can't I see you properly? You're coming and going like the Cheshire cat. Is it because we— I mean, is this something to do with what happened last night?'

His mouth didn't move, but his eyes – when they were visible – bore into me in a most unnerving way. I couldn't *hear* anything, but I became aware that Hector was somehow speaking to me. Goosebumps sprang up all over my damp skin as I realised he must be letting me read his mind.

You can't see me because I'm using such power as I have to ignore your summons. And your need.

'But why?'

My own voice startled me, then once again Hector's thoughts penetrated my confusion.

Because there's no future for us, Ruth. Because what happened last night should not have happened. I displayed weakness and selfishness. Such a lapse must not occur again.

'You mean you're deliberately keeping yourself invisible?'

Aye. At least, I'm trying... You caught me unprepared by emerging from the bedroom. Half-naked.

'I was hoping to remind you what you're missing!'

Pale lids closed over his tortured eyes, then opened again. *I've not forgotten. Nor am I likely to.*

'But I don't understand! Are you abandoning me?'

No, never. But we cannot be lovers.

'We *are*!'

Your future doesn't lie with me, Ruth.

'I don't care about my future, I care about *you*!'

You know it's madness to think about me in this way. I'm dead. I've been dead for almost a century. I was blown to smithereens by a shrapnel shell. It reduced me to bloody gobbets of flesh and bone, caught on the wire in No Man's Land. There wasn't even a body to bury, Ruth. That's the man you now desire.

'Hector, don't! Please... I still want you!'

I know, lassie. I can sense how much. Och, it's very nearly as much as I want you! But I'm not meant for you. There'll be another. Some day.

'I don't want another, I want you!'

It cannot be. You must see that. Our relationship... He shook his head, seeming at a loss. *"It was begotten by Despair upon Impossibility."*

'Don't give me that crap!' I shouted, fighting back tears. 'Get your act together and get into that bedroom. Just hold me, Hector! For one minute. Touch me. *Please.* I can't bear this!'

No more can I. That's why it must end. Here. Now.

'Then I shall leave *Tigh-na-Linne.*'

No!

'So you want me to stay, but you're going to ignore me! Or are we going to indulge in some form of head-sex from now on? Do tell, Hector, what you have planned for us.'

It's not what I have planned, Ruth. I'm only an instrument.

'Instrument? But not one I'm allowed to use!' As I waved my arms angrily, my towel slipped and I clutched at it automatically, covering myself again.

As I glared at Hector, he became clearer. His body appeared more solid, so that, after a few seconds, he was in the form I recognised. He looked like a man again. I took an eager step toward him, but he raised a warning hand and this time, addressed me using his voice.

'Stay there, Ruth. If you approach me, I swear I shall marshall such meagre resources as I have left to remove myself from your sight.' He paused, allowing the threat to sink in, then said, 'I want you to listen to me. Will you do that?'

'Yes, if it means I can look at you. See you as I know you. Yes, I'll listen. Listen all night.'

'We belong to different worlds. There can be no future for us together. I am not a man. I *appear* to be a man because that's the form in which I can best serve you. If I thought our carnal relationship was a novelty of which you would eventually tire, the indulgence would perhaps be forgivable. But I have grown to love you. And I very much fear you love me, or are in danger of loving me. How can I allow you to throw yourself away on... a *spectre*? A dead man who cannot give you children, or support you? Who cannot satisfy you physically in a normal way?'

'Oh, don't trouble yourself on that score. Believe me, I had no complaints.'

'Your future doesn't lie with me, Ruth. I *have* no future, only a past.'

'But you promised me "wonders". Don't you remember? You said there would be wonders for both of us.'

'And there will. Believe it.'

'But we won't be ... *together* somehow?'

'No. It's impossible, you know that. What happened between us was... an aberration. You offered yourself to me and I – I should not have given in to my desire. I bear the responsibility for your present unhappiness. To see you like this, to witness your misery, is punishment enough for what I did.'

Deflated, despairing, I shivered and hugged my bare arms. Hearing a soft, swishing sound behind me, I turned and saw the patchwork quilt from my bed creeping across the threshold of my bedroom. It gathered itself at my feet, slid up and over my body, then draped itself around my shoulders like a cape. As I watched, open-mouthed, the quilt moulded itself to my chilled body, like a lover's embrace. I looked up at Hector to thank him for this tender gesture, but his eyes were fixed on some point on the floorboards, his brow deeply furrowed, as if at any moment, his struggle might finally overwhelm him.

'You won't desert me altogether, will you?' I pleaded. 'You'll still appear? And talk to me? Will things be as they were before?'

He didn't look up, but said, dully, 'How can they ever be as they were when you know I love you? That you love me? Its impossible, Ruth.'

'Oh, stop using that word! Can't we at least *try*? I've lost so much this year. David. My father. Janet. I just can't bear to lose anyone else! Please don't leave me.'

Hector didn't reply and appeared to be wrestling with his

151

emotions. Eventually he sighed and said, 'There will come a time when I have to leave, but until then, I shall remain your faithful servant.'

'And friend?'

'Of course. Now away to your bed. You're cold and tired.'

Turning, I began to trudge along the passage, dragging the quilt behind me, then I stopped and looked back over my shoulder. Hector was still there.

'Will you wait outside my door tonight? As you used to?'

'Aye.'

'All night?'

'Aye.'

'But you'll be gone in the morning?'

'Aye, I will.'

As I turned away, I sensed him following me to the door and could smell the damp earth that clung to his boots. I'll never know how I commanded my feet to take me in the opposite direction. Hesitating in the doorway, I laid trembling fingers on the handle.

'Hector, we—'

'Goodnight, Ruth.'

I turned and looked into his pale eyes and said, 'I know you're right. In my *sane* mind, I do know that what you say makes sense. It's just that, I don't think I want to be sane. I preferred the madness. It made more sense to me. And it was much more fun, you have to admit.' I was rewarded with the slightest of smiles and a lightening of Hector's stern expression. 'Do you know what Janet said once? She said, "A creative artist needs to keep sanity in check".'

'Did she now?'

'Yes. And I'm sure she was right.' Quite unaccountably, tears sprang into my eyes and Hector became a blur. 'I miss her so much!'

'Och, wheesht now!' he murmured softly. Without touching me, he reached down and wrested the door handle from my fingers. 'Away to your bed now. You'll sleep.'

It sounded like an order and, as Hector closed the bedroom door, I obeyed. I cast off the quilt and my wet towel, put on a warm nightie and got into bed. Miserable and angry,

I assumed sleep would elude me, but I fell into a doze almost immediately, lulled by the sound of Hector's low voice reverberating gently in my aching head, like a sort of spoken lullaby. His words seemed familiar, but it took me a while to place them. He was reciting the last verse of the Marvell poem, the one he'd set to music – music that Janet had appropriated.

Therefore the love which us doth bind
But Fate so enviously debars,
Is the conjunction of the mind
And opposition of the stars.

Chapter Fourteen

The following morning, I saw with startling clarity that I must leave *Tigh-na-Linne* and as soon as possible. I would leave my car on Skye, fly down to London and embrace normality once more. Tom could be put in charge of looking after the house. He could even live in while I was away. If I went back to London, I would be doing us both a favour. Admittedly, there was a danger he might sell the contents of the house in my absence, but my instincts told me Tom might just have turned a corner. Every time he looked in the mirror (and I suspected he did that quite often) he'd see the evidence of his stupid and selfish behaviour. He would be reminded that I'd trusted him and (perhaps foolishly) continued to trust him. If he had any remnant of conscience left, Tom wouldn't let me down again. He needed all the friends he could get.

Stan could be cancelled – *had* to be cancelled, since Janet's professional integrity had been called into question. It seemed there *had* been some plagiarism and, whatever her motives, they'd never withstand the harsh scrutiny of the academic world. Much as I wanted my aunt's musical legacy to reach a wider audience, I didn't want her to be pilloried or misunderstood. Stan himself had suggested Janet might have collaborated with another uncredited composer, but even if I could persuade *him* Janet's partner in crime was actually a ghost, there was no way we'd be able to convince anyone else. Janet herself would surely have agreed obscurity was preferable to ignominy.

So after breakfast, I sat with my laptop, attempting to compose a musical *Dear John* letter to Stan, informing him that changed circumstances dictated my immediate return to London and, since I couldn't be sure of my future plans, I must reluctantly withdraw my offer of hospitality.

Saving the email in draft, I felt a total coward and

154

wondered how long it would take me to pluck up the courage to send it. I also wondered if Hector would try to prevent me leaving.

He didn't have to. The weather did it for him. When I went online to book a flight to London from Inverness, I found the airport had been closed by snow. It never took much to close that airport and looking at the Met Office long-range forecast, it looked to me as if it might be closed for at least another twenty-four hours, maybe longer.

I decided I would have to risk the five hour drive to Glasgow and leave the car there, so I checked the AA's website. In view of local weather conditions (high winds, drifting snow, blizzards) they advised motorists not to travel unless their journey was essential.

I wondered briefly and paranoiacally if this was all Hector's doing, but there was no evidence he had any meteorological powers. Locals had predicted a long, hard winter in the Highlands and it seemed it had begun. So perhaps, I thought, searching for the silver lining of this particular dark cloud, Stan wouldn't even attempt the journey to Skye. But a Canadian was unlikely to be daunted by a spot of bad weather. No, I would just have to put Stan off. He would never know if I'd gone back to London or not.

But in the event, I didn't have to send my email. When I returned to my inbox, I found Stan had got there before me. It was only then, as I read his desolate apologies, that I realised how much I'd been looking forward to meeting him and talking about Janet.

Crestfallen, I shut down my laptop. So much for all my jolly Christmas plans. And so much for Hector's promised "wonders".

My dear Ruth

Forgive an email, but as I type, you will, I'm sure, be tucked up in bed – perhaps dreaming of your ghost!

155

I'm sorry to say I have a domestic crisis here and it affects my proposed Christmas visit. My father has had to be admitted to a nursing home and I've been told that's where he's likely to stay now. I've also been told his stay might not be a long one.

I'm his only close relative, geographically speaking, so for some years now his care has fallen to me, which means my visit to Skye might have to be cancelled or postponed. Dad could stabilise, in which case I can come over. He might pass away, in which case I would be free to travel some time after the funeral. But he might just remain poorly, in which case, I don't think I can consider making the trip.

The next 48 hours are critical. If Dad rallies, my trip could be feasible as I'm not due to fly out for a couple more weeks. But if I did come, I'd need to be on stand-by in case he deteriorated. My trip could therefore turn out to be a short one. This degree of uncertainty is, I know, most unsatisfactory, so I think it's probably best if I cancel. That way you're free to make alternative arrangements for Christmas.

Before he took a fall, Dad was encouraging me to visit "the Old Country" and I have to admit, I was really hoping to meet Hector the Spectre. (My plan was, if I didn't make the bestseller lists with my study of Janet Gillespie, I would sell the story of my spook encounter to *Haunted Times* magazine.

Perhaps I could come over in the spring, when things have settled down here? I have plenty of preparatory work to do on Janet's book in the meantime.

With very best wishes

Stan

Both hugely relieved and hugely disappointed, I drafted an email to Stan, expressing regret about his father's health. When I read my response through, it was clear Sane and Insane Minds were still at loggerheads. I'd assured Stan we could keep things flexible – it was far too soon to think about cancelling his trip – but I'd also informed him I'd encountered problems with Janet's archive which had led me to re-think the extent to which I wished to participate in his researches.

Vague and non-committal, yet sufficiently worrying to throw the poor man into a panic about the fate of his proposed book. So I deleted the paragraph about Janet's archive, let my invitation stand, but informed Stan I might be returning to London shortly for work meetings. (Chance would be a fine thing. I doubted I'd even get a Christmas card from the BBC.)

This, I thought, would give me plenty of options. I could flee Skye if I had to, but I could also keep Stan lined up as a possible fall-back plan for avoiding spending Christmas alone. And there was always Tom. Not to mention Hector. In fact it seemed pretty unlikely I'd get to spend Christmas alone.

But I still couldn't tell if I was relieved or disappointed about Stan.

I pressed *Send* anyway.

The temperature plummeted. I offered up a prayer of thanksgiving to the inventor of the Aga and kept a fire going all day in the sitting room. The pond froze over, then disappeared under several inches of snow, so I now had a rickety bridge to nowhere. Eventually it was too cold for snow to fall and Tom took advantage of the clearer, colder weather to make a spectacular job of removing the bridge.

Using his harness, he attached himself to a big willow that overhung the pond. He descended like a spider on to the ice, lowering himself gingerly to see if it would take his weight. I stood by anxiously with blankets, brandy, my mobile and the number of the Mountain Rescue team, listening for the sound of cracks, but the ice held and Tom was able to tiptoe across the surface, sawing through rotting timbers. Then he tied long ropes to the sections of bridge, attached the ends to the back of his van, got in and started the engine.

Standing well back, I watched as the ropes went taut and then began to strain. There was a creaking and rending noise as the wood fell, followed by sounds like gunshots as the ice cracked and then split open. The old timbers slid across the frozen pond, piling snow as they travelled. When the remains of the bridge reached *terra firma*, I signalled to Tom, who stopped the van and ran back down, grinning like a schoolboy.

'It worked then?'

'Brilliantly. Destruction is definitely your forte. Many thanks. I'm glad to see the back of that eyesore.' I looked at the black holes now disfiguring the pond's white surface. 'Shame it's made such a mess of the pond.'

Tom looked up at the sky, which was beginning to darken. 'There's more snow on the way. And the water's freezing over already. You wait, by tomorrow it will look like a Christmas card again. You'll forget the bridge was ever there.'

Remembering how I'd fallen in and how I'd nearly drowned, I found I didn't share Tom's view. Even with the bridge gone, I doubted I'd ever forget the black and muddy depths of that pond.

Tom was right about the weather. The combination of wind and snow meant we were plunged into white-out conditions for a couple of days. Even if I'd had the energy to clear the driveway to use the car, I wouldn't have been able to see where I was going. I worked my way through the tinned soups Janet had always kept in stock and I made soda bread when the ordinary bread ran out. I sat tight, waiting for the weather to improve, so I could get back to London.

For that was surely where I belonged. Hector was avoiding me and Stan hadn't rung or replied to my email. If I was going to be spending Christmas alone, it would surely be better to spend it in London, with thousands of other lonely people, than on Skye, in a large, empty house – empty, that is, apart from a resident ghost.

I'd considered offering hospitality to Tom, but as he was unable to reciprocate or even contribute financially, I wondered if another invitation to eat and drink at my expense might seem humiliating. He forestalled me anyway by saying he was going to spend Christmas in Inverness with a Gamblers Anon mate. They'd volunteered to work at a night shelter over Christmas, which Tom said would "keep him out of trouble". I wasn't surprised he'd made arrangements to be away from home. If you were a father who'd lost touch with your only child, I imagined Christmas could be a difficult time.

Tom didn't know my own Christmas plans had probably fallen through. I didn't tell him because I knew he might be concerned about me coping on my own. I let him think my Canadian professor was still expected and that my Christmas was both well organised and eagerly anticipated.

It was neither of these things.

I waited, but Stan didn't ring or email. And Hector didn't appear.

Time seemed to grind to a halt. I sat slumped by the fire, staring out the window at the hysterically whirling snowflakes, watching as the familiar contours of the garden disappeared, until in the end, I didn't recognise my world; didn't recognise myself.

I finally came to the decision that I *must* leave *Tigh-na-Linne* after a morning spent poring over photograph albums. I should have guessed what would happen, but as one snowy day merged into another, I had a lot of time on my hands and pictorial research for my project seemed like a good idea at the time.

I adjourned to the study where I at least had a different view of the arctic wasteland the garden had become. Janet had of course organised the many leather-bound photograph albums in date order, so it was easy to find what I was looking for.

The pre-1914 photographs were heartbreaking. The Munro family were pictured outdoors on summer picnics, hiking, riding, fishing and swimming. Life appeared to have been one long summer, even on inclement Skye. By referring to the family tree in the old Bible, I could guess at the identity of those pictured.

Hector was easily recognised. In black and white, the splendour of his hair was not apparent, but I was surprised to see how Byronically thick and curly it was before he'd been shorn for the army. In most of the photos he was smiling or laughing. It struck me that I'd rarely seen Hector smile, let alone laugh.

He was often pictured with his siblings: his two brothers, Archibald and Donald (who appeared to be twins, about ten years younger) and his little sister, Grace (younger still), who was often captured gazing up at Hector instead of the camera.

By the time Grace was twenty, all three brothers were dead. No shadow of the loss she was to experience darkened her laughing face, but someone – Hector's father perhaps? – had written a quotation underneath a formal portrait of the four Munro children in which a solemn teenage Hector held baby Grace on his knee, flanked by the twins.

No sense had they of ills to come,
Nor care beyond today.

There were formal commemorative photographs – studio portraits taken before the brothers went off to war. As they stood, proudly uniformed, under a fake, cloudless sky, beside what looked like a *papier mâché* stone balustrade, the brothers' eyes were fixed on a distant horizon. The twins were young, fresh-faced and innocent; Hector, at thirty-four, had seen something of the world, but none of them could have imagined the horrors that lay in store.

I just couldn't bear it. Afraid my tears might fall and damage these precious photographs, I shut the album and put it back on the shelf. Then I snatched it down again and carefully removed one of the photos of Hector. It was one of him standing by the pond at *Tigh-na-Linne*. He looked as if he might be about to jump in. It was an informal shot of a young man, perhaps not yet 30, grinning at the camera – handsome, carefree, looking very solid. Much of his body was revealed by his modest Edwardian swimsuit and you could see that he was fit, his pale arms and legs slim, but sinewy. As I stared avidly at the photograph, I tried to imagine what it would feel like to hold this young man in my arms. And I'd have to imagine it for I never *would* hold him. When I clung to Hector's phantom form, it was like trying to hold on to water, or a memory: the harder you tried to grasp it, the more it dispersed.

I cast an eye round the study, looking for a frame to fit the photo. I spied a picture of me as a girl, dressed in my new school uniform. I removed my photo from the silver frame and inserted Hector's. He smiled back at me, meeting my eyes in a way he seldom managed in our encounters.

It was then, as I stood weeping over a photograph of a long-dead man – the friend I'd always known; a man I never knew – that I realised things had gone far enough. As soon as the weather allowed, I must leave.

Clutching the frame, I went upstairs to pack.

I stood the photograph of Hector on the bedside table and took a suitcase down from the top of the wardrobe. I packed all the clothes I thought I'd need for winter in London, but I didn't pack everything – partly because there wasn't room in the case and partly because I wasn't prepared to face up to the idea of quitting *Tigh-na-Linne* for good. As I folded clothes and laid them in my case, I composed an explanation to Stan. I also tried to think what to say to Tom. I couldn't just leave without asking him to look after the house. If he was spending Christmas in Inverness, I either had to drain the water system completely or leave the heating on. I decided I would deal with all this tomorrow, when I was feeling more on top of things; when I wasn't trying to avoid catching sight of a photograph of a dead man who smiled at the camera as if he had his whole life in front of him.

I walked over to the bedside table, opened the drawer and took out Hector's journal. There was no point in taking it to London, especially as I still felt it would be an invasion of privacy to read it, but I could think of nothing else that was

Hector's, nothing that would make me feel as if the connection between us wasn't entirely severed. Holding the journal, I gazed once again at the photograph in its silver frame. I picked it up, walked back to my case and buried frame and journal deep among my clothes.

I filled a holdall with shoes and boots – randomly, they might not even have been pairs. By then I couldn't see because I was weeping again. I zipped up the holdall and set it outside the bedroom door, then went back to the wardrobe to collect my smart winter coat and the velvet fedora I could never wear on Skye because of the wind. I lay the coat over my arm and wheeled the case across the room and out into the hallway.

Where, standing in front of the memorial window, Hector was waiting.

'You're leaving.' It wasn't a question and he didn't look surprised. 'I'm sorry.'

Trying to keep my voice level, I said, 'What are you saying sorry for?'

'For driving you away. Out of your home.'

'You aren't. I have to go to London,' I said briskly. 'For work. I have some important meetings to attend.'

Hector didn't reply at once, then, after a moment, he said wearily, 'Ruth, we surely don't need to *lie* to each other, do we? I understand the impossibility of... what we did. What I feel.'

'What *we* feel, Hector.'

He turned away and stared at the window, the colours brilliant now the snow reflected so much more light. 'Is that what you see?'

'I'm sorry?'

He gestured toward the angel in the window. 'Is that what I look like? To you?'

'Yes. Well, you're not dressed like that, obviously, but the face is a good likeness.' It dawned on me then why he was asking. 'Oh! You can't ever see yourself, can you?'

'No. I sometimes imagine I see myself reflected in your eyes. Very faintly. But it's just a trick of the light.'

'So when did you last see yourself?'

'Whenever I last shaved, I suppose... September 1915.' He continued to stare at the window. 'Is my hair really that colour?'

'Yes. It's glorious.'

'I'd forgotten... Someone once asked for a lock of my hair. Before I went to the Front. She said she knew she'd forget the colour while I was away. Of course, what she meant was, she wanted something to remember me by. In the event of my death.'

'And did you—?'

'I bought her a silver locket. She disliked gold. Thought it vulgar. And I put a lock of my hair inside.'

'What was she called?'

'Frieda. Elfriede von Hügel. Her mother was a Scot, but her father was German. So there was no question of our marrying. My mother was frail and it would have finished her. The Hun had killed her two younger sons and might yet kill her eldest, so marriage was quite impossible. But I'd proposed anyway... And Frieda had declined. For the sake of my family. She said they'd suffered enough. And I think she feared there would be more suffering. She was right about that... My eyes are surely not that colour?'

I dragged my brain back to the window and stared at the face of the glass angel. 'No. They're paler. But brighter. The colour of delphiniums. The light blue ones.'

Hector nodded slowly, as if filing away the horticultural reference for future use, then he turned and looked at me. 'You remind me of her sometimes. Though I confess, my memories of Frieda are dim after almost a hundred years. Perhaps what I mean is, you enable me to remember her a little. Though I find I don't really want to think of Frieda any more...'

He laid the slightest emphasis on the name and there followed a long silence in which I thought my legs would give way beneath me. I fervently hoped they would, so Hector would spring forward and catch me, take me in his arms and prevent me, forcibly, from leaving. But instead I said, 'I'm glad you gave her the locket.'

'Aye, so am I. I hope it was some comfort to her.'

'I'm sure it must have been.'

'I regret there's nothing I can give *you*. To remember me by.'

'There's not the slightest chance I'll ever forget you, Hector. I've known and loved you since I was eight.'

He tipped his head back suddenly and appeared to examine the ceiling, then he closed his eyes. He put a white hand to his temple and clasped his forehead. Eventually, he said, 'Is there anything I can say that would make you reconsider?'

I dropped my coat and hat onto the suitcase. 'You could try explaining why you want me to stay.' He didn't reply, nor did his eyes meet mine. 'What do you know that I don't, Hector?'

'Nothing. I know nothing.' His chest rose and fell with a great sigh. 'But I sense... *everything*!' He stepped forward and took my hand. The chill surprised me, but no longer shocked me. It seemed you could get used to anything. 'You must stay, Ruth. Until it's finished. Or until it begins.'

'*Which?*'

'Both.'

'Oh, don't be so exasperating, Hector! You *must* know more than you're letting on.'

'No! Only that something will end for me. And begin for you.'

'Something has already begun for me!'

'Something *real*.'

'What I feel *is* real!'

'Och, will you no' stay then!'

As I stared into his wide blue eyes, there was a pounding in my ears and my lungs seemed to stop working. As the room began to spin, I gasped, 'Hector, please, I beg you... I just can't *bear* it!'

He didn't appear to move, but all at once I smelled earth and blood, then cold water seemed to engulf me, knocking me off my feet, sweeping me away in a raging, icy torrent. As I sank down and down, I felt Hector's limbs tangle with mine and gradually darkness closed over us. Then his body, like a surging current, buoyed me upwards until finally, gasping for air, I burst into the light and found myself beached, naked and half-drowned, among the twisted sheets of my storm-tossed bed.

Chapter Fifteen

When I woke, I felt as if I'd been in a deep sleep, possibly for a long time, but the level of daylight in the bedroom hadn't changed. As I surfaced, I clawed at the sheets and blankets, drawing them automatically round my naked body, though I wasn't actually cold. A faint crackling noise and a comforting smell of wood smoke told me that either I was hallucinating, or Hector had performed one of his pyrotechnic miracles before leaving.

Rolling over to check the fireplace, I discovered Hector hadn't left. He was lying beside me, propped up on one arm, apparently naked, regarding me with an enigmatic smile. I was so astonished to see him there, I sat up with a start, clutching the bedclothes.

'You're still here!'

'Aye, so I am.'

'Have you been watching me for long?'

'A wee while.'

I looked round the room and saw a phantom fire in the grate and my discarded clothes folded neatly on a chair, but there was no sign of Hector's kilt or tunic. Then I remembered. A ghost wouldn't wear real clothes. Through the open door, I could see my packed suitcase, standing in the hall like a rebuke.

I rubbed my eyes. 'Have I been asleep for long?'

'Not long.'

'Did you sleep?'

'No.'

'Do you ever sleep?'

'No.' As I blinked in astonishment, he added, 'I rest occasionally.'

Aware he might fade away at any moment, I stared, trying to fix Hector's image in my mind. He seemed relaxed. He looked like a man, not someone from a battered photo album. My hand moved toward him, seemingly of its own accord and traced the map of fine, auburn hair that curled on his chest. My fingertips sensed undulating muscle beneath skin that was neither warm nor solid, but still made me want to touch. It seemed a shame I had no clear memory of how we'd ended up in bed together. I thought I might have enjoyed recalling the details. Minutely.

My palm came to rest on Hector's chest. 'There's something I want to ask you. And I want you to give me an honest answer.'

His look was guarded. 'What d'you want to know?'

'I'd like to know if – well, if there's any *satisfaction* for you. In what we do.'

His auburn brows shot up, then he smiled, rolled on to his back and put his hands behind his head. 'Och, plenty!'

Relieved, I lay down beside him and ran my hand over the ripples of his ribcage, letting it come to rest in the shallow concavity below. I spread exploratory fingers, twining them in the tendrils of soft, curling hair they eventually found. Hector closed his eyes and arched his spine. I explored further. He moaned softly.

'What I'm seeing, Hector... what I'm touching... now. That's just what I *want* to see?'

'Aye. And it's what *I* want you to see.'

'So do you present yourself in a flattering light?'

He opened his eyes and looked at me candidly. 'There's no need. Your loving eyes do that for me. I simply present myself to you in human form.' His expression darkened a little. 'As the man I once was.'

I swallowed and said, 'Hector, I wish—'

He raised a hand and laid his fingertips on my mouth. '*This* is why we cannot be lovers. If I present myself to you as a man – *fully* as a man – you'll think of me as a man. And I'm not. And can never be.'

'Never?'

'I can work wonders, Ruth, not miracles.'

'Are you sure?'

'If you ever got the miracle you desire, it wouldn't be my

167

doing.' He lifted my hand and pressed it to his lips. 'But it can never be. We both know it.'

I rolled away from him, sat up and hugged my knees, thinking it would be easier to accept Hector's words if I didn't have to look at him. It wasn't.

Keeping my back turned to him, I said, 'Will I always be able to *see* you?'

'You see me when you need to.'

'Only if you co-operate,' I retorted.

Ignoring me, he went on. 'So, no, perhaps you won't always be able to see me.'

There was a long silence while I contemplated the misery of this, then I said, 'Can anyone else see you?'

'Not unless they want to. Or need to.'

The question had already formed in my mind, but I was reluctant to ask, as if Hector's answer might confirm, once and for all, his existence or, alternatively, my madness. I moistened my lips and, my voice barely more than a whisper, said, 'Did Janet see you?'

'Aye, she did.'

It was now or never, I supposed. 'Hector... You composed *In Memoriam*, didn't you? And it was you who dedicated it to Frieda.'

'Aye.'

I bowed my head and rested it on my raised knees. 'Why on earth would Janet pass off your work as hers? I can't believe she'd do such a thing. Not Janet!'

Something cool trickled down my spine. Hector's fingers. 'Poor Ruth. So many things you can't believe. Just like Alice.'

I lifted my head, and swivelled round to look at him. 'Alice?'

'*Through the Looking Glass*. She tells the White Queen she can't believe impossible things. The Queen says that's because she hasn't had much practice. "*Why, sometimes I've believed as many as six impossible things before breakfast*".' Despite myself, I smiled at Hector's haughty, English falsetto. 'I used to read that book to your grandmother – my wee sister, Gracie. It was her favourite. Grace had no trouble at all believing impossible things! And she was the first to see me, the first to allow me into her life. Her pain and loneliness provided a portal, so I could get back. Then one day she met a young man who became a good friend. Then something more. And I didn't see Gracie again... I wasn't forgotten. But I was no longer *needed*.'

I stretched out my hand and touched his cheek. 'I do believe in you, Hector. Even though you're impossible. In all senses.'

He grinned. 'I find it easy to believe impossible things now. I suppose I've a vested interest in believing in myself. Discovering I'd become a ghost was some small consolation for finding myself dead.' He sat up and, with his mouth close to my ear, said, 'D'you not believe what happened to you a while ago, Ruth? The evidence of your own eyes? Your own body?'

'Yes. I believe what I feel. Well, most of the time. But I just can't believe my aunt was capable of deceit!'

'There was a good reason for the subterfuge and you'll not be surprised to hear Janet's motive was entirely unselfish. She'd no reason to believe my music would be any more successful than her own. It belonged to an earlier age. We thought it would be deemed old-fashioned. But it was taken up by a popular soprano who made a recording of it. The piece became a great success – critically and with the public. It was played on the radio and in concert halls all over the world. Which was exactly what we'd hoped for.'

'What do you mean?'

'I'd helped Janet. Supported her. A long time ago. When she lost her wee brother to scarlet fever. And I was there again when she lost her parents. Janet and I had quite a history... So she wanted to help me. Help me find someone. But how could I search for anyone when I couldn't leave *Tigh-na-Linne*? When I could only speak to people who believed in me? So Janet suggested we use my music.'

'I don't understand, Hector. Start at the beginning.'

His arm slipped round my shoulders and he drew me back down on to the bed, so that we lay side by side. I stretched myself along the cool length of him and relaxed. It felt very pleasant. Something like floating.

'When you were a wee girl,' Hector said, 'I told you I wasn't able to rest because there was something I needed to do. Someone I needed to find. So that I could set things right.'

'Yes, I remember. Is that why you're here now?'

'Aye. It's why I've been here all this time.'

'But surely everyone you knew must be dead by now?'

'Oh, aye. But *then* – we're talking fifty years ago now – then, the people I wanted to find could have been alive. It's even possible one of the people I was trying to find is still alive now.'

'Who were you looking for?'

'I was looking for Frieda.'

'But you knew her name. And where she lived, presumably?'

'The last time I heard from her, she told me her father had gone into hiding to avoid persecution. Her mother was long dead. It looked as if the war was going to last forever, so Frieda said she was going to go abroad and change her name to something thoroughly Scots. She was born and bred in Edinburgh and she *was* a Scot,' Hector added, unable to keep the note of anger from his voice. 'But she was a Scot called Elfriede von Hügel.'

'And she didn't tell you where she was going?'

'No. But in her last letter, she gave me another piece of news. News that made it all the more imperative for her to go away and begin a new life.'

Received letter from Frieda. This is a very bad business. I am in Hell.

'She told you she was expecting your child.'

'Aye.'

'Oh, *Hector...*'

He didn't say any more, but lay very still while I watched his chest rise and fall. Eventually, his voice quite level, he said, 'Frieda lived in Edinburgh with her father. He was a retired singer of some renown. Before the war he gave singing lessons. She kept house for him and accompanied his pupils on the piano, but she was a fine singer herself. We'd met in a choir and had become friends. Frieda cherished hopes of becoming a professional singer one day and we used to give the odd wee recital together. I played the piano and she sang. Occasionally she sang pieces I'd composed. Her favourite was called *The Definition of Love*. It was my setting of the Marvell poem.'

'And that was the piece Janet published as *In Memoriam*?'

'Aye... Frieda and I planned to marry, but we hadn't told our parents. Then war broke out. It was not a good time to bear a German name. Then both my brothers died in the first year. Frieda and I agreed we couldn't make my parents suffer any more. Or Grace. We wanted to remain friends but... well, that was impossible. So I said we must stop seeing each other. I thought it for the best. I expected to be killed at the front and I was sure Frieda would find a new love. She was a beautiful young woman... But I hadn't taken into account her fidelity. Or the strength of her feelings.'

Hector's body seemed to become cooler and less solid. Fearful he was about to de-materialise, I felt for his hand and twined my fingers with his, hoping to keep him with me. With what sounded like an effort, he continued.

'The night before I was due to travel to London on my way back to the Front, Frieda came to my lodgings late at night... I'd thought never to see her again. We were so happy!... But what happened was beyond reason and I alone must bear the blame. She asked me – *begged* me to love her. And I begged her to leave. I should have been stronger. I should have compelled her to leave, told her I didn't love her, *anything*, rather than besmirch her name and leave her alone, unprovided for, with the burden of my child.'

'But if that was what she wanted? The path she chose for herself? Maybe she wanted your child.'

'She said she did. She said she wanted to have our child because she wished to give my parents another Munro son. I think she cherished hopes that a child might change their minds about our union. She also gave me to understand that in the event of my death, a child would be a consolation to her.'

'Well, she had that, at least.'

'Aye. If it lived.'

'You don't know?'

'No. Her last letter told me only of her condition. I didn't have the opportunity to reply. We went into battle and I was killed. I don't know if the bairn lived. I don't know where Frieda went or what became of her. *In Memoriam* was my attempt to locate her. She'd sung that music many times and the words had come to have a special meaning for us. If she'd ever heard it played, she would have recognised it as mine and known it had been plagiarised. And if I knew Frieda, wherever she was, she would have made contact with Janet to demand why she was passing off Hector Munro's music as her own.'

'But that never happened?'

'No.'

'So do you think perhaps Frieda was dead by then?'

'Aye, perhaps.'

'But you still didn't give up hope of tracing her?'

'No. I thought she might have told the child something about me. About my family. My music. There was the silver locket – the only thing I'd ever given her. And the song that had meant so much to us... It was little enough on which to pin my hopes, but it was all I had.'

'What exactly were you hoping for?'

'I wanted my child to know – *somehow* – that in the seconds before I died, he – or she – was in my thoughts. When that shell came screaming over and I saw it land, I knew I was a dead man. As it exploded, my only thought was, I wanted that wee bairn to know it was my dying regret that we'd never know each other, never even meet... And I still want that, Ruth! In death as in life. I cannot rest – *will* not rest – until I've made my peace. Until I've made some kind of reparation. For my absence.'

'Don't you think Frieda would have explained? As best she could, as soon as the child was old enough to understand?'

'Maybe. Maybe not. If she'd married, our child would have been raised as another man's, with another name. The child might have known nothing at all about me.'

'Would Frieda have learned of your death?'

'She might have contacted mutual friends. She could have contacted the school where I taught before I enlisted. Or she

172

could have checked the casualty lists. My body would never have been identified. There was nothing to bury,' Hector added in a matter-of-fact voice that made me cling to the pale, naked form that lay beside me. As my hand curved around his shoulder, Hector's flesh yielded to my touch and I thought of the white, waxen petals of magnolia blooms – how they felt firm, but fragile. And were so short-lived.

'I would have been posted "Missing, presumed killed",' Hector explained. 'But my parents would not have informed Frieda of my death. In their eyes, she was the enemy. They had no idea how much she meant to me, nor that she probably bore them their first grandchild. But even if I'd lived, I doubt I could have discovered what happened to her, or where she went. Her alias would have made that impossible.'

'And yet...'

'And yet?'

'You still believed – *believe* – there's a connection? That there's some way you can contact your child? In life or in death?'

'Aye. I have to believe, Ruth. I *feel* it! I've felt that connection for nearly a hundred years. Unbroken. Even though Frieda died many years ago. The connection's not with Frieda, but with the child. Members of my family have called me back again and again. When they're unhappy. When they're bereaved. When they are *about* to be bereaved. I recognise the summons of grief and I have to obey. I'm a messenger of death, but I'm also a companion in sorrow. I bring consolation. And, I hope, comfort.'

'Yes, you do. You *did*! I don't know how I'd have coped with my mother's death if I hadn't had you to talk to. I couldn't talk to my father. He couldn't handle his own grief, let alone mine.' I propped myself up on the bed and looked down at Hector's sad, ravaged face. It was the face of a young man, but his eyes reflected a century of suffering. 'It's not fair. You've been the repository for so much grief and sadness. It's more than any man should have to bear.'

'I'm not a man, Ruth. Not any more. But whatever I am now, I'm glad to be of service to my family. Especially if it means there was some meaning in my meaningless death.' He looked away and, as I studied his profile, I racked my brains to think of something to say, but could think of nothing that would comfort a ghost.

Eventually, I said, 'I know you're not a man, Hector – and I do try to remember that – but what exactly *are* you?'

His laugh was short and mirthless. 'Damned if I know! I'm a father looking for his child. I'm a lover looking for his sweetheart.' He sighed. 'Sometimes I think I'm every man who ever lost someone he loved. Someone he believed he could never live without. Sometimes I think that's all I am: a personification of grief.'

'You've been more than that to me. Even when I was a child, you were so much more. You helped me come to terms with losing my mother. You helped me see past her suffering. And my own. You showed me the natural world and encouraged me to explore. You showed me the consolation to be found in a garden, a wood, a pond and all the plants and animals that lived there. You taught me about *life*, Hector. Not death.'

'Och, it was Janet did that!'

I fixed him with a look. 'And who taught Janet?' He didn't reply, but I noticed the muscles round his mouth relax a little, so I pressed on. 'Best of all, you taught me to have an open mind. Open to the natural world. And *other* worlds. You did all that for me, Hector. And for the generations before me.'

'Aye, maybe... But you'll be the last.'

'The last?'

'The last of the Munro line. You're my sister's grandchild. There's no one else left now.'

'Unless your child lived.'

'Aye. Unless it lived.'

'And if he or she *did*—'

'There's nothing more I can do but wait. And hope. As I've waited and hoped for almost a century.'

With that, he rolled away from me. I'm sure I only blinked - – I certainly wasn't nodding off – but when I opened my eyes again, he was sitting, dressed, on the edge of the bed, with his back to me. Unusually for Hector, his spine curved forward and his shoulders sagged. His head hung, as if he couldn't

174

summon the strength to raise it.

'I sense my time is drawing to an end, Ruth. And God knows,' he added wearily, 'I've had enough of waiting! I long to *sleep*. Not when I'm with you, nor when I was with Janet. Or Gracie. When there was companionship to enjoy, a sense of purpose, time didn't hang so heavy. It was something like being alive again. But when I'm alone, when I'm... not in the form of the man I once was, the tension and the damnable *boredom* are indescribable! It's like being in the trenches again, waiting for an assault to begin.'

I sat up and, resting my chin on Hector's shoulder, I saw he was clasping his hands tightly in his lap, as if he were trying to prevent them from shaking. His silence began to bother me. Sensing his suffering, I began to wonder what right I had to expect this extraordinary being to inhabit my world?

But he'd said time spent with me was bearable. More than bearable. He'd said – I hadn't dreamed it, surely? – that he loved me. But it wasn't a man's love, even if it felt something like a man's love. Even if my lover expressed it with something that looked and felt like a man's body. But it *was* love, of that I was certain. Just love of a different kind.

And what I felt for Hector? That too must be love. How did I know? Because if there was one thing worse than contemplating Hector's absence, it was knowing that I might be making him suffer. He had a mission and he longed to complete it. Then he just wanted to sleep. For ever. If I loved him – *really* loved him – then I would have to find the strength to let him go.

Was *that* what Hector had meant when he'd said I would know what to do?...

I slid my arms round his waist and laid my cheek between his shoulder blades. His tunic should have felt rough against my skin but it felt like the rest of him. Cool. Soft. Moist. I synchronised my breathing with his and wondered how long we had. Weeks? Perhaps only days?...

Unable to bear the silence any longer, I ventured a question. 'Hector, what was it like in the trenches? Can you bear to talk about it? I mean, I just can't imagine...'

His ribs swung out as he inhaled, then sank again, like a bellows. 'Life was very boring. And very dangerous. And the boredom made it more dangerous. The unutterable tedium caused many a lad to put his head above the parapet, just to get a glimpse of a different view. But Jerry would always be waiting. Waiting with a sniper's bullet to transport the curious to that "undiscovered country, from which no traveller returns".'

Hector fell silent again. Clinging to his back, I said, 'Tell me more. Please. If you can bear it. I want to know as much about you as possible.' I didn't say the words, but the thought hung in the air between us: *Before you leave me.* 'Tell me more about your life. About when you were a man. An officer looking after your men. I like to think of you doing that. I'm sure you'd have been very good at it. And very popular.'

'I take it,' said Hector, with a sidelong glance at me over his shoulder, 'that you don't wish to hear about foot inspection?'

'Was that one of your responsibilities?'

'Aye, when I was a junior officer.'

'What were you looking for?'

'Trench foot. Gangrene.'

'Oh...' The conversation languished again and I made another attempt to engage him. 'You said the waiting reminded you of being in the trenches.'

'Aye. Waiting for something to happen. Or waiting for it all to be over.' He laid a hand on mine. 'If you *really* want to know—'

'I do!'

'Then I'll tell you about stand-to...' He paused and the silence was so prolonged, I thought perhaps he'd changed his mind about speaking to me, but eventually, in a voice so weary, I hardly recognised it as Hector's, he said, 'Troops were required to stand-to on the fire-step. That was a ledge on the forward face of the trench. We stood for an hour at dawn and an hour at dusk, in case Jerry chose that time to attack. The grey light was thought to be the most favourable for mounting an attack. So that's how almost every day began and ended. With waiting. Waiting while our nerves frayed.

176

Waiting for a few nervous shots along the length of the trench – theirs or ours – as men got the wind up and fired at nothing. We stood-to until it was full light or full dark. Men sat on the fire-step, while sentries stood looking over the parapet. And on the other side of No Man's Land, Jerry was doing exactly the same. Waiting. Waiting for the war to end... Waiting for our lives to end.' Hector was silent, then his body heaved with a great sigh. The sound that issued from his throat was broken, a murmur only, like the last words of a dying man. 'I've had a bellyful of waiting.'

I tightened my arms around his waist, at a loss to know what to say. As I did so, his spine straightened and he lifted his head, suddenly alert.

'What is it, Hector?'

'Your waiting is over.'

'What do you mean?'

'You were waiting for something. It's here.'

'I'm not waiting for anything.'

'You were.' He twisted round to look at me. 'A message of some sort? It's come.' He lifted his chin and looked past me, as if watching something, something invisible. His eyes narrowed and a frown crumpled his smooth, pale brow, then he announced, 'He's out of danger.'

'Who is?'

He shrugged. 'I don't know. Someone you were concerned about?'

'Tom?'

Hector's eyes flashed momentarily and he looked back at me, his frown deeper still. 'Och, I cannot tell. It's not clear, it's only... a feeling. Something distant. *Very* distant.'

'Oh – that'll be Athelstan!'

'Athelstan?'

'My professor. I've been waiting to hear if he's coming to visit. His father's very ill, so Stan probably won't be able to come.'

'You weren't concerned about Tom?'

'I *am* concerned about Tom, as it happens, but he's not ill. Well, not in the way you mean. And I certainly wasn't waiting to hear from him.' Hector's expression told me he was still unconvinced. 'Tom's no more to me than – well, than a very old friend. He's a throwback to my childhood.'

'So,' said Hector pointedly, 'am *I*.'

'You're different.'

'Aye, I suppose you might say that,' he conceded. 'And this professor? What is he?'

'Stan? He's a new friend, I suppose. A musicologist. He wants to examine Janet's manuscripts. He's been pretty persistent. So I've got to find a way of explaining to him that my aunt wasn't a plagiarist, she was just following a ghost's instructions.'

'Och, what does it matter who wrote the damn music? All that matters is what the music *does*, the effect it has on folk. How it makes them *feel*.'

'Well, I have some idea how it made Stan feel. He wrote to me about *In Memoriam*. He said it was one of the finest and most underrated pieces in the twentieth century classical repertoire. He's a big fan of yours. Or would be, if he knew you.'

Hector wasn't listening. His eyes had swivelled toward the bedside table and he was gazing at the phone. My own eyes followed and then the phone started to ring. My naked skin broke out in goose bumps.

'You must answer,' he murmured.

'No, not now! It could be nothing. Someone selling something.'

'It isn't,' he replied, getting to his feet. He strode to the bedroom door, his kilt swinging and unhooked my dressing gown. He returned and held it open for me. As I got out of bed, my eyes never left his face, but Hector's wandered over my naked body with a look of such guilty longing, I covered myself quickly to spare him.

'If I answer the phone, you won't disappear while my back's turned, will you?' Still his eyes didn't meet mine. 'Promise me, Hector.'

'Answer the telephone, Ruth. It's important.'

'Not if it means you'll leave!'

He ignored me and stared at the fireplace. The blaze in the grate began to dwindle and then died, revealing the ugly metal bars of the old electric fire. When I looked back at Hector, I could see the other side of the room through him, as he began to fade.

'Hector, please don't go!'

'You haven't seen the last of me, Ruth. Not quite. Speak to your new friend. He has something to tell you.'

I lunged, clutching at the remnants of Hector's body, but there was nothing there, just currents of cold, moist air that eddied around me as the phone continued to ring.

Chapter Sixteen

The phone stopped ringing. Relieved, I belted my dressing gown and scanned the room for signs of Hector, but could see nothing, nor could I sense anything. As tears began to prick the back of my eyes, the phone rang again. With one last despairing look round the room, I picked it up.

A voice – I didn't recognise it as mine – said, 'Hello?'

'Ruth! At last! I was beginning to think maybe you'd already gone to London. It's Stan.'

I sank onto the bed and tried to gather my teeming thoughts. 'Oh, hello, Stan. I'm sorry, I was just talking to someone. On my mobile,' I added hastily. 'Work stuff. It was urgent.' (How many more superfluous lies was I going to tell before normal service was resumed?)

'That's OK. I didn't really want to disturb you, so I sent an email a while back, but then I decided I should speak with you right away as I haven't been in touch. It's about my father.'

'Not bad news, I hope?'

'No, on the contrary! He's made a good recovery and there are no immediate concerns for his health – though the winter's always a trying time for the elderly. But Dad's a fighter! He's rallied and settled well into the nursing home.'

'Oh, good! You must be so relieved.'

'Indeed I am. I was ringing to ask – it's a liberty, I know – but I wondered if it would be possible for me to visit *now*?'

'Now?'

'Well, as soon as possible. Now Dad's out of danger, I think I have a window. I couldn't stay long. I want to be back in Toronto for Christmas, to spend it with him. So I wondered if it would be convenient for me to bring my visit forward? But please don't let me impose on you. This is really short notice and I know you had other plans.'

'No, that's OK. There was nothing that couldn't be

postponed,' I answered vaguely. 'But I thought term didn't end until December 7th?'

'It doesn't, but I've requested leave to do research in the UK and it's been granted. I only had one more lecture to give this term and I'll make that up early next year. The department has been very accommodating.'

'So you're free now? You can come over straight away?'

'In a matter of days. If it suited you.'

I was thinking fast. Sane Mind and Insane Mind were slugging it out again and, as usual, Insane Mind was winning.

'So you're saying, if you don't come now, you won't be able to come later.'

'That's right. But if I *do* come, it will only be a short visit.'

'Oh, that's not a problem. I was looking forward to your visit.'

Was I?... Yes, I *was*. And then I remembered why Stan mustn't come.

I took a deep breath and heard Insane Mind say, 'But there's something I think you ought to know, Stan. In case it affects your decision to travel. I'll be straight with you, but what I'm about to say is said in confidence. You see, I haven't come to terms yet with – well, with the full implications.'

'Is this about Janet?' Stan sounded wary.

'Yes, it is... Stan, she didn't write *In Memoriam*.'

'She *didn't*?'

'No.'

'Then who did?'

It was now or never... 'The ghost. When he was alive, I mean.' There was a long silence, as if the line had gone dead. 'Stan? Are you still there?'

'Yes, I'm here. I'm stunned, but I'm still here. Are you *sure*, Ruth? I mean, how do you know?'

I recalled Aunt Janet lecturing me as a child, pointing out that one of the advantages of telling the truth is that you don't have to remember the lies you told. I took Janet's advice.

'I know because the ghost told me.'

'Well, I'll be damned!'

'It wasn't exactly plagiarism,' I insisted. 'Well, not plagiarism at all, technically. Janet had Hector's permission.'

'So, let me get this straight... Hector – that's the ghost, right?'

'Stan, you're not laughing at me, are you?'

'Not at *all*! How could I laugh at something so serious? And so exciting? Tell me, how did you establish that Janet had the ghost's permission?'

'Hector told me that too. He explained everything. It was all part of a quest. To find someone. His lost love,' I added lamely.

There was another silence while I waited, heart sinking, for a change in Stan's voice, for him to hang up or say something that indicated we'd moved out of his credibility comfort zone.

'Well... I don't know how the hell I'm going to incorporate all this into an academic study,' he said slowly. 'But I guess I'll cross that bridge later. Maybe we'll make a movie instead,' he added brightly. 'If you could contrive to fall in love with this ghost, it would be more commercial.'

I swallowed and said faintly, 'Now you *are* laughing at me.'

'Not at all! But I admit, excitement is getting the better of me. You know, unless you expressly forbid it, I'll be on the next plane out of Toronto that's headed in the general direction of Scotland.'

To my surprise, I found I was absurdly pleased. 'Oh... I thought you'd be upset! Or that you wouldn't believe me.'

'Why wouldn't I believe you? And why would you lie? If you were lying, would you have concocted *quite* such an outrageous story? No, either you're completely insane or you're telling the truth. And I'll know which, just as soon as I meet you. Now I *am* laughing at you, Ruth. At *us*.'

If he'd been present, I think I might have thrown my arms round Stan and given him a hug, so relieved was I to share the burden of Hector's existence. 'I know it does sound quite mad. Believe me, there have been moments when I've doubted my sanity! It's been awful at times. Yet also... very wonderful. But all this is going to ruin your study, isn't it?'

'Probably,' Stan replied, sounding unruffled. 'I don't really know. I'll keep an open mind. But what the hell? If Janet didn't compose *In Memoriam*, I'd certainly like to meet the man who did.'

'He's dead, Stan. Long dead. He's a ghost.'

'Oh, I won't hold that against him. In fact I sincerely hope to shake him by the hand and pay my respects. Do you think he'll appear to me?'

'I don't know. He says the only people who can see him are those who want to—'

'Oh, I want to!'

'And those who *need* to.'

'Why would anyone need to see a ghost?'

'It's complicated. I'll explain when you get here.'

'So I can come then?'

'Of course! On the understanding that I still haven't decided what to do about Janet's archive. I mean, you can go through it all, but I don't know what I want to do about it yet. Whether I should go public about *In Memoriam*. I don't see how I can without Janet's reputation being damaged. She passed off the work of a dead man as her own. No one – apart from you – is going to believe the dead man instructed her to do so. They'll assume she was delusional. Or that *I'm* delusional. Maybe they'll think it's hereditary insanity... Perhaps it *is*.'

'Don't worry about all that now. Let's just take a look at Janet's archive and see what we've got. We can worry about falsifying the evidence later.'

'Stan, I wouldn't *dream* of asking you to—'

'It's OK, I was joking! Though I happen to know a few authors with a reputation for academic rigour founded on more dubious studies than mine is likely to be.'

'I feel dreadful. As if I've sabotaged your work. Your career even. I know this book must be very important to you.'

'It is, but what's more important to me is to understand Janet's creative process. Hector's too, I suppose. Remember, Ruth, I'm a composer primarily. My academic work subsidises that. If my book about Janet creates a stir in musical circles, well, that could be bad for me as an academic, but good for me as a composer. A reputation for eccentricity hasn't done Schumann or Satie any harm. But it doesn't really matter to me who wrote *In Memoriam*. It's the music that's important.'

'Oh...' I couldn't help expressing surprise at the echo of Hector's words.

'Did I say something wrong?'

'No, not at all. You just said something I heard someone else say. Quite recently.'

Stan paused for a moment, then said, 'Hector?'

'Yes. He said all that really mattered was what music does. The effect it has on people.'

'Sounds like we're all in agreement then! So I can come over?'

'Yes, please do. But beware – the weather's awful here. I'd offer to come and meet you at Glasgow airport, but I couldn't actually guarantee I'd get there. The snow's thick and there's no thaw forecast.'

'That's OK, I'll hire a car at the airport and drive up.'

'Conditions will be pretty bad.'

'Ruth,' Stan said gently, 'I'm Canadian. We never go anywhere in winter without snowshoes. Igloo-building is in our DNA. I'll be *fine*.'

'Well, you'll need Satnav when you get to Skye. *Tigh-na-Linne* isn't easy to find and landmarks have disappeared since the snow fell.'

'It must all look very beautiful'

'It does, but in a dangerous sort of way. It doesn't do to underestimate Highland weather.'

'Don't worry, I won't. Look, I'll email you details of my flight, so you know when to expect me.'

'The drive from Glasgow takes five or six hours on a good day, but it will take you longer now.'

'Duly noted. OK, I have a lot to organise and I'm sure you do too, so I'll spare you any more of my schoolboy enthusiasm. Thank you so much for allowing me to come – and at such short notice.'

'You're very welcome. I'm so pleased you still want to pursue your study of Janet. I thought you might want to abandon it, once you knew. About Hector, I mean.'

'No, Hector is one of the main attractions. And this memorial window. You say it's a good likeness?'

'Oh, yes. Very.'

'Well, if I don't get to meet the spook himself, the window will be my consolation.'

As it will have to be mine, I reflected, once Hector ceases to appear to me. He'd already hinted at his imminent departure and I knew I must prepare for the worst. But when I could no longer touch Hector, no longer even see him, I would still have the window. If I could bear to look at it. Was that why Janet had placed the wardrobe in front of the window? When Hector no longer visited, did Janet miss him badly? Was the window too painful a reminder of the friendship they'd known?...

Stan was talking but I wasn't listening. I tuned back in, just in time to hear him say goodbye, then he hung up.

I put the phone down. Sitting perched on the edge of the bed, I thought of all the things I needed to do before Stan arrived. Unpack my suitcase for a start. As the mental list grew longer, I found myself curling up on the bed. The room was chilly now without Hector's phantom fire, so I pulled the quilt over me and lay still, staring up at the window. As the afternoon light faded, more snow began to fall. The large flakes were of the slow, relentless variety, the kind that settle and form thick drifts. Watching them as they sank past the window, I faced facts.

Hector would leave me. He would perhaps never leave *Tigh-na-Linne*, but he would leave *me*. I understood why and knew it was for the best. For both of us. But that didn't make the loss any easier to bear. I'd hoped the prospect of Stan's visit might drag me back into the real world, but pleased as I was he'd decided to come – and that I'd decided to let him – it did little to assuage my loneliness and the gnawing despair I felt when I contemplated a future without Hector, my lover and friend.

When finally it was dark, I switched on the bedside lamp and sat up. Throwing back the quilt, I got off the bed, went into the hall and dragged my suitcase back into the room. I unpacked the contents, putting Hector's precious journal back in my bedside drawer and his photograph on the table, facing the bed. These and the old family albums would soon be all I

185

had of him, apart from my memories. I stared at the photograph for a few moments, then decided I couldn't cope. It joined the journal in the drawer, which I slammed shut. I lay down on the bed again, turned out the light and then slept.

I dreamed of Hector – not the Hector I knew, but the warrior angel in the window. But in my dream Hector wasn't made of glass. He was made of ice and as I clung to him, he melted, until eventually my wet and frozen arms held nothing.

Chapter Seventeen

There was a lot to do, for which I was thankful. I now had an excuse to clean the house from top to bottom, which I did in a frenzy of resentment – not resentment of Stan, but Hector. When I tried to work out why I was so angry with Hector, I came to the conclusion it was not so much because he was about to terminate our relationship, as that he was *dead*. As I scrubbed and polished, it struck me Hector must also be pretty angry about being dead and he'd been angry for a lot longer than I had. Disgusted with myself for being so self-centred, I cleaned the oven as an act of penance.

I braved the snow to do a big shop at the Co-op. I cooked and filled the freezer with hearty casseroles and pies. I even bought a haggis since it looked as if Stan might be here in time for St Andrew's Day.

I wanted to give him something as a Christmas gift, even though he wouldn't actually be here for Christmas Day. I thought I could let him have one of Janet's bottles of Talisker as a souvenir of Skye, but I also wanted to give him something that had belonged to Janet, so I spent some time in the study, going through her things, trying to find something suitable.

I settled on her gold fountain pen. I'd wavered when I recalled that the sight of Janet's pen and pen top lying casually on her desk had been the first indication of Hector's presence, but that seemed reason enough to give the pen away to a good home. I would never use a fountain pen, but it would be difficult to think of anything more personal that I could give to a man who'd never met Janet, but in a way, *knew* her. The pen would make an excellent gift. I found a box to put it in and wrapped it in some left-over Christmas paper that Janet had put away last year.

Given the weather, there was little Tom could do to earn his wages, but I did give him the back-breaking task of clearing the drive – something I'd put off doing because it would remind me of witnessing David's sudden death at the beginning of the year. He also chopped me a mountain of firewood and cleared the snow off the greenhouse roof. When I explained that Stan would be visiting, Tom suggested digging up a sapling fir to serve as a Christmas tree as it was too early to buy one. He put the small tree in an old metal bucket which I disguised with one of Janet's grotesquely festive tablecloths.

It took me a while to find her Christmas decorations. When I finally opened the box of treasured glass ornaments that had been carefully preserved for generations, it was all I could do to suppress a tear. The sight of them nestling in their cardboard compartments brought back happy memories of Christmases past, memories now tinged with sadness, because Janet would never share my Christmas again.

Tom had put the tree in the sitting room in front of the French windows and despite my sombre mood, I made a good job of decorating it. I used tinsel, angels, robins, fairy lights, the works. When I switched on and regarded the illuminated tree, framed in the window against a background of thick snow, my spirits lifted and I was glad I'd made the effort. Something told me Stan would appreciate all the joyous kitsch. After all, he'd expected to lose his father and now it looked as if he'd get to spend another Christmas with him. That was worth celebrating. So was the fact that I would soon have a convivial house-guest who'd distract me from brooding about Hector's departure.

Well, that was the theory.

On the day Stan was due to arrive, I put clean, aired sheets on his bed, gave the room a final dust and chose a selection of reading matter (mostly Scottish) for his bedside table. I found a volume of the collected ghost stories of M R James and placed that on top of the pile. Stan would appreciate the joke.

Looking round the slightly shabby guest room, it struck me there was nothing living in the room. No houseplants. No flowers. Flowers from the garden were no longer an option and it didn't seem worth driving up to Broadford in search of any, so I decided to cut some evergreens to stand in a jug. Perhaps I might even make a welcoming wreath for the front door, as Janet had done every year. Even though she wouldn't be present in person this Christmas, there was no reason why, if I maintained some of her traditions, Janet shouldn't join us in spirit.

I checked my watch and decided I probably still had an hour before Stan arrived. Plenty of time to have a walk round the garden in search of holly, ivy and laurel, though I doubted the birds would have left many berries. It was already proving a hard winter and it was still only the end of November.

I wrapped up warm, pulled on my wellingtons, dropped a pair of secateurs into my coat pocket and ventured out into the snow.

It was like walking into a freezer, but bracing. After the initial shock to my sluggish system, it felt good to be outdoors, breathing the fragrant, icy air, surrounded by the stark beauty of snow and ice – so much more spectacular close-up than viewed through grubby panes of glass.

I kept to the paths as much as possible, but still my wellingtons sank deep and the snow went over my feet. As I cut sprigs of holly, some with a few ice-frosted berries, I saw a movement out of the corner of my eye. I spun round in time to see a startled robin fly away. I smothered my disappointment with a resolution to put out scraps for the birds. Almost all the berries were gone and there was nothing for them to eat.

But there I was wrong. As I rounded a corner I came upon the old covered bird table that stood outside the French windows. The roof and floor had been swept clear of snow and scraps of food had been set out. It looked like the remains of someone's breakfast – pieces of toast and bacon. Tom had been taking care of the birds.

I stood and stared at the table, feeling vaguely guilty – about the hungry birds and about Tom – when the robin which had evidently been following me, landed on the table, snatched a piece of bacon rind and flew off.

I remembered Hector helping me to string half a coconut from this very bird table, over thirty years ago... I must have been ten or eleven. Hector would have been thirty-five. Hector would always be thirty-five. I would age and he would not. And when I died? What then? Was there an afterlife where I'd catch up with Hector, my parents, Janet and David? Would my father be any more affectionate in death than he'd been in life? And just how would I explain Hector to David?...

It was all nonsense, of course. I had no religious or spiritual beliefs to console me. As a teenager, I'd rejected my father's nominal Anglican faith in favour of Janet's brisk atheism. (She used to quote John Buchan with glee: "An atheist is a man who has no invisible means of support.") Then I'd trained as a scientist. I'd built enough compost heaps in my time to know that matter decomposed and returned to the earth, from which new life grew. Death was the end. That was what I'd always believed. Until Hector had reminded me of his existence...

I hadn't seen him for days and suspected he'd departed this world without leaving a forwarding address. But it was unlike him to shirk responsibility. I'd been expecting a formal farewell, or at least some indication that this would be our final meeting, but perhaps that was expecting too much of a ghost. I should have learned by now. Hector was a law unto himself and was unlikely to be bound by mortal conventions of politeness.

I was standing, staring aimlessly at the bird table, waiting for the robin to return, when I felt an odd, but familiar sensation that centred on the back of my neck. I was being watched.

I spun round and, shocked to find Hector so close, I dropped my bunch of holly. I bent to retrieve it and found myself crouched at his feet. Hector's boots had made no impression on the snow. There was only one line of footprints – mine – and nothing to indicate where he'd come from.

The holly gathered up once more, I rose to my feet. Despite the freezing cold, Hector was dressed as usual, in his khaki army tunic and kilt, his red head bare. Whatever sensations ghosts were able to feel, cold didn't appear to be one of them.

We stood facing each other and I waited for him to speak. He looked down at the ground for a moment, then lifted his head and said, 'There's no easy way to say this, Ruth.'

'Say what you have to say, Hector. Let's get it over with.'

'I've come to say goodbye.'

'I know. And you've chosen to do it outdoors so there's no possibility of us ending up in bed again. Very wise.'

He gave me a long look, then said, 'D'you think that's not what I want too? But each time we make love, it just makes it harder for you to come to terms with my leaving. With my being a ghost, not a man. So I thought it best we say our farewells outdoors. Where we first met. In the garden that has meant so much to us both.'

I bit my lip in an attempt to prevent myself from asking, but it was no good. I said it anyway. 'Hector, will I ever see—'

'I don't know, Ruth. I suspect not. We were brought together for a purpose and that purpose has been served.'

'Has it?'

'Aye.'

'How do you know?'

'I don't know how I know. But I know.'

'Well, I'm damned if I know what the point of it all was.' I hadn't meant to sound quite so bitter. I was losing control of my voice as well as my emotions.

'You are reconciled,' Hector said gently.

'What do you mean, reconciled?'

'To your loss. David. Your father. Janet. Your grief is less now. You feel less lonely. Less... abandoned. And you're reconciled with Tom. You've forgiven him. Even though he doesn't deserve it,' Hector muttered.

'I think Tom might be a good friend. Eventually.'

'And I think you know now that *Tigh-na-Linne* is your real home. That you're meant to be here.'

'I can't afford to keep it on, Hector.'

'You'll find a way. What's for you will not go by you.'

'Oh, don't go all cryptic and Highland on me! What would

191

be the *point* of staying here?'

'This is the Munro family home. You're a Munro. You're Janet's niece. She wanted *Tigh-na-Linne* to be your home. Your future. And so do I.'

'The house should have gone to your child.'

'Who must be dead by now. But in any case, the house was bequeathed to Gracie, as my parents' only surviving child. Grace was your grandmother, so the house is rightfully yours. Use it. Make something of it. Make something of its story, of the people who lived here. And loved here,' Hector added. '*Tigh-na-Linne* has known a deal of love. And it will know more.'

'Did Janet love Tom's mother?'

Hector nodded. 'Aye, she did. And that love was reciprocated, but... impossible. Impossible to acknowledge publicly.'

'Poor Janet.'

'Aye. Poor Janet.'

'Hector, I can't do this.'

'What do you mean?'

'I mean, I can't do *this*. Say goodbye. Stand around making small talk about a future in which I have little interest. I can't watch yet another loved one *leave* me. I won't hold another dead person in my arms and then try to say goodbye!'

He nodded slowly. 'I understand... Och, I'll just go. But you'll care again, Ruth. And you'll be cared for. Believe it.'

'I don't.'

'You *will*.'

'You make it sound like an order.'

'It is.' His lips curved in a slight smile and I cracked.

'Go, Hector! Now, please. I don't want your last sight of me to be red-nosed and weeping. I want you to remember me at my best. Remember what you're *missing*.'

'There's not the slightest chance I'll ever forget you, Ruth. I've known and loved you since you were eight.'

As the echo of my own words returned to me, I tossed the holly onto the ground. I pulled off my gloves and dropped them too. I took hold of Hector's cold face – the face of a dead man – and I stared into his icy blue eyes for the last time. He bent his head and I felt the touch of his chilled lips. Closing my eyes, I tried to throw my arms round his neck, but there was nothing there. When I opened my eyes again, I saw that he was walking away from me, his red hair bright against the snow, his booted feet leaving no footprints. His stride was unhurried and his kilt swung in time with his paces. I wondered why he'd decided to walk away rather than simply de-materialise. Perhaps allowing me to watch him go was his final gift to me.

Hector had always walked away. Or I had. When I was a child, there had been none of the supernatural comings and goings I'd witnessed as an adult. He hadn't wanted to alarm a little girl, I suppose. He'd presented himself tactfully as my faithful, if enigmatic friend, a surrogate uncle. So he appeared to come and go like an ordinary man, the man he once was, the man he no doubt longed to be. And now he was walking away from me like a man, not a ghost – not just because he thought that was how I'd want to remember him, but because that was how he wished to be remembered.

I stood and watched for as long as I could bear, then I gave up and followed. Unable to skim the surface of the snow like Hector, I plodded through it, sinking in over my ankles. I trudged through a garden I no longer recognised as my childhood playground. Its geography had vanished. The features that remained distinguishable – trees and tall shrubs – seemed to have doubled in bulk where snow had accumulated on their branches, disguising their familiar, much-loved forms. This arctic landscape was alien. It had become a nowhere place, a No Man's Land and I ploughed on, following Hector, a dead man, as he strode across it.

He was heading downhill through the garden, toward the sea. I wondered whether, when he eventually met it, he'd just keep walking. Unable to close the gap between us, I broke into an ungainly run. The going suddenly got easier as I hit firmer ground and my boots got a better purchase. I called out to Hector, desperate to get him to turn round and look at me for what might be the last time.

He ignored my cries and walked on steadily. Behind me, I heard the sound of a car pulling up at the house, then a door opening and closing, but I didn't look back. Anxious he might suddenly vanish, I didn't take my eyes off Hector for a second. I kept walking until I was stopped dead in my tracks by a sound like a gunshot. Hector wheeled round. He saw where I was, then yelled at the top of his voice, but I couldn't understand what he was saying. He started to run toward me, shouting and waving his arms. It sounded like "Lie down!" As he came closer, I could hear him quite clearly, bellowing, "Ruth, for God's sake! Spread yourself *flat*!"

I had no idea what he meant. Lie down in the snow? Had he taken leave of his senses? As Hector approached, almost flying across the snow, I ran forward, laughing, crying with joy that he'd decided to come back to me. Then there were more sounds like shots, louder now. I looked round the garden, startled and disoriented. Too late, I recognised where I was.

Then the ground gave way.

I'd walked on to the frozen pond. The ice had borne my weight for a while, then, in the centre where the ice was thinner, it had cracked, then shattered.

I fell through the ice into the freezing black water below. The cold was so intense, the shock such a physical pain, that I screamed in agony as much as terror. My cries were quickly stifled as my mouth and throat filled with pond water and fragments of ice. Choking, I tried to kick my legs to stay afloat, but my wellingtons had already filled with water and I couldn't move my feet. I thrashed around with my arms, grabbing at the ice, but it just broke off in my hands. There was nothing for me to hold on to and no way I could pull myself out. If I didn't drown, I would be dead of hypothermia in ten minutes, maybe less.

In between choking coughs, I screamed Hector's name. Scraping hair and pondweed out of my eyes, I saw him standing, motionless and white-faced at the edge of the pond, his skin the same colour as the snow. But he wasn't looking at me. He was looking past me, across the pond, as if someone were standing there. He suddenly raised his hands and held them up, palms flat. 'Go back!' he barked. 'You can do nothing! Leave this to me.'

I had no idea who he was talking to and realised I didn't care. What did it matter? What did *anything* matter any more? My limbs had stopped feeling heavy. I couldn't feel them at all now. I couldn't feel anything. Just an overwhelming desire to sleep, to cease this pointless struggle. As the foul, black water covered my face and the stench of mud filled my nostrils, I thought perhaps it was all for the best. This way, at least I would be with Hector. For ever.

When I opened my eyes again, it was much darker. But I didn't feel cold any more and the pain in my chest had stopped. Hector wasn't yelling now and neither was I. I couldn't see him. I couldn't see anything much, but there was light above me – not bright, but I could see it was lighter on the other side of the impenetrable barrier above my head, like a ceiling. A glass ceiling. Only this one wouldn't break.

I'd stopped pushing at it and punching it with my fists. It was too much effort. I was content just to drift down, away from the light. Maybe when it was completely dark I'd finally be able to sleep. Perhaps I'd dream of Hector...

I *was* dreaming of Hector. He was there, right beside me, his eyes wide. Wide with horror. I tried to smile, to reassure him I was OK, but something came between us, obscuring my view. Fronds of something dark. Silky. Tangled. I thought it was my hair, then I recognised it as vegetation, curling round my limbs. I waved my arms to free myself from the weed and saw Hector again. His pale skin was luminous in the gloom and he appeared to be naked. I tried to lift my arms to embrace him, but they were too heavy.

Hector's arms went round my waist and he started to drag me upwards, toward the light. But something was pulling at my feet. I felt one of my wellingtons slide off, freeing one leg. Hector let go of me, then disappeared. I felt something pull hard at my other boot, then I lurched and floated upwards, until my head hit something hard. The light... But the light was solid and I couldn't pass through it.

I didn't care. I could feel Hector's arms around me once more and when I turned my head I found his face close to mine. I gazed into his eyes, looking for the love that was usually there, but instead I saw something strange. At first I thought it was pain. Then I realised it was *indecision*. Hector looked as if he was on the rack.

And then I understood.

I know I didn't speak the words. I couldn't. I only thought them. But thought was enough.

Let me go, Hector. It doesn't matter.

This is not what was meant to happen!

I don't care. It's what I want. And it's what you want.

No!

It's the only way! How else can we be together?

We aren't meant to be together. Fight, Ruth! Fight, God damn you! Don't give in! You're meant to live. And I'm meant to leave. It's finished. I've seen your future – and it isn't this!

Hector took my face in his hands and fastened his mouth on mine. His lips were warm, warm in a way that his body had never been. I lifted my hands and laid them on his bare arms. They felt warm too and hard, not like Hector's at all, but like a man's. I could feel firm muscle, bone beneath the muscle, rigid strength where once there had just been flowing energy. I wrapped my arms round Hector's naked body and clung to him, rejoicing in his warm solidity.

But I knew what this transformation meant.

I wasn't afraid. This was the end and I was about to join him. I knew all this, but I felt no fear. The fear was all Hector's.

I raised my head from his shoulder and looked into his tortured eyes. I tried to smile, but couldn't find the strength. He gripped my arms and opened his mouth wide in a long, silent scream. Then I saw something move swiftly across his face, like a shaft of light. Indecision was replaced by a fearful resolve. Grim-faced, Hector folded me in his arms and crushed me to his living, breathing body.

Goodbye, Ruth. Live! Be happy.

I felt his muscles tense as he crouched, as if ready to spring. Then there was a rushing sound in my ears and we seemed to move very fast through the darkness. There was a sudden, bone-shattering impact, then an almighty crashing sound. Shards of something hard and sharp scraped my head, tearing my skin.

The last thing I remember is being enveloped by warm air, bathed in a light so dazzling, my eyes hurt. I tried to breathe, but my mouth and nostrils were full of stinking mud. Blood trickled down my forehead, into my eyes, all but obliterating my view. When I finally looked up, I saw a pale and terrified face hanging over me. Snowflakes fell slowly out of a bruised grey sky, spiralled and settled like confetti on curling red hair.

'Hector?', I croaked.

Then the daylight went out.

I surfaced into light again. And noise.

Traffic?...

A wailing siren...

I was numb. And horizontal. I tried to move, but nothing happened, so I concluded I was dead. I thought about this for a while and decided I didn't really mind. Living had become a chore and I didn't seem to have much of a future. It might be nice just to sleep for a very long time. For ever, in fact. And surely, if I was dead, I could now spend eternity with Hector, which I vaguely remembered was the thing I'd wanted most before the ground gave way and everything had gone black.

I tried to focus on the light, but it was a world away, on the other side of my eyelids. I could sense it though. Movement too. So perhaps I wasn't dead? I could feel vibrations coming up through the floor, or whatever it was I was lying on. (Where *was* I?) I tried to raise my eyelids, but they were too heavy. How could eyelids possibly be this heavy? They must be frozen over. Sealed shut. With ice.

I gave up on my eyelids and was lying there, doing a

creditable imitation of a corpse, when I heard voices coming from a long way off. Male. One man sounded a bit like Hector. But that wasn't possible. Hector didn't *chat*. And he didn't really sound like Hector. For a start he wasn't Scots. But the other man was.

I realised they were talking about me. I thought about my eyelids again and the logistics of opening them, but it all seemed too much effort. I couldn't actually remember how you did it.

After pondering the problem for some time – it felt like hours – I managed to peel one eyelid back far enough to view my surroundings through a slit, like a letterbox. Things were blurry and the light hurt. It seemed I was in hospital. A *mobile* hospital. Equipment rattled and occasionally swayed about. It was weird. What was weirder was, I appeared to be wrapped in tin foil, like a roasting turkey.

Hector was talking to the other man. I knew it was Hector straight away, because of his hair – so bright, it dazzled. The other man was pointing at me, which struck me as very rude. Hector turned round and both men leaned forward to peer at me. Just before my leaden eyelid collapsed, my brain took a snapshot of the two men. One of them I'd never seen before. The other was Hector.

Except that he *wasn't*.

Straining, I wrenched one eyelid open again and then the other. Hector wasn't in uniform. His legs were near my face and they appeared to be clad in denim. I swivelled my eyeballs upward. He was wearing a green polo neck and a fleece jacket. The jacket was filthy and smelled of mud. But not Hector's mud.

My eyes travelled laboriously upward, toward Hector's face. That was wrong too. His chin was shadowed with auburn stubble. (Hector hadn't needed to shave since 1915.) His hair was different too. It was still the same astonishing colour, but it had grown. It now curled over his ears and flopped over his forehead, so he looked very like the angel in the memorial window. Apart from the stubble, that is. His expression was the same as the angel's, too. Worried. As if something awful was about to happen. Or *had* happened.

I tried to say Hector's name, but my tongue lay inert in my mouth, like a dead thing. He must have realised I was trying to speak, because he leaned forward again and spoke close to my ear – softly, but it was still too loud.

'You're going to be OK, Ruth. These guys are taking us to Inverness – at about 100 mph, just like in the movies! Don't try to talk now. And don't be scared. Everything's going to be just fine.'

But everything *wasn't* fine. Something was wrong. Very wrong.

This wasn't Hector.

The vehicle swerved suddenly and Hector's face swung out of my eye line, then back again. The other man said something I didn't catch. Hector nodded, then looked back at me, smiling, but it was the kind of smile that didn't reach the eyes. I suddenly felt frightened and wanted to go home, to *Tigh-na-Linne*. I just wanted to sleep.

Hector appeared to read my mind. (So maybe it *was* Hector?...) 'You're in good hands, Ruth. Dougie here has everything under control – isn't that right, Dougie?'

'Oh, aye,' came the laconic reply from a long way off. That was followed by a whimpering noise that sounded like an attention-seeking puppy. I realised it was me.

Hector leaned forward again, his voice sounding urgent now. 'Hang on, Ruth! I've come a long way to be with you. Don't go giving up on me now!'

My eyelids abandoned the struggle and crashed. As everything gradually faded to black, my brain processed an avalanche of new information.

The smiling man looked like Hector, even sounded something like Hector. But he didn't *talk* like Hector.

Yet he talked like someone I knew. Someone I knew, but... not someone I'd *met*.

I knew that voice. And I knew that face.

But they didn't go together.

As darkness engulfed me and I began to drown again, I realised the man at my side, holding my hand, reassuring me in a warm Canadian baritone was – dear God in Heaven, *would wonders never cease?* – Dr Athelstan Blake.

Chapter Eighteen

When I woke, there was an angel at my bedside. The glass guardian was sitting perched on a chair beside my bed, in a room that wasn't my bedroom. I assumed I must be dead and was surprised to find the Afterlife lit by fluorescent tubes. Clearly, this couldn't be Heaven. Perhaps I was in the other place.

I closed my eyes. When I opened them again, the angel was still there. He was dressed in white. At least, what I could see of him was white, but as my eyes began to focus, I saw no folds of classical drapery, just a simple white Henley T-shirt, unbuttoned at the neck, with the sleeves pushed up to the elbows, revealing a chunky watch.

I tried, but could think of no possible reason why an angel might require a watch. I began to re-assess.

'Hector?...'

The angel leaned forward, put his glorious auburn head on one side, and looked down at me. 'Hector's not here, Ruth. At least–' He looked over his shoulder, glancing round the room. 'I don't *think* he is.'

And then I began to remember...

I'd almost drowned. Hector had nearly let me, then evidently changed his mind, since the next thing I could recall was opening my eyes and seeing the sky partially occluded by his familiar, beloved face. But it hadn't been Hector. It had been *Stan*. Stan, who appeared to be a Hector clone.

Studying the man at my bedside, I could see now that there were some subtle differences. Stan's eyes weren't as uncannily pale as Hector's and they weren't as sad. His brows weren't as thick and his nose wasn't quite as straight, but the mouth was identical. So was the hair colour. I doubted their own mothers could have told them apart.

But who *was* Stan's mother? Or for that matter, his father?

My voice, when I finally managed to construct a sentence, sounded alarmingly frail. 'You aren't Hector in *disguise*, are you?'

'Indeed, I'm not.' The erstwhile-angel smiled and extended his hand toward me. 'Athelstan Blake. I'm delighted to meet you at last. Albeit under such sorry circumstances.'

'You're... *Stan?*'

'Yes.' His smile faded. 'If that's OK?'

'Oh, yes. Perfectly OK. Just... *confusing*, that's all. You see – well, you're not going to believe this, but I assure you it's true – you're the absolute living image of...' I swallowed and then said, '*Hector.*' Stan didn't look surprised, so I assumed he hadn't understood. 'Hector is the ghost,' I explained. '*My* ghost. And you look exactly like him.'

'I know.'

'You *know*? How can you know?'

A fleeting look of apprehension passed across Stan's face, then he seemed to square his shoulders (which I noticed were broader than Hector's) and said, 'Because I saw him.'

I reeled mentally, as if he'd dealt me a blow. '*Who?*'

'Hector. I guess.'

'You *saw* him?'

'Well, I saw *something*. I thought maybe it was just some kind of... snow mirage or something. Some kind of reflection. Because – well, because—'

'Because it was like looking at yourself?'

'Well, yes. Apart from the kilt.'

'Did Hector speak to you?'

'Why, yes, he did!'

'What did he say?'

'He didn't *speak* exactly...'

'But you heard what he said. Inside your head.'

'That's right!' The fearful look passed across Stan's face again and I watched as his Adam's apple moved up and down convulsively. Then, his voice scarcely more than a whisper, he said, 'You get that too?'

'Sometimes. In a crisis. I think perhaps it takes more energy for him to speak. And he doesn't actually need to. He just does it so he seems... more like us. I mean, like a mortal.

What did he say?'

'He told me not to go in after you.'

'Good grief, Stan! Were you going to? You could have died!'

'So could you. I thought maybe if I lay down on the ice and spread my weight evenly, I could reach you and if you were anywhere near the hole in the ice, I might be able to grab hold of you.'

'But you'd never have been able to haul me out! The ice would have broken up.'

'Well, I couldn't just stand and watch you drown, could I?'

'Some people would!'

I thought of Tommy and the accident long ago, then felt a pressing need to cry my eyes out. Stan appeared to read my mind and in a pre-emptive strike, handed me a box of tissues from the bedside table.

'Hey, don't go getting upset. You're OK. Everything's going to be fine now. You just need to rest. You've had a hell of an ordeal.'

I plucked a tissue from the box. 'So have you – coming face to face with a ghost. When Hector reappeared at *Tigh-na-Linne*, I thought I must be going mad.'

'Well, you know, that thought *did* cross my mind.'

Stan smiled. I blew my nose and felt a little better. I lay back on my pillows and tried to order my teeming thoughts.

'You said Hector told you not to go in after me?'

'That's right. He said – don't ask me how – "Leave this to me." Then he just... disappeared! Well, then I started to crawl on to the ice, because I assumed I'd just been hallucinating, that I was in shock, or something. And then...' Stan's pale skin seemed to turn even paler, as if he'd suddenly recalled some horrific detail. He passed a hand over his face and moistened his lips. 'Ruth, I don't mind telling you, it scared the bejesus out of me. Feeling the ice vibrate. Sensing you trapped underneath! I thought I could hear you *knocking*. Or maybe that was Hector?'

I surveyed the backs of my hands, bruised and blood-crusted where I'd punched frantically at the ice. 'No. It was me... How did I get out? I don't remember much. Just Hector holding me.'

Holding me and saying goodbye... I reached for another tissue as Stan resumed his account.

'Well, I hadn't got very far across the pond, when there was an almighty explosion of ice. It just erupted! And then you suddenly appeared. It was terrifying. The most terrifying thing I've ever seen. You were *black*, Ruth. Black with mud and trailing weed. And Hector was carrying you in his arms. But he *wasn't* black. He wasn't kilted either, not any more. He was naked. And kind of... *transparent*. I couldn't really see where Hector ended and the snow began. But I could see his face and I'll never forget it! I was convinced you must be dead. If you could have seen his expression, Ruth... Broken-hearted doesn't begin to describe it.'

I thought perhaps I *had* seen that expression. As I struggled to control my emotions, I murmured, 'What did he do?'

'Well, I'd crawled back on to *terra firma* by then, so I rang for an ambulance. Hector handed you over and I took off my jacket and wrapped you in it. You weren't breathing, but Hector told me you weren't dead. Well, he didn't tell me, I *heard* him. In any case, I knew you had a chance because people have been revived twenty minutes after a near-drowning incident.'

'Really?'

'Oh, sure. Low temperatures slow down body functions. It can take you sixty minutes to drown in freezing water. So I started on CPR.'

'Lucky for me you knew what to do.'

Stan smiled and seemed to relax a little. 'Oh, I've picked up some basic First Aid over the years. I go canoeing and white-water rafting when I get the chance. It blows away a few musicological cobwebs.'

'But I gather an ambulance must have come?'

'Yes, but it was pretty tense, waiting. When you started to breathe again, you coughed up a lot of muddy water, then I carried you indoors and laid you down beside the stove. I'm afraid there's mud all over your kitchen floor.'

'Oh, don't worry about that! The ambulance brought me

here? Where am I? Is this Broadford?'

'No, Inverness. Raigmore Hospital.'

'Good Heavens! And you came all that way with me?'

'I said I was your husband. I hope you don't mind. They let me travel with you and they've let me sit by your bedside. They think I'm family.' (Now didn't seem the moment to inform Stan that, in all probability, he *was*.) 'While they were loading you into the ambulance, I tried to find a key to lock up the house. Then a big blond guy arrived at the door. He seemed to know his way around.'

'Tom Howard.'

'That's right. He said he'd take care of things at the house, so I jumped in the ambulance and they drove us to Inverness.'

'It was very good of you to come.'

'You didn't think I was going to stay behind on my own in that big old house with a *ghost*, did you?'

I peered up at Stan and saw the teasing light in his eye. 'Well, thank you anyway. I'm glad you're here.'

We were both silent for a moment and then I started to cough. I struggled to sit upright, still coughing, but I seemed to have no strength. Stan stood up and put an arm round my shoulders, supporting me. He handed me a glass of water from the bedside table and I took a few sips, then he lowered me back on to the pillows.

When I'd got my breath back, I said faintly, 'Did you see Hector again?'

'No, which was a pity, because I wanted to thank him. And if we'd had more leisure, I'd have liked to ask him why he looks like my twin brother. Does he always look like that? Or was that some kind of "welcoming committee" *doppelgänger* effect?'

'He always looks like you.'

Stan's eyes widened. 'You're kidding me?'

'No. When I opened my eyes in the ambulance, I thought you were Hector. With longer hair.'

Stan's look of consternation was almost comic. 'So... this is just some bizarre coincidence, right?'

'You didn't see the window, I suppose, before we left? The stained glass memorial window upstairs?'

'I didn't move from your side. You were breathing, but unconscious. I wasn't taking any chances. I opened the stove doors and covered you with all the coats and towels I could find.'

'Well, if you'd seen the window, you'd have realised it's you who look like Hector, not Hector who looks like you.'

'But how? I mean, *why*? Do you think I could be related to the family in some way?'

'I think you must be.'

Stan seemed to sway a little on his chair, blinking several times as he tried to assimilate this new information. 'Then... that would mean I'm related to Janet Gillespie! *Oh, my...*'

'Stan, didn't you tell me you had a grandmother who emigrated from Scotland to Canada?'

'That's right. Dad's mother was a Scot.'

'*Your* dad? You mean, the man who's now in the nursing home?'

'Why, yes.'

I struggled up onto one elbow. 'And he's still OK? I mean, he's still alive?'

'Well, last I heard he was doing fine,' Stan replied, looking puzzled. 'Pretty tired, but the old guy is ninety-four. His white-water rafting days are long gone.'

'Ninety-four? You're sure?'

Stan spread his hands, perplexed. 'Ruth, he's my Dad.'

'So he must have been born in... Oh my God! 1916?'

'That's right. Why? Is this important?'

'Stan, you have no idea *how* important. What was your grandmother's name?'

'Effie Blake.'

'I mean, before she married.'

He thought for a moment. 'I think she was Effie Dunn.'

'*Dunn?* You're sure?'

'Yes, I'm sure. It just took me a moment to recall her maiden name.'

'Oh...'

My face must have fallen because Stan said, 'That wasn't the name you were hoping to hear, was it?'

'No, I'm afraid it wasn't.'

'What should my grandmother have been called?'

'Ideally, Elfriede von Hügel.'

'*Von Hügel?* That's German.'

'I know.'

Stan was thoughtful for a moment, then said, '*Hügel*... That's German for "hill".'

'If you say so.'

'Well, that's a strange coincidence.'

'What is?'

'Well, *Hügel* means hill in German. And in the Scottish vernacular, I believe a *dun* is–'

'A *hill*! "Effie Dunn" was the name Frieda adopted when she went to Canada!'

'Frieda?'

'Elfriede. Your grandmother! That was her real name.'

'My grandmother was German?'

'Half-German on her father's side. But her mother was Scots and Frieda was born in Edinburgh. Do you know when your grandmother emigrated? Or when she married?'

'No, not offhand. But I'm sure Dad would know.'

'I think you'll find she emigrated to Canada some time after 1915 and that she'd changed her German name to something Scottish.'

'Wait a minute. Are you saying Effie – Elfriede – emigrated without the father of her child?'

'He was dead. Killed at the Battle of Loos in 1915.'

Stan let out a long whistle. 'Hector was the father of her child?'

'Yes.'

'Then that means my father is... Hector's *son*!'

'Yes.'

'And I am–'

'Hector's grandson.'

'Holy moly!... You mean to say, my grandpa is a *ghost*?'

'Yes. And Janet was some sort of distant cousin.'

'Why then,' Stan exclaimed, 'So are you!'

'Yes, I suppose I must be.'

Stan beamed. 'Well, this is the best Christmas present anyone could have! A new cousin and my own personal ghost!

Do you think maybe he'll haunt me some more? I mean, seeing as I'm a close relation?'

'I don't know. I think now you're here and he's seen you, Hector might think his work is done.'

'Are you saying Hector *brought* me here?'

'No, I don't think so. But he was expecting something... Something wonderful, he said. But I've no reason to suppose he was expecting to meet his grandson.'

'Did Hector even know of my father's existence?'

'Frieda wrote and told him she was pregnant. He got the letter at the front, shortly before he was killed. He was very upset by it. You see, he'd wanted to marry her, but she'd refused, for the sake of his family, who viewed her as the enemy. Then a few days after he got the letter, he was killed, before he could reply. So he's never known if his child lived... He thought so. He said he felt a sort of connection, even after he knew Frieda must be dead. He told me he had to know what had happened to his child before he could... *rest*. But I think we might not see him again now. He'd already said his final goodbyes to me.'

'Well, thank God that final goodbye wasn't final for another reason.' Stan took my hand. 'You know, I hope you won't think it over-familiar of me, but I would really like to give you a hug. I was pretty glad Hector saved your life before, but now I know who you are – well, I'd really like to shake that guy's hand!'

Stan's voice was thick with emotion and his eyes – so similar to Hector's – were now sparkling. I suspected *he* might be in need of the tissues shortly, so to save his embarrassment (and for other reasons, which weren't entirely clear to me) I spread my arms wide, inviting him to put his arms around me and said, 'Greetings, cousin.'

He sprang up from his chair beside my bed and enveloped me in a hug. For a moment I felt the sexual frisson I'd experienced whenever I'd touched Hector, then I remembered this wasn't Hector, this was someone else. Someone real. A new friend. And someone who'd helped save my life.

Completely confused now and in a highly emotional state,

I released Stan and we sat regarding each other, grinning foolishly, then he let out a joyous whoop of laughter. He looked just like the photo in my bedside drawer, the one of Hector as a young man in his bathing suit, taken by the pool, the pool that was almost the death of me. *Twice*.

I looked at Stan laughing, at his bright blue eyes and even brighter hair and I felt an odd mix of sensations, the least comfortable of which was guilt. Could I really be so fickle?... Was I actually sitting up in bed after a near-death experience, thinking how attractive my stuffy Canadian academic was? Or had I just projected what I felt for Hector onto Stan? Surely I was just feeling emotional, not to mention grateful that Stan had looked after me. Maybe I was just glad to be alive, glad to have a newly-discovered family member sitting by my bedside, *caring* that I was alive.

I couldn't tell. But a new thought struck me and I gave up the futile struggle to stave off tears. Stan leaned forward, his sunny smile gone, his pale forehead creased by a frown.

'What's wrong, Ruth? Are you OK? Should I ring for a nurse?'

'No, I'm fine. I just thought of something.'

'Something bad?'

'No, something nice. But so nice, it's made me cry.'

'What was it?'

'It just struck me suddenly. You coming to stay at *Tigh-na-Linne*... It means it's going to be a real family Christmas now.'

A slow smile lit up Stan's face until he was grinning at me. 'Why, so it is!' Then he took my hand, leaned forward and kissed me on the cheek. 'Merry Christmas, Ruth!'

Chapter Nineteen

The hospital wanted to keep me in for forty-eight hours' observation. Complications can occur after a near-drowning apparently – pneumonia, infection, even heart failure – so I had to stay put. When I wasn't sleeping, I was showering, trying to get mud out of my hair and the smell of death out of my nostrils. Stan went back and forth on the bus and shopped in Inverness, buying a change of clothes and toiletries for me and Christmas presents for his family (including a Loch Ness Monster T-shirt for his younger sister, the particle physicist.)

Stan wouldn't countenance going back to Skye without me and, to tell the truth, I was glad to have him around. Left to my own devices, I had a pathetic tendency to turn my face to the wall and mope. I suppose it was reaction setting in, but I was also missing Hector. I didn't know if I'd ever see him again. I thought it unlikely. But when Stan was with me, I found I didn't miss Hector quite so much. Whether that was because he reminded me of Hector, or because he was just nice to have around, I couldn't tell, but I found myself looking forward to conversations with Stan, in which we swapped details about our lives and families.

He was thirty-eight, single and, as he mentioned an ex-girlfriend, I assumed he was straight. He said he was tired of academic teaching and wanted to devote more time to research and composition. He wanted to take a sabbatical to write his book and decide on his direction in life, but since his father had gone into the nursing home, he felt life was on hold. His father's health remained uncertain, there was now a big house to be sold and a lifetime's possessions to be disposed of. It was a scenario familiar to me and I sympathised.

Sitting together over a cup of tea in an anonymous day room, I'd asked Stan how he'd first become interested in

Janet's music. He narrowed his eyes and was silent for a while, as if struggling to remember.

'I don't rightly know any more. Janet and I go *way* back... But I guess it must have been when I was a music student... No, it was earlier than that! It began with something Dad told me about his mother. About Frieda. Long after she died.'

'What did he say?'

'He told me she had a favourite poem. By Andrew Marvell.'

'*The Definition of Love.*'

'Right. So you know where this is headed then. I didn't think anything of it at the time. I didn't even check out the poem, but I remembered the title and when I was a music student I came across an obscure Scottish composer who'd set this poem to music. I was intrigued enough to find the music and listen to it. Well, I was blown away. *In Memoriam* really spoke to me. So did the words for some reason. I wondered why this had been my grandmother's favourite poem? But she wasn't around to ask, so I just listened to the music, over and over. Then I got hold of some more of Janet's work. I liked a lot of it, but no other piece seemed to me in quite the same league as *In Memoriam*. That seemed like a one-off.'

'Which of course it was.'

Stan nodded. 'Nevertheless, Janet became something of a hobby-horse of mine. I was very interested in the Scots connection – probably because I had Scottish roots.' Sipping his tea and settling back in his armchair, Stan said, 'Do you happen to know why Hector asked Janet to publish *In Memoriam* after all that time?'

'It was meant to flush out Frieda. It was a long shot, but Hector thought that if by any chance she heard the music, she'd be so outraged by the plagiarism, she'd contact Janet and complain.'

'Frieda knew the piece?'

'It was dedicated to her. She and Hector had played it together many times. Hector played piano and Frieda sang. It was their "song" if you like.'

'So the piece I heard and loved was actually *created* by my grandparents.' Stan's smile was nothing short of beatific. 'It's all pretty wondrous, don't you think?'

'Yes, I do.'

'But you know, Hector's plan could never have worked.' Stan shook his head slowly. 'If only the poor guy had known.'

'What do you mean?'

'Frieda never would have heard the piece.'

'How do you know?'

'The recording was made in the late 1950s, right?'

'Yes. And it was very popular. On the radio all the time apparently. But as Frieda never got in touch with Janet, Hector assumed she must have died.'

'No, she wasn't dead. She was deaf.'

'*Deaf?*'

'Yes. I never met her – she died before I was born – but Dad said she gradually went deaf in her sixties. By the time *In Memoriam* was recorded, Frieda was no longer listening to music, so she never could have recognised Hector's piece.'

'Of course! We never thought of that! But how very sad. For someone so musical to lose their hearing. Poor Frieda.'

'But the plan still worked. Partially at least. *In Memoriam* didn't locate Frieda. But it did eventually find me.'

'And if you existed, Hector would know his child must have lived. Did you ever share *In Memoriam* with your father?'

'Yes. Dad was a historian and although it wasn't his specialism, he was interested in World War I. Maybe he suspected his father had been a soldier who'd fallen in battle. He knew Frieda's husband wasn't his father – she'd never made any secret of that – but Dad could never find any evidence of an earlier marriage, even though Effie – Frieda, I mean – referred to being the widow of a "Mr Dunn". So Dad assumed his mother's sweetheart had been a war casualty. He didn't want to embarrass her by asking for details and who knows, maybe he didn't want to establish for a fact that he was born illegitimate.'

'That would have been quite a stigma in those days.'

'I reckon so. Anyway, he said he didn't like to ask. But he was always interested in military history and the battles fought by Scottish regiments. So that was why I shared *In Memoriam* with him. It was a memorial to the fallen of World War I and it seemed to be about a pair of lovers who'd been driven apart in life, then finally separated by death. Dad figured something like that might have happened to his parents.' Stan was silent, then added with a sad smile, 'I suppose they just weren't meant to be together.'

I fixed him with a look. 'Do you believe that?'

'What? That Hector and Frieda weren't destined to be together?'

'Yes. And that some people are.'

'I don't know. I can't say I've ever really thought about it.'

'Hector believes it. *Believed* it. Oh, for Heavens' sake!' I said, setting my tea down with a bang and spilling some on the table. 'What tense is one supposed to use when talking about a ghost?'

Stan gave me a shrewd look and said, 'You're missing him already.'

'Of course I'm not,' I lied. 'How can you miss a *ghost*?'

'Well, from what you say, it seems like Hector wasn't your average ghost.' I avoided Stan's eye, refusing to be drawn. 'So what is it he believes?' I still didn't reply, but Stan persisted. 'Something that... upsets you?'

I picked up my tea-cup again and was dismayed to see my hand was shaking slightly. Taking hold of the cup in both hands, I said, 'Hector believed there was some sort of rosy, pre-destined future for me.'

'Without him?'

I looked up, shocked by the accuracy of Stan's guesswork, but I said nothing. He was giving me another appraising look and I began to think that, for all their gentle humour, those eyes didn't miss much.

'You and Hector,' Stan continued. 'Were you... *close*?'

I hesitated before answering, then, avoiding Stan's eye, said, 'Yes, we were. I first saw him when I was eight. I thought he was real. And I thought of him as my friend. Other people called him my *imaginary* friend.'

'But not Janet?'

'No.'

'Because she'd seen him too.'

'I presume so. She was always sympathetic anyway. If I asked, she'd lay another place at table, in case Heckie "dropped in for tea".'

'Heckie?'

'That was my pet name for Hector when I was a child... He disappeared from my life when I was about ten or eleven and I seemed to just forget all about him. Until this year, when I saw him again at *Tigh-na-Linne*.'

'Do you know why you were suddenly able to see him again?'

I watched Stan, still apprehensive about his reaction to my story, still thrown by the fact he seemed to take me perfectly seriously. Looking into his eyes as they regarded me calmly and kindly, I decided he could probably cope with the truth if I could cope with telling it.

'I believe I started to see Hector again because I needed to. I needed *him*. Well, I needed a friend. I'd recently lost Janet and earlier in the year, my father. I'd also lost a very close friend. One I might have married. There'd been so much death!... I was very lonely. And unhappy. I think that's why Hector came back to me. He also seemed to think I could be instrumental in furthering his purpose.'

'Which was to find out if his child had lived?'

'And what had happened to Frieda. He and Janet had tried and drawn a blank, but Hector seemed to have some sort of confidence in me that I'd be able to help him. That we could help each other. He said... I would know what to do. '

'Which was graciously agree to open up Janet's musical archive to the scrutiny of a persistent and curious academic on the other side of the Atlantic, even though visitors must have been the last thing you needed.'

'Well, I did want to sort through Janet's stuff. And for some reason, I knew I'd like you.'

Stan looked surprised. 'Even though we'd never met?'

'I liked the sound of you. Whenever we spoke on the phone, I always felt better. My heart felt lighter.' Despite Stan's candid smile, I felt I'd said too much and I attempted to backtrack. 'And of course I didn't relish the thought of spending Christmas alone.'

'Tom?...' Stan queried, raising an auburn brow in a gesture of exquisite tact.

I shook my head. 'Tom's just an employee. Well, he's also an old family friend, but nothing more. I was planning to spend Christmas at *Tigh-na-Linne* on my own, so it seemed like a good idea to invite you. Or something *made* it seem like a good idea, because most of the time, what I really wanted to do was cut and run. Shut up the house, put it on the market and go back to London.'

'But Hector wouldn't let you?'

I shook my head. 'He said there was some sort of process going on and we mustn't get in the way.'

Stan spread his hands. 'Well, he was right, wasn't he? And you *did* know what to do.'

I stared at him and said, 'You know what? I think you must be as crazy as I am.'

'You think so?' He shrugged. 'Maybe it's something genetic.'

'Seriously though, you said on the phone that you had an open mind about most things. Is it really *this* open?'

'Well, I don't know quite what I thought about destiny before I embarked on this adventure, but since I discovered I have new family and that I'm descended from a Scottish bloodline that includes not one composer, but *two*, I think I'm prepared to admit there may be something at work here that we simply don't understand. Either that, or we're talking about coincidence on a massive scale.'

'Seeing a ghost isn't a coincidence. But it could be a delusion.'

'And we happen to share the same delusion?... You never told me what Hector looked like and I haven't seen the window. But when I saw him, it was like looking in a mirror.'

'And when I met you–'

'You thought I was Hector. That isn't coincidence, Ruth. And it can't really be a shared delusion, can it? Of course, one of us could be lying... Are you?'

'No. Are you?'

'No. So what is it then?'

'I have no idea.'

Stan was pensive for a moment, then announced cheerfully, 'Me neither! But you know what? I really don't mind. Do you?'

As I pondered my answer, it was if a heavy burden was suddenly lifted from my shoulders. 'No, I don't think I do. I don't think I actually need to understand.'

'No, neither do I.' Stan grinned at me, his eyes bright with amusement. 'Now *there's* a coincidence...'

Stan and I caught the bus back to Skye. We sat side by side in enforced intimacy for a couple of hours as I pointed out the sights he hadn't see on his drive up from Glasgow. As we drew up on the shore of Loch Ness to drop off and pick up tourists, Stan exclaimed like an excited schoolboy, pointing to the snow-clad ruins of Urquhart Castle. 'Oh my – just wait till I tell Dad about this! Everywhere you go in this country, you bump into history!' He tore his eyes away from the outrageously picturesque ruins to smile at me. 'I'm *so* glad I came.'

'I'm glad too.'

'And I'm glad you're glad. Are there going to be any more castles? I'm not sure I can cope with much more architectural excitement.'

The time passed quickly and easily. I felt relaxed in Stan's company and I put this down to the fact that I was constantly confusing him with Hector, but the truth of the matter was, I'd rarely felt *relaxed* in Hector's company. After love-making perhaps, but at all other times I'd felt apprehensive, disturbed or simply unhappy. Being with Stan reminded me rather of how I *used* to feel with Hector. As a child, I hadn't known what he was and had just accepted him as a friend, an uncle, an eccentric but loving extension of my family, like my Aunt Janet.

Stan was also – it turned out – an extension of my family. Also somewhat eccentric. And loving? Warm and attentive, certainly, but I attributed that to my recent near-death experience and his delight in discovering a new branch of the family. There could surely be nothing more to it than that?...

As we approached Kyle of Lochalsh and the bridge that would take us over to Skye, I realised it would still be daylight when we arrived at *Tigh-na-Linne*. Stan would get to see the glass guardian in all his technicolour glory. But would he see the window's ghostly counterpart again?

Would I?...

I'd ordered a taxi to meet us off the bus and we were driven back to *Tigh-na-Linne* by a driver who appeared to know more about my accident than I did. I presumed Tom and the Skye jungle drums had spread the word.

The driver deposited us outside the back door. I'd been carted off to hospital without my handbag, but as I kept a spare house key under a flower pot, we were able to let ourselves in. I was braced for the worst. Stan had said he'd left mud and pondweed all over the floor, but we found the kitchen clean and tidy. Tidier than usual in fact. I guessed Tom had cleaned up, but he'd left a note on the kitchen table confirming it and explaining he'd left some milk in the fridge. He also said I was to call him straight away if I needed any help.

I was touched by his thoughtfulness. I wondered if, when he'd met Stan, he'd noticed his resemblance to the stained glass window. I thought it unlikely. Tom's attention would have been on the mud-covered body deposited in front of the Aga. Since he'd removed the decaying bridge, Tom must have wondered how I'd come to fall through the ice. Had he also marvelled at my good fortune, being hauled out of the pond by a stranger for the second time in my life?...

I'd prepared a guest room for Stan on the same corridor as the memorial window. There was no way I could show him to his room without his seeing the portrait of his grandfather. In any case, I knew Stan was anxious to view the window and eager to confirm that the vision he'd seen of a figure bearing my apparently lifeless body was in fact the ghost of his grandfather.

So I turned to him and, my heart beating slightly faster,

said, 'I imagine you'd like to meet your grandfather?'

Stan rubbed chilly hands together, grinned and said, 'You bet!'

I led the way upstairs. My legs felt leaden, partly through lack of exercise, partly through fear of meeting Hector at the top of the stairs, or finding him in front of the window, waiting for me. But when I got to the top of the staircase, I had no sense of him and when Stan and I stood and looked along the hallway, all I saw was the window, brilliantly illuminated by the bright winter sunshine, its strength magnified by the reflective power of the snow.

Stan stood and stared. I couldn't bear to look at the window, so I watched Stan (which amounted to much the same thing.) He seemed to straighten up as he looked. He stood taller – perhaps as some mark of respect? Eventually he cast his eyes down and passed a hand over his face, then he exhaled and slowly shook his head, as if he couldn't believe the evidence of his own eyes. When he finally lifted his head again, Stan looked even more like Hector. His expression had somehow taken on the sad weariness I associated with Hector, the palpable sense of loss.

Stan emitted a guttural noise and I wasn't sure if he was trying to speak or maybe just clear his throat. He pointed to the window and said, his voice gruff with emotion, 'Looks like he was one hell of a guy.'

'Yes, I think he probably was. In fact, I *know* he was.'

Stan turned to me, his eyes brimming and now as bright as Hector's. 'Would you excuse me, Ruth? I have to call my Dad. I want him to know—' His voice tailed off and he stood looking helpless for a moment, then fixed his eyes on the window again.

'Yes, of course,' I replied. 'I'll go and put the kettle on.'

'No, no – you don't have to leave. In fact, I'd rather you didn't. I'd quite like you to have a word with Dad. And perhaps you might want to have a word with Hector's son?'

'Do you want to do that *now*? I mean, what time is it in Canada?'

Stan glanced at his watch. 'It's OK. He'll have finished having breakfast a while ago.'

I stood and watched as Stan got out his phone and pressed a few buttons. His face was tense as he waited for a reply, then he began to walk toward the window. He took up a position with his back to me, in front of his almost life-size twin.

Stan's head shot up suddenly. 'Dad? Hey, it's me... No, I'm fine. I'm in Scotland... That's right, the Old Country! I wanted to share something very special with you, Dad. Are you sitting down?... Well, listen to this... *I've seen your father.*'

I was shocked that Stan was prepared to tell his father he'd seen Hector's ghost, then I realised he was referring to the window. As he listened to his father's response, Stan turned and smiled at me over his shoulder, giving me a thumbs-up.

'Well, I'm standing in front of a memorial window in the family home of—' Stan bent to read the inscription on the window. 'James Munro, who was born in 1880 and died in 1915 at the battle of Loos, in France. He was your mother's first love, Dad. You were right! He *was* a soldier and he died before they could marry. Effie named you James after him but,' – this with a look at me – 'I have it on good authority that he was actually known as Hector.'

Stan was silent for a few moments while his father replied, then he continued. 'No, I've been talking to a member of the family. In fact I'm *staying* with a member of the family. It turns out Ruth Travers is some sort of distant cousin of mine. Can you believe that?' Stan listened again, then continued. 'Well, I said I'd *seen* him, because this memorial window is a stained glass portrait of James Hector, made after he died. Ruth assures me it's a good likeness... What?... Well, I suppose she's seen old photos... What does he look like?' Stan laughed. 'A lot like me, Dad!'

He turned round again, but as he did so his wide smile vanished and the hand holding his mobile to his ear began to drift slowly down. I realised Stan wasn't looking at me, but *past* me. I spun round, but I already knew what I would see.

Hector, dressed as usual in his uniform, wasn't looking at

me either, but at his grandson. His mournful eyes followed Stan's hand as it sank down, then rose as Stan put the phone to his ear again.

Unsmiling now, his eyes fixed on Hector, Stan said, 'Dad, seeing this window and thinking about your father as a young man – you know, it's got me wondering. About Grandma Effie... I never knew her when she was young... That's right, it was a long time ago. But can you still remember what she was like as a young woman? She used to sing, right? And play piano?...' With the phone still pressed to his ear, Stan walked back along the hall until he faced Hector. He took the phone away from his own ear, then, his hand trembling slightly, he held it up to Hector's.

As he listened to the sound of his son's voice, Hector's form seemed to thin until he was almost transparent. As Stan stepped back in alarm, Hector reappeared and snatched the phone from his hand. The two men's fingers touched briefly and I saw Stan recoil as he registered the temperature of Hector's ghostly flesh.

They continued to face each other as the old man talked, reminiscing about his mother, Elfriede. Stan was probably close enough to hear the words, or at least get their gist, so when Hector handed him the phone, Stan spoke into it as if resuming a conversation.

'Thanks, Dad. I didn't know all that about Effie. You never talked about her much. Not young Effie. And now standing here, actually looking at your father—' Stan gazed steadily into Hector's eyes, but didn't miss a beat. 'Well, I thought it would be good to talk about the old days and the girl who fell in love with this fine young man... What?... That's right, almost a century ago...' Stan listened for a few moments more, then said, 'It was great to talk to you too, Dad. You have no *idea* how good it was to hear your voice... Look, I have to go and unpack now, so I'll just say goodbye, OK?'

Without waiting for a reply, Stan thrust the phone at Hector's ear and gave him a curt nod. Understanding, Hector's mouth moved, but no sound emerged. Stan whispered, 'Go on!'

Without taking his eyes off Stan, Hector worked his lips

until a few dull syllables emerged. 'Goodbye... Dad.'

From a few feet away, I heard James Blake's hearty farewell. 'Goodbye, son. Thanks for calling. You take good care now.'

For a moment we all stood listening to the silence, then Stan switched off his phone and put it back in his pocket. He took a step away from Hector and glanced across at me. Still none of us spoke. I watched Hector and waited, but his attention was on his grandson. He drew himself up to his full ghostly height, extended his hand and said, 'James Munro. I was known as Hector.'

Stan took Hector's hand, but this time, his face betrayed no surprise. 'Athelstan Blake. Everybody calls me Stan.'

'I'd like to thank you for—'

As Hector faltered, Stan butted in. 'My pleasure... You know, your son is a grand old man.'

Unable to speak, Hector lifted a pale hand, laid it on Stan's shoulder and bowed his head. Then, as he released Stan, Hector turned to me. After what seemed like a very long time, in which nobody moved, he said, 'It's finished, Ruth.'

'I know.'

'I must away.'

I nodded, no longer trusting myself to speak.

'Thank you... For believing in me. Goodbye.' He paused, then murmured the traditional Highland farewell. 'May your god go with you.'

As I sprang forward, Hector was already fading. By the time I'd covered the few paces between us, he was gone. I heard myself scream his name in a voice that seemed to rend me in two, then, as I sank toward the floor, Stan's arms went round me and pulled me up again. I lay my head on his chest and sobbed for a long time, during which Stan said not a single word, but simply held me.

Chapter Twenty

Afterwards, Stan and I didn't say much to each other. I was relieved he didn't try to console or explain, nor did he intrude on my grief. He was just *there*, a solid presence (unlike Hector) and for that I was grateful. Only by sharing the experience with someone sane could I convince myself I hadn't gone barking mad.

Stan suggested I go to bed and try to sleep. I felt exhausted with crying and I was probably still a bit weak from my experience at the bottom of the pond, so I didn't take much persuading. While I undressed and got into bed, Stan busied himself in the kitchen. He reappeared at the bedroom door (for just a second I thought it was Hector) with a laden tea tray. He'd made two kinds of tea which he presented in his characteristic breezy fashion, but I knew he was only talking to save me the trouble.

'Now, I know how seriously you British take your tea, so I made two kinds. There's a strong Assam brew there, if you feel in need of fortification. Alternatively, if you require something soothing, there's also camomile, which gets my vote for universal cure-all. And unlike chicken soup,' he added, 'You can actually apply it to open wounds.' He shot me a look. 'Of all varieties.'

'Camomile, please, Stan. Just what I need.'

He set down the tray on top of a chest of drawers and, as he poured, said, 'Can I get you anything to eat?'

'No, thanks. I'm not hungry. But *you* must be. I'm sorry, I'm being a lousy hostess. This isn't *at all* what I had planned.'

'Please don't concern yourself! I have a tin of emergency shortbread in my luggage and just now I spotted eggs and bacon in the fridge.'

'There's plenty of bread in the freezer. Help yourself. And you can choose dinner if you like. There's a variety of frozen pies and casseroles. All home-made.' His eyes lit up. 'I stocked up before you arrived.'

'Oh joy! Home cooked food! My *batterie de cuisine* consists of one well-used wok. If it can't be stir-fried, I'm afraid I don't know how to cook it. Sad, but true... OK now, drink your tea, then try to get some rest while I go and unpack.'

'I've put you next door. There's a bathroom opposite. If there's anything else you need—'

'I'm sure I'll be able to find it. I feel right at home already.'

'Maybe that's because this *is* your home. Your family home. When you think about it, you have more right than me to be here.' Stan blinked at me, astonished, as I continued. 'Hector's son should have inherited *Tigh-na-Linne*, but no-one knew he existed. By rights, this is your father's house.'

'Well, I suppose if you look at it like *that*...' Stan said doubtfully. 'But this was Janet's home for her entire life and she left it to you. I'm just a guest. And very happy to be one.'

As I sipped my tea, he drew the curtains, then left, closing the door quietly behind him. I managed a few more mouthfuls, then set the cup down, too weary even to drink. As I drifted off to sleep, I heard the distant sound of someone playing the piano, very softly. My heart turned over and I was instantly wide awake again. I thought it must be Hector, then I realised it was Stan, seated at Janet's piano, paying homage – something he'd travelled three thousand miles to do. The thought was comforting in an odd way. My breathing steadied and eventually I slept.

If I found it hard adjusting to a new family member and the absence of Hector, Stan must have found it even harder to embrace his new family history – one that included a ghost. I'd already got the impression nothing much fazed him, but after his second meeting with Hector, in front of the window, Stan seemed a little subdued and we spent the rest of the day quietly, chatting and poring over old photograph albums.

The following morning he took a photo of me on his phone to send to his father and then asked me to take one of him, standing in front of the memorial window. He sensed my unease and apologised. 'I know it's a lot to ask, Ruth, but I'd really like Dad to see us side by side. Hector and me, I mean. I think he'd be so thrilled. And I know he'd love to see his father. He's never mentioned having seen a photo of him before.'

'I'm sure he hasn't. If he had, he couldn't have helped commenting on how much you take after your grandfather.'

'Exactly. So that's why I'd like to send him a photo of the window. As soon as possible. If you could bear to take it.'

So I took a photo of Stan standing beside the glass version of Hector. He immediately sent it to his father and received a delighted text in return. After he'd read me the text, Stan thanked me again and said, 'Dad's ninety-four. I never put off doing anything that might give him pleasure. Not now...'

Stan set up a work station in the music room and spent a couple of days going through Janet's papers, so I found myself at something of a loose end. It still seemed too soon after the accident to face walking alone in the garden, so I returned to my notes and re-considered the ideas I'd had for a book about my family. So many more pieces of the jigsaw were now in place, I felt the need to re-assess the material.

Now Hector was gone for good (I repeated that phrase in my head over and over, in an attempt to brainwash myself into accepting the truth of it), I thought it was now permissible for me to read his journal. Stan was still busy in the music room, so I went upstairs, intending to sit in my bedroom, reading the journal.

I remembered that I'd put it in my bedside drawer when I unpacked after my abortive attempt to run back to London. I hadn't looked at the journal since. I steeled myself to open the drawer, fearing I might feel overwhelmed, not only by the smell of mud that emanated from the pages, but also by the sight of Hector's handwriting. And his blood.

I told myself to stop being so ridiculous and pulled open the drawer. The photograph of Hector that I'd put into one of Janet's silver frames lay on top, but it was facing downwards, so, mercifully, I wasn't confronted by Hector as a laughing, very alive young man. But even as I removed the frame and rifled through the accumulated junk of my bedside drawer – pens, medicines, a notebook and several seed catalogues – I knew something was wrong. The journal should have been on top. That's where I'd put it. The journal and photograph had both been on top in the drawer. I was in too much of a state that day to have done anything other than just shove them in. But now the journal wasn't there.

I knew it wasn't there, but I still took every single thing out, tossing it on to the bed, just to make absolutely certain.

Hector must have taken it.

He could hardly have taken it with him to wherever he'd gone to, so he must have removed it and put it somewhere else. Presumably somewhere I wouldn't find it. But *why*? Was it for my own good? Did he think he could stop me brooding about his absence by taking away his journal, when I had a shelf full of photo albums cataloguing his entire life? What could he be thinking of?

By the same token, I told myself, attempting to be reasonable, the journal going missing wasn't really such a tragedy. I had lots of other mementos, including a photo of Hector in his uniform. But that thought didn't relieve the pain I felt at the loss of his journal; the book that had seen him through the last few dreadful days of his life; the book that was perhaps the last thing he'd held, apart from his rifle. Of all the keepsakes, Hector's journal was the most precious, the one I wouldn't wish to lose.

But that was the one he'd taken.

I considered turning the house upside down to find it, but assumed Hector, with his supernatural powers, could have made that impossible. In any case, I could hardly begin a major hunt for the book while Stan was my guest. So I sat on the bed, miserable and angry that Hector should have behaved in such a devious, unfathomable way.

I don't know how long I'd sat there when I heard Stan come upstairs and go into his room, next door to mine. I looked at my watch and realised it was lunchtime.

I struggled to my feet and went and knocked on his door.

'Are you ready for some lunch?' I called. 'Soup and a

sandwich be OK?'

He appeared at the door at once. 'Sounds great. Can I help prepare it?'

'No, there's nothing much to do. I'll just get some soup out of the freezer and thaw it in the microwave. Did you have a good morning's work?'

'Yes, I did, thanks. How about you? You don't look as if *you've* had a good morning.'

'Really?... Oh, I've just had a bit of a frustrating time,' I said, deliberately vague. 'Looking for something. I wanted to show it to you, but it seems to have disappeared.'

'What was it?'

'Just Hector's war journal,' I said airily, hoping that if I sounded as if I didn't care, I wouldn't. 'The one he wrote in the trenches.'

Stan put his head on one side and treated me to an indulgent smile. 'Had you forgotten? You left it by my bedside. And that was so thoughtful of you. It makes fascinating reading – not just the anecdotes about his music, but the—' He broke off and peered at me. 'Did I say something wrong?'

'I didn't put it by your bedside.'

'You didn't?'

'No. I put it in my bedside drawer. I made a particular point of putting it there. For safe keeping.'

'So... you're saying somebody moved it?'

'No, not somebody. Hector.'

'*Hector?*'

'There's no one else it could be. I promise you, it wasn't me. Hector must have taken it out of my drawer and put it in your room.'

'But... why?'

'Because he wants you to have it. And he wanted me to *know* that's what he wanted.' For once, Stan was at a loss for words. 'Hector's absolutely right of course. You *should* have it. You can take it back to Toronto to show your father. He'll be thrilled,' I said, sounding far from thrilled myself.

Stan shook his head. 'No, I couldn't possibly deprive you of a precious family heirloom!'

'You forget, Stan – *you* have as much right to these things

225

as I do, possibly more. In any case, I don't see any point in trying to go against Hector's wishes. He's made himself quite clear, hasn't he? And it was his journal.'

Stan considered for a moment, then said, 'You know, we could always photocopy the whole thing. Make a duplicate.'

'That's a good idea. But I'd still like you to have the original. And clearly so would Hector.'

'Well, in *that* case,' Stan said, retreating into his bedroom and unzipping a holdall. 'I'd like *you* to have this.'

He extracted a black velvet pouch, gathered up with a silk drawstring ribbon. He opened the pouch, tipped the contents into the palm of his hand and a silver chain slithered out. Attached to the chain was an oval locket. It took me only seconds to realise what it was.

'Frieda's locket! The one Hector gave her before he left for France!'

'Is that so? Dad knew it was Effie's, but he never knew for sure who gave it to her. The inscription is a little ambiguous. And he thought the lock of red hair might be his own, cut when he was a baby.'

'Hair?' My mouth went dry as I remembered. 'The locket still contains Hector's hair?'

'I think we can assume it's Hector's, yes. It's the exact colour.'

'We don't have to assume. I know. He told me. He didn't expect to return from the front and he gave Frieda the locket as a parting gift. She'd asked for a lock of his hair. To remember him by.'

Stan flipped open the locket and held it out for me to see. One half was engraved with words that I didn't stop to read. In the other half, a lock of dark auburn hair curled round the oval of silver, hair the same colour as Stan's, but dull after almost a hundred years.

I took the locket and examined the hair – its colour and texture – before I allowed myself to touch it. When finally I did, I found myself unable to speak, but Stan seemed to have plenty to say and I realised I should probably be listening.

'...so I brought it over, hoping to find out more about the piece. Dad gave it to me shortly before I left. He said I could

226

keep it, but he asked me to see what I could find out about it. He'd established that the locket was nineteenth century and he knew it had belonged to his mother, but she'd never spoken about it. I was going to take it to a jeweller's in Edinburgh to see if they could tell me anything more about its provenance, but actually I don't think I'll bother now. I think I'd rather give it to you. As a Christmas gift. Because if the journal belongs to Dad as Hector's son, then I think by rights that locket belongs to you as the last woman Hector Munro loved.' As I gaped in astonishment, Stan said, 'You haven't read the inscription, have you?'

'No.' I peered at the tiny letters, trying to focus. They said, *"This is my beloved and this is my friend.* Song of Songs V, 16"

'Oh... That's *beautiful!* That's what they were to begin with. Just friends. Music brought them together. And then... then they fell in love.'

'So the locket commemorates both friendship and love. And that's why you must have it, Ruth. As a gift from me and from Hector. I'm sure it's what he would have wanted. And what will *I* do with a silver locket?'

'You could keep it until you— well, until you find someone you want to give it to.' I floundered. 'Someone *special*,' I added, extending my open palm toward Stan, offering him the locket.

Without meeting my eyes, he folded my fingers around the locket until they enclosed it completely, then he held my fist in both hands and looked at me. 'Consider it done.' Stan's usual mischievous twinkle was absent and his regard was serious now, almost solemn. His bright blue eyes searched mine for a moment before he released my hand and turned away. 'Well, I think we can say Christmas has already begun if gifts are being exchanged. I'm delighted with mine. I shall treasure it as a memento of a very happy – and *momentous* – time. Thank you, Ruth.' He cast his eyes up at the ceiling. 'And thank *you*, Hector. Wherever you may be.' He raised a hand in salute. 'God bless.'

I didn't know whether to laugh or cry. Laughter won – just – and I said, 'Shall we go and hit the sherry? I was going to tip some into the beef consommé, but I don't see why we shouldn't tip some down our throats as well. Come on – I refuse to drink alone.'

'Now you're talking! You know, I just can't get enough of these quaint British habits.'

Stan followed me dutifully downstairs and dutifully drank two large glasses of sherry. So did I, after which, things looked *much* brighter. I very nearly forgot about Frieda's silver locket burning a hole, deep in the pocket of my cardigan.

As the level of sherry in the bottle went down, we covered a lot of ground, nibbling roasted almonds and cubes of Manchego. We then wolfed down the soup, after which, in the absence of pudding, I suggested we open a bottle of Prosecco "because it was almost Christmas", which, as it was still the first week of December, was a feeble excuse to drink in the middle of the afternoon. But Stan offered no objection and agreed that Prosecco was the sort of wine you could drink any time of day.

The alcohol appeared to have little effect on him other than to make him more loquacious and hilariously funny. Or perhaps the latter was the alcohol's effect on *me*. Whichever, Stan was extraordinarily good company, whether he was telling stories about vicious rivalry in the academic world or treating me to his collection of deadpan Canadian jokes. ("How many Canadians does it take to change a light bulb?" "None. Canadians don't change light bulbs, we accept them as they are.")

In the end we got to the helpless stage where, if one of us had shaken a stick at the other, we would have howled with laughter. I don't know about Stan, but it was as if I hadn't laughed for a year and needed to catch up.

When we'd calmed down a little, I shared my own stories of the rampant misogyny and ageism in television. Stan sympathised and encouraged me to pursue my hare-brained idea of a book about the family. *Our* family. He even offered to help me write it.

I told him I had to return to London, either to live in my flat or sell it, so he asked what I was going to do with *Tigh-na-*

Linne. Suddenly sober, I hedged and said I might let it, or more probably sell it.

He was too drunk to disguise his horror. 'Sell up? How can you think of doing that? This is your family home! And it's so... *beautiful.* And in such a beautiful place. How can you bear to sever your connection with Janet? And Hector?'

'Severing my connection with Hector is something of a priority, actually. I need to get on with my life, Stan. With *real* life. And frankly, I need the money. I've trodden water, living off savings for the last year. Janet left me the house, but she didn't leave much cash. I *have* to sell up or try to turn the house into a business of some sort.'

'Let me rent the house.'

'*What?*'

'I'd like to rent the house for a year.'

'What on earth for?'

'Well, I told you I was planning to take a sabbatical. A year to write and research. And maybe compose. Here's as good a place as any. It's quiet.'

'Oh, it's certainly quiet.'

'There's a piano, a library, a musical archive. Instead of shipping all that over to Toronto, I could come here. And now I know who Janet is – in relation to me, I mean – I would dearly love to buy her piano, if you'd sell it to me.'

'Please - have it! It's rightfully yours. Or rather your father's. Hector told me his parents bought the piano for him. If you take it off my hands, it would save me the heartbreak of seeing it go out of the family.'

Stan shook his head. 'I don't have room for it in Toronto. I live in a tiny apartment, most of which is taken up by a baby grand. I need a carpenter to adapt it so I can eat on it and sleep under it.'

'So you can't take Janet's piano off my hands?'

'Not if I'm selling Dad's house. He would have had room, but the poor guy won't be going home again and I need the cash from the sale of his house to pay for his care... So you see, it would suit me very well to take a lease on a house like this for a year. And I know my sister would love to come here for a holiday with her family. The place is ideal for kids.'

I paused to consider Stan's suggestion. 'You think you'd want to live here for a year? Alone?'

'I live alone anyway.'

'There are no near neighbours. Or shops.'

He shrugged. 'I live a pretty quiet life outside term-time. I'm really a wilderness person. I have to work in a city, but I like to hike and fish. And I do a bit of climbing when I get the chance.'

'Skye would be Heaven for you then.'

'I guess it would.'

'Stan, this is going to sound like I'm a total control freak, but if you rented the house, would you keep Tom Howard on?'

'The handyman?'

'Well, he's more of a gardener really. He's looked after this garden for a while now and I'd hate to see it go to rack and ruin. And... well, I don't really know what else Tom would do. There's not much work on the island. And he badly needs a job.'

'If I lived here, I'd certainly need a gardener, so I don't foresee that as a problem.'

'You're serious about this?'

'I certainly am.'

'Because your plan would buy me some time. And I think that's what I need. I don't want to sell up, but I can't afford not to. Equally, I can't face the idea of strangers occupying the place. I suspect I'd have to pay for major renovations before I could persuade someone to rent it anyway. And I doubt they'd stay on for winter, which is when I really need the house to be occupied. So you see, if you *are* serious, you're offering me a bit of a lifeline.'

'And if *you're* serious, you're offering me the opportunity of a lifetime.'

'Well, I am.'

'And so am I.' He grinned and raised the remains of a glass of Prosecco. 'I think we might have struck a deal!'

'But we're both drunk!' I exclaimed, laughing.

'Oh, you noticed? Being Canadian, I was of course too polite to draw attention to the fact... Do you think inebriation presents a serious obstacle to our reaching an understanding?'

Stan was looking at me intently now, with an unfamiliar expression on his face and I suddenly wondered if he was talking about something else entirely. I played his last words over again in my head as I watched him watching me. His frank, appreciative stare unsettled me. When he stopped performing the all-singing, all-dancing Canadian cabaret, his focused stillness and those candid blue eyes had a disturbing effect.

Flustered and definitely the worse for wear, I said, 'Please don't look at me like that, Hector.'

I detected a slight sigh as his long golden eyelashes drooped and masked his eyes. 'Stan,' he said softly, his voice quite neutral.

My hand flew to my mouth. 'Oh, God – I'm sorry!'

'That's OK. Serves me right for staring at you in what must have been a disconcerting fashion. But I was pretty disconcerted myself.'

'Oh, bloody hell, I get so *confused*! Please forgive me, Stan. I'm not sitting here thinking of Hector, really I'm not! I'm enjoying your company very much. In a way I never enjoyed Hector's.'

'So what made you think of Hector just then?'

I hesitated, wondering just how honest I could or should be. 'The way you were looking at me.' He looked a question. 'As if...'

'As if what?'

'Oh, I don't know!'

He put his head on one side and nailed me with a look. 'I think you do.'

'Well, as if you... as if you wanted to go to bed with me, I suppose. I thought I saw... *longing* in your eyes. And that made me think of Hector. How he used to look at me. Sometimes.' I looked down, unable to meet Stan's eyes and murmured, 'I'm really sorry.'

'No, *I'm* sorry. For not disguising my feelings better.' I looked up again. He was smiling genially now and whatever it was I'd seen, was now veiled. 'I hope I haven't spoiled the

231

afternoon? I promise to be better behaved for the rest of the holidays. And I'll steer clear of your lethal sherry.'

'I didn't mean it like that. I'm not offended or anything. Just… *perplexed*.'

'By me?'

'By my *feelings*.'

'Feelings for Hector?'

'Yes… And my feelings for you, I suppose.'

'Which feelings,' Stan said carefully, 'would those be?'

The silence that followed was broken by the jingle of a mobile. Stan reached into the pocket of his trousers, drew out his phone and looked at the screen.

He frowned. 'It's the nursing home, but it's not Dad. I have to take this, Ruth,' he said quickly, standing up. 'Would you please excuse me?'

Without waiting for a reply, he strode out of the kitchen, speaking into his phone.

I put the kettle on and began to clear away the remains of lunch. It wasn't until the kettle came to the boil that it occurred to me why the nursing home might be ringing Stan.

My stomach and its contents seemed to surge upwards, as if I was descending too fast in a lift. I laid a steadying hand on the back of a chair and closed my eyes. When I opened them again, I felt calmer. Resigned. If I was destined to spend Christmas alone, then so be it. Things were getting far too complicated anyway.

I made a pot of tea, set crockery out on a tray, then sat down and stared at it, waiting for Stan to return. When he didn't, I got to my feet, preparing myself for the news that I'd lost another family member, one I'd never even met.

But I could be useful now. I knew all about death and loss. And, if the worst *had* happened, Stan could no doubt use a friend. I left the cooling tea on the kitchen table and went in search of him.

Chapter Twenty-one

I found Stan in the sitting room, standing by the French windows, looking out into the garden. His arms hung loosely by his side and he still had his phone in one hand. I stood in the doorway for a moment, holding the door handle, uncertain whether to enter or speak. Without turning, Stan said, 'He's gone, Ruth. In his sleep... It was a good death. As these things go.'

'I'm so sorry... Would you prefer to be left alone?'

He ignored my question and said, 'You know, even though it's half-buried in snow, you can still see what a lovely garden this is. It must have been an inspiration to Janet, don't you think?'

'Oh, yes, I'm sure it was.'

'Do you think it would be an inspiration to me?'

'I don't see why not. Generations of your family have lived here. And this house has been filled with music. And a great deal of love.'

He turned round then. His cheeks were wet and his skin looked grey in the fading light. Grief had transfigured him and he looked shockingly young. 'I'm the older generation now, Ruth... Isn't that strange? I just turned thirty-eight and now I'm head of the family. Somehow that feels... oh, I don't know – it feels...' he broke off, struggling to find a word.

'Lonely?'

'Yes, that's right. It *does*.' He gripped his phone and stared at it. 'I mean, now, when something *good* happens – or just something crazy, something stupid! – who'm I going to call?' He sounded angry, but I understood.

'I hope you'll think of calling me.'

His head shot up and he looked at me, his eyes bright with fresh tears. 'Could I do that?'

'I really wish you would. I used to love getting your calls.

They often made my day. I didn't realise it at the time, but I do now. Please call me, Stan. Whenever you need to. Any time.'

He managed a wan smile. 'Thank you. I'll do that.' He rubbed at his eyes and said, 'Right now, I have to ring my sister. Let her know.' He turned away and looked out the window again. 'They said he'd been very excited the last couple of days. Happy. Telling people about his son's great discovery in the Old Country. He told one of the nurses it made him feel closer to the father he'd never known...' Stan was silent for a few moments, then with a note of anguish in his voice he was unable to disguise, he said, 'Do you think they're together now? Jim and Hector?'

'I think they might be.'

'That's a good thought, isn't it?' He clutched his phone. 'A good thought to hang on to.'

'Yes, it is.'

He looked at his phone again. 'OK, I'm going to ring Edie now... Her name's really Eadgyth. Sister of Athelstan, the first king of a united England. They were the grandchildren of Alfred the Great, did you know that?... No, nobody knows that. But Dad just *loved* his history.' Stan shook his head and smiled. 'He didn't foresee a lifetime of spelling out your name over the phone.'

Stan didn't seem anxious to make the call, so I said, 'Can I get you anything? Coffee? A drink of water? At times like this, the British make copious pots of tea. Which we never actually drink.'

The remark wasn't remotely funny, but Stan gave a sort of choked laugh. I could see he was close to cracking, but he smiled – in a way that nearly broke my heart – and said, 'You know what I'd like, Ruth? What I'd *really* like?'

'What?'

'A hug.'

'Of course!' I replied, moving quickly across the room and taking him in my arms.

We stood like that for some time. As the afternoon light faded rapidly, I thought for one moment that I saw Hector, wraith-like, standing out in the snow, his red hair glowing. Then I realised it was Stan's reflection in the window.

~

After Stan had made his call, I lit a fire and turned on all the table lamps to banish the darkness. He switched on the Christmas tree lights and we sat on the sofa, drinking tea. Conversation was desultory and painful. For both of us.

'Ruth, I'm afraid I have to leave. Straight away.'

'Yes, of course. I'll drive you to the airport.'

'Thanks, but that won't be necessary. I have the hire car, remember.'

'Oh, I was forgetting... But I can come with you anyway. If you'd like the company. I can get the bus back from Glasgow.'

'I couldn't possibly put you to all that trouble.'

'No, I'd like to come. And it would give me a bit more time with you. I mean, as your visit has been cut short. But I wouldn't want to intrude. If you'd rather do the journey on your own?...'

Stan set down his tea and swivelled round to face me. 'Now don't reject this idea without thinking about it first. Hear me out... I'd like you to come to Toronto with me. And I'd like you to come to Dad's funeral. I know you never met him, but he was your kin. And Hector's son.'

I didn't reply – *couldn't* reply – but it didn't matter because Stan carried on talking.

'Then I'd like you to spend Christmas with me. I'd like you to meet Edie, my brother-in-law and nephew. My family. *Our* family. You'd like them. And they'll *love* you.' I opened my mouth to speak but Stan forestalled me. 'And before you start telling me you can't afford the flight, may I remind you that earlier today you were offering me a grand piano as a *gift*? A gift I couldn't possibly accept unless you allow me to treat you to a winter holiday in Canada. Edie and Doug live in Vancouver. You'll love Vancouver. *Everyone* loves Vancouver. It's the kind of place people go to for a holiday and forget to go home. Seriously.'

I stared into my empty cup, trying hard not to cave. But Stan was merciless. 'Of course, you might prefer to spend a quiet Christmas alone. And I realise most people hate travelling at Christmas. But if we went now, we'd be going

235

before the Christmas mayhem begins.'

I still didn't reply and he began to lose heart. 'I suppose you're worried about leaving the house empty in the depths of winter? If you drained the system, the pipes wouldn't burst.'

Finally, I found my tongue. 'I wouldn't need to do that. I could ask Tom to move in while I was away. It would be doing him a big favour, actually. His place is just a renovated hovel, right by the sea. I don't know how he survives the winter. I could ask him to move in while I'm gone. He could do some decorating. It badly needs doing...'

I ground to a halt and gazed at Stan helplessly. He still looked drained, but happier.

'So that's settled, then. I'll book our flights and tell Edie to expect you for the funeral. Oh – do you need to shop for an outfit?'

'No. That's one thing I won't have to do. I have a selection of funeral outfits, all bought recently.'

Stan swore under his breath and seemed to crumple. 'I'm sorry. That was unforgivable. I wasn't thinking.'

I took his hand and squeezed it, deriving an odd sort of comfort from the warm, hard bones. 'Don't be ridiculous! You've just suffered a major bereavement! You're stressed out. And tired. And doing bloody well, if I may say so.' I let go his hand with a certain reluctance – a reluctance that made me question the wisdom of Stan's travel plans for me. 'Look, can I take some time to think about all this? I think you should too. Talk to Edie about it. She might not think it's such a good idea... Can I let you know later on tonight whether I'm going to come? After dinner? Would that be OK?'

'Of course. I have to fly back straight away, but you don't. You could take a day or two to think about it.'

'I'll sleep on it and tell you my decision in the morning.'

'Fine.'

'Would you like some fresh tea?'

He eyed the empty pot with suspicion. 'Is it possible to O.D on tea?'

'I don't think so. Though you can get serious withdrawal symptoms.'

'We'd better have some more then.'

As I gathered up the tea things, Stan sprang up from the sofa, strode over to the door and opened it for me. As I passed him, he said, 'Ruth?'

I stopped in the doorway and looked at him. He stood looking awkward and seemed at a loss for words. Then reaching for the tray, he said, 'Here, let me take that.' He stared at the tray as if memorising its contents. 'I just wanted to say, if you do decide to come... there'd be no strings.'

'Stan, I really didn't think—'

He looked at me then, his expression earnest. 'You know, what you said earlier – about the way I was looking at you? When you confused me with Hector?'

'Oh, *please* – don't remind me!'

'We're friends, Ruth. And family. And that was all I meant when I said I wanted you to come. Though I won't pretend something more hasn't crossed my mind. Forgive me for being frank, but I'm a little too tired to be diplomatic.'

'That's all right. I understand. And I did realise your intentions were entirely honourable.'

'You did?'

'You're *Canadian*, Stan.'

He beamed. 'And fast becoming addicted to British tea. Time for the next fix...'

While Stan was booking flights and speaking to the nursing home about funeral arrangements, I prepared supper. As it was probably his last night on Scottish soil, I dug out a haggis from the freezer and peeled quantities of potatoes and "neeps". (Turnips to Scots, but, confusingly, swede to the English.) It was a high risk meal, perhaps. Haggis is something of an acquired taste, but the ultimate in comfort foods, second only to porridge. I thought we both needed all the comfort there was going.

As I worked my way through the veg preparation, I decided I probably shouldn't go to Toronto. It was just too complicated. But then I wondered if I wanted to stay on at *Tigh-na-Linne* in the hope that Hector would re-appear? I was sure he wouldn't, not now Jim Blake was dead. I didn't think anyone would be seeing Hector ever again. *'It's finished, Ruth'.* That's what he'd said. And Hector wouldn't lie to me.

That thought depressed me utterly until I realised *why* no one would see him, which was that the poor man had finally found peace – everlasting peace, I hoped. I was very glad for Hector and glad he'd met his grandson. And what a splendid grandson he'd turned out to be. One who had to be warned against trying to rescue drowning women from frozen ponds. One who wasn't afraid to shake hands with a ghost...

As I looked at my own hands peeling the veg, I remembered the chill of Hector's fingers and then the warmth of Stan's as I'd held his hand in the sitting room. I hadn't wanted to let go. Nor had I wanted to let go when he'd asked to be hugged after the news of his father's death. I couldn't kid myself I was confusing the two men when they both felt so very different – even *smelled* so different. Stan didn't smell of mud and blood and his flesh didn't yield under pressure. Stan was solid. Fit. *Alive.*

I started to feel rather warm and tried to change the direction of my thoughts – without much success.

Hector had said, *"You'll care again, Ruth. And you'll be cared for. Believe it."* He surely couldn't have meant his own grandson, could he? And how was I to distinguish my feelings for Stan from my feelings for Hector? They had very different personalities, but looked like identical twins. How could I possibly separate my feelings for these two men?

Except that they weren't two men. One was a man and one was a ghost. One was alive and the other was very dead.

As I lobbed peeled potatoes into a pan of water, I continued my self-interrogation. Why would I go to Canada to spend Christmas with a man I'd met only a week ago?... Well, because he was family – some sort of distant cousin – also a friend I'd been emailing and speaking to on the phone for months, that's why. And I'd never been to Canada... It would be just a holiday. With a funeral thrown in. Stan was inviting me to stay as a friend. That's all. Why did I have to go and *complicate* things?...

It occurred to me, the reason I was so hot was because I

was standing beside the Aga. I dried my hands and took off my cardigan, flinging it over the back of a chair. Something fell out on to the tiled floor and landed with a metallic clink. I bent down to retrieve Frieda's locket. Anxious it might have been damaged by the fall, I flicked it open to check the mechanism still worked. Bracing myself for the sight of Hector's hair again, I found my eyes were in fact drawn to the inscription opposite.

This is my beloved and this is my friend.

David had been a friend and probably should never have been more.

Tom was a friend, one who'd wanted to be something more.

Hector had been a friend, one who'd become *much* more.

And now there was Stan. Who was just a friend. *So far.*

It had to be said, my track record for distinguishing between friends and lovers was not impressive. I shut the locket and fastened it round my neck for safe-keeping, patting it absently as it settled against my breast-bone.

Complicated? Too damn right it was complicated.

Stan was understandably subdued for the rest of the day and, as I hadn't yet said whether I was going back with him, conversation was a little stilted. He appeared to enjoy the haggis and after dinner he sat staring into the fire, nursing a glass of Talisker, saying little. He retired early and after I'd cleared up the kitchen, I too turned in.

Perhaps it was the haggis or maybe too much wine, but I woke some time in the night after one of my nightmares. I couldn't remember much about it, only darkness and a sense I was choking to death. I sat up and switched on the bedside lamp. By its dim light I surveyed the bedroom. I don't know what I was looking for. Hector probably. But I saw nothing.

I looked at my watch and groaned. 3.30am. Still hours to go until daylight, but I was no longer tired, so getting back to sleep would be difficult. I stared at the closed door, remembering all the times I'd been comforted as a child by the thought of Hector on sentry duty at my door...

It wasn't a dare exactly. It was just that I wanted to prove once and for all that Hector was gone. Gone for good. I needed to know he wasn't coming back and I couldn't think of any other way to be certain. So I summoned him. I concentrated my heart and mind on calling Hector back. Because I needed him. Or rather, I needed to *know*.

Nothing happened of course. Hector was a man of his word. It was finished.

I settled down in bed and was just about to turn out the light when there was a light tap at my door. I sat up again, my heart hammering.

'Come in.'

The door swung open to reveal a ghostly white figure, standing in the doorway.

'Ruth?... Are you OK?'

It was Stan. Stan dressed in crumpled white linen pyjamas. Stan, monochrome in the dim light, apart from his bright, tousled hair.

'Yes, I'm fine. I wasn't, but I'm fine now.'

'Oh... That's good.'

'Are *you* all right?'

'Me? Oh, I'm fine.' His smile was bleak. 'In a sad sort of way. Sad about my father. Sad to be leaving Scotland so soon... But he had a good life. And a long one... And Scotland will always be here, won't it?... Sorry if I disturbed you.'

'You didn't. I was already wide awake. And thinking.'

'What about...?'

'About Christmas. And Toronto.'

'Oh...?'

'I've decided I *would* like to come. I'd like to spend Christmas with you and your family. And I'd like to be present at your father's funeral. I think that's what Hector would have wanted. And Janet... And it's what *I* want too.'

His pale face broke into a smile. 'You're sure? That's really what you want to do?'

'Yes. That's really what I want.'

His expression changed again and was suddenly grave. 'Well, I won't trouble you now with the hideous fate Edie promised me if I failed to persuade you to come, but, let me tell you, boiling in oil would have been a softer option. Good night, Ruth. Sleep well.'

He grasped the door handle and was about to close the door when I called out, 'Don't go! I want to ask you something.' He turned round and took a step back into the room. 'Stan, why did you come and knock on my door? Did you *know*?'

'Know what?'

'That I... That I wanted someone to be with me?'

He thought for a moment, then dragged a hand through his already untidy hair and frowned. 'I don't rightly know why I came... It seems a strange thing to have done now. But at the time, it seemed like the *only* thing to do.' He took another step forward, so he was standing almost at the end of the bed. 'I guess I just knew this was where I needed to be. By your side... And it was where I *wanted* to be.'

I said nothing, but stared – not at Stan, but past him, at the open door behind as it began to swing, very slowly on its hinges. As it shut with a click, Stan wheeled round. He stared at the door, then turned back to me, looking shaken.

'Don't worry,' I said, smiling. 'It's Hector. I think he's giving us his blessing.'

'He *is*?'

'Yes. But he's gone now... Gone for good.'

'And... is that OK?' Stan asked, peering at me.

'Oh, yes. That's OK.' I looked up at him and smiled. 'It's finished, Stan. He won't be coming back.'

And I was right. We never saw Hector again.

~~~

ACKNOWLEDGEMENTS

I'd like to thank the following people for their help and support during the writing of this book:

Tina Betts, Jill Broderick, Amy Glover, Philip Glover, Lynn Latimer, Michelle Moore, Laura Ramsey & Colin Richardson.

For more information about Linda Gillard and her books visit
www.lindagillard.co.uk

Follow Linda Gillard on Facebook:
https://www.facebook.com/LindaGillardAuthor

Other books by **Linda Gillard**...

EMOTIONAL GEOLOGY

A passionate, off-beat love story set on the bleak and beautiful island of North Uist in the Outer Hebrides.

Rose Leonard is on the run from her life.

Haunted by her turbulent past, she takes refuge in a remote Hebridean island community where she cocoons herself in work, silence and solitude in a house by the sea. A new life and new love are offered by friends, her estranged daughter and most of all by Calum, a fragile younger man who has his own demons to exorcise.

But does Rose, with her tenuous hold on sanity, have the courage to say "Yes" to life and put her past behind her?...

REVIEWS

"Haunting, lyrical and intriguing."
ISLA DEWAR (Keeping up with Magda)

"Complex and important issues are played out in the windswept beauty of a Hebridean island setting, with a hero who is definitely in the Mr Darcy league!"
www.ScottishReaders.net

"The emotional power makes this reviewer reflect on how Charlotte and Emily Brontë might have written if they were living and writing now."
NORTHWORDS NOW

A LIFETIME BURNING

Flora Dunbar is dead. But it isn't over.

The spectre at her funeral is Flora herself, unobserved by her grieving family and the four men who loved her.

Looking back over a turbulent lifetime, Flora recalls an eccentric childhood lived in the shadow of her musical twin, Rory; early marriage to Hugh, a handsome clergyman twice her age; motherhood, which brought her Theo, the son she couldn't love; middle age, when she finally found brief happiness in a scandalous affair with her nephew, Colin.

"There has been much love in this family – some would say too much – and not a little hate. If you asked my sister-in-law, Grace why she hated me, she'd say it was because I seduced her precious firstborn, then tossed him on to the sizeable scrap heap marked 'Flora's ex-lovers'. But she'd be lying. That isn't why Grace hated me. Ask my brother Rory".

REVIEWS

"An absolute page-turner! I could not put this book down and read it over a weekend. It is a haunting and disturbing exploration of the meaning of love within a close-knit family... Find a place for it in your holiday luggage!"
www.LoveReading.co.uk

"Probably the most convincing portrayal of being a twin that I have ever read."
STUCK-IN-A-BOOK's blog

"Disturbing themes, sensitively explored... An emotional avalanche."
LOCHCARRON READING GROUP

STAR GAZING

Short-listed for *Romantic Novel of the Year 2009* and *The Robin Jenkins Literary Award*, the UK's first environmental book award.

Blind since birth, widowed in her twenties, now lonely in her forties, Marianne Fraser lives in Edinburgh in elegant, angry anonymity with her sister, Louisa, a successful novelist. Marianne's passionate nature finds expression in music, a love she finds she shares with Keir, a man she encounters on her doorstep one winter's night.

Keir makes no concession to her condition. He's abrupt to the point of rudeness, yet oddly kind. But can Marianne trust her feelings for this reclusive stranger who wants to take a blind woman to his island home on Skye, to "show her the stars"?...

REVIEWS

"This was a joy to read from the first page to the last... Romantic and quirky and beautifully written."
www.lovereading.co.uk

"A read for diehard romantics with a bent towards environmental issues."
ABERDEEN PRESS AND JOURNAL

"A story of love, music and nature, with touches of the supernatural and a very engaging and believable heroine."
ADÈLE GERAS (Facing the Light)

HOUSE OF SILENCE

Selected by Amazon for *Top Ten BEST OF 2011* in the Indie author category.

"My friends describe me as frighteningly sensible, not at all the sort of woman who would fall for an actor. And his home. And his family."

Orphaned by drink, drugs and rock'n'roll, Gwen Rowland is invited to spend Christmas at her boyfriend Alfie's family home, Creake Hall – a ramshackle Tudor manor in Norfolk. Soon after she arrives, Gwen senses something isn't quite right. Alfie acts strangely toward his family and is reluctant to talk about the past. His mother, a celebrated children's author, keeps to her room, living in a twilight world, unable to distinguish between past and present, fact and fiction.

When Gwen discovers fragments of forgotten family letters sewn into an old patchwork quilt, she starts to piece together the jigsaw of the past and realises there's more to the family history than she's been told. It seems there are things people don't want her to know.

And one of those people is Alfie...

REVIEWS

"HOUSE OF SILENCE is one of those books you'll put everything else on hold for."
CORNFLOWER BOOKS blog

"The family turns out to have more secrets than the Pentagon. I enjoyed every minute of this book."
KATHLEEN JONES (Margaret Forster: A Life in Books)

UNTYING THE KNOT

Awarded a Medallion by the *Book Readers Appreciation Group* (**www.bragmedallion.com**)

Marrying a war hero was a big mistake. So was divorcing him.

A wife is meant to stand by her man. Especially an army wife. But Fay didn't. She walked away - from Magnus, her traumatised soldier husband and from the home he was restoring: Tullibardine Tower, a ruined 16th-century castle on a Perthshire hillside.

Now their daughter Emily is getting married. But she's marrying someone she shouldn't.

And so is Magnus...

REVIEWS

"This author is funny, smart, sensitive and has a great feel for romance... Highly recommended!"
RHAPSODYINBOOKS blog

"Daring to write characters like this is brave. And it works. Beautifully."
Cally Phillips, INDIE EBOOK REVIEW

"Another deeply moving and skilfully executed novel by Linda Gillard. I am totally in awe of this author. Once again, she had me committed to her characters and caught up in their lives from the first few pages, then weeping for joy at the end."
Tahlia Newland, AWESOME INDIES

Made in the USA
Lexington, KY
30 June 2014